THE VERY LONG,

VERY STRANGE LIFE

OF ISAAC DAHL

Books by Bart Yates

LEAVE MYSELF BEHIND

THE BROTHERS BISHOP

THE LANGUAGE OF LOVE AND LOSS

THE VERY LONG, VERY STRANGE LIFE OF ISAAC
DAHL

And writing as Noah Bly

THE THIRD HILL NORTH OF TOWN

THE DISTANCE BETWEEN US

Published by Kensington Publishing Corp.

WHITE CREEK: A FABLE
Published by Citadel Press

THE VERY LONG,

VERY STRANGE LIFE

OF ISAAC DAHL

a novel

Bart Yates

JOHN SCOGNAMIGLIO BOOKS
KENSINGTON BOOKS
www.kensingtonbooks.com

JOHN SCOGNAMIGLIO BOOKS are published by

Kensington Publishing Corp.
900 Third Avenue
New York, NY 10022

All Kensington titles, imprints and distributed lines are available at special quantity discounts for bulk purchases for sales promotion, premiums, fund-raising, educational or institutional use.

Special book excerpts or customized printings can also be created to fit specific needs. For details, write or phone the office of the Kensington Special Sales Manager: Kensington Publishing Corp., 900 Third Ave., New York, NY, 10022. Attn. Special Sales Department. Phone: 1-800-221-2647.

The JS and John Scognamiglio Books logo is a trademark of Kensington Publishing Corp.

Library of Congress Control Number: 2024934896

ISBN: 978-1-4967-5045-7

First Kensington Hardcover Edition: August 2024

ISBN: 978-1-4967-5047-1 (e-book)

10 9 8 7 6 5 4 3 2 1

Printed in the United States of America

ACKNOWLEDGMENTS

Great thanks and love to:

— My fabulous editor, John Scognamiglio, and all the talented people at Kensington Books.

— Gordon Mennenga, Prince of Tales.

— Marian Mathews Clark, the better angel of my nature.

— Tonja Robins, dreamer and soothsayer; believer in neurotic novelists and odd books.

— Lisa and Edward Leff, creators of lovely moments and great memories.

— Abraham Assad, unrepentant goofball and occasional genius.

— Angel and Lindsey Dean, babysitters extraordinaire of wayward winos in Napa Valley.

— Debbie and Jacob Yarrow, the kindest souls in Sonoma County.

— Adrian Repasch, website guru and slayer of Demon Glaag.

—Pena Lubrica, Dave Dugan, and Allison Heady, gifted members of the Iowa City Show-And-Tell Society.

—Michael Becker, for sharing his knowledge of the mating habits of gastropods.

—My family and friends, for making my life both rich and strange.

I also owe a debt of gratitude to the following excellent historical resources:

—*THE WORST HARD TIME: The Untold Story of Those Who Survived the Great American Dust Bowl,* by Timothy Egan

—*SHIP OF GHOSTS, The Story of the USS* Houston, *FDR's Legendary Lost Cruiser, and the Epic Saga of Her Survivors,* by James D. Hornfischer

—*FOR THE GOOD OF MANKIND, A History of the People of Bikini and Their Islands,* by Jack Niedenthal

—*THE BOMB,* by Theodore Taylor, a meticulously-researched and moving novel about the Bikini people in the final days before the destruction of their home.

DAY ONE

February 17, 1926. Bingham, Utah.

Each day is a story, whether or not that story makes any damn sense or is worth telling to anyone else. If you live a long time, and your memory doesn't completely crap out, you end up with enough stories to fill a library; it's nearly impossible to pick and choose a mere handful to write about—a stupid, arbitrary stricture I've been cowed into accepting by a dead bully. Why I lack the testicular fortitude to just say no is a vexing question, but what aggravates me even more is the fact that I have no idea where to start.

Okay, I'm lying.

I actually do know, but it irks me beyond belief to give Aggie the satisfaction of following her advice. That she now only exists in my head is beside the point: I'd like to maintain at least a smidgeon of autonomy in my own skull, for God's sake. Is that so much to ask?

Sadly, in this case, it is.

You're very unattractive when you whine, Isaac.

That's what she'd say, of course, if she were still here. I find it both irritating and oddly comforting that I can hear her voice so clearly, without even trying. She may as well never have died, given that she's every bit as exasperating in my imagination as she ever was in person.

Just get on with it and tell them about the giant.

Agnes and I were getting ready for bed—and fighting, of course, about whose turn it was to stoke the woodstove—when our mother lifted her head and told us to shush. Agnes was my twin sister, and Mama always claimed we came out of her womb mad as weasels, screaming hell and death at each other, same as every day afterward. (The midwife hauled me out only a few minutes ahead of Aggie, who no doubt thought the whole sordid business was my fault, and something I should have warned her about.)

"Shush, both of you," Mama repeated. She was nursing Hilda, our baby sister, by the woodstove. "Did you hear that noise?"

"What noise?" Agnes asked.

"The giant," I said.

"Don't be ridiculous," Agnes said. "Giants aren't real."

"Shush!" Mama insisted.

I was eight and had just read *Jack and the Beanstalk*. I was a timid kid with a perverse imagination, and long before the story of Jack and his magic beans came into my life, I was jumping at phantom faces in every shadow. I believed the large rock beside our house was a troll turned to stone, waiting for the next dark of the moon to become flesh; I swore I could hear nymphs and demons battling for dominion in the restless water of Bingham Creek; I dreamt almost every night of warty, jaundiced witches, lumbering ogres, and pallid ghosts with milky eyes. Yet the old fairy tale about Jack the giant-killer—a murderous, thieving boy who not only got away with his sins, but was actually rewarded for them—unsettled me in a way few things did. Whatever my mother may have heard that night, *I* heard a vengeful relative of Jack's slain giant, rousing to wrath somewhere up the canyon.

Agnes and I had just finished bathing in the claw-foot, cast-iron tub Father bought for Mama at Christmas. There was no privacy in our one-room house. Agnes and I shared a cramped bed on one side of the room, next to Hilda's crib; Father and Mama's bed was on the opposite wall, a few feet from the kitchen table. It was the only home Agnes and I knew, and we couldn't imagine not bumping into each other every time we hunched over to tie a shoe. The two of us used the same towel to dry ourselves before slipping into our matching night-shirts—cut and sewed from the same bolt of blue flannel by Mama—and the smell of rye bread, fried onions, and boiled cabbage was still in the air from supper, three hours before.

"Oh," Agnes said, cocking her head. "I hear it now, too, Mama."

The winter cold was slithering like rattlesnakes through every crack in the walls and floors that night, and I tugged on gray wool socks and listened to the strange rumbling in the dark world beyond our walls. The only light in the room aside from the fire in the woodstove was from two candles on the kitchen table, flickering in the frigid draft blowing through the house. We lived in the Carr Fork area of Bingham with all the other Swedes, and nobody in Carr Fork had electricity. (Nor indoor plumbing, for that matter: For baths, Aggie and I had to cart in a few buckets from the outdoor water pump that Mama then heated on the stove.)

"The giant's getting closer," I whimpered.

Agnes rolled her eyes. "There's no such thing as—"

"HUSH!" Mama cried, rising from the rocking chair, and it bronco-bucked on the floor behind her.

The entire population of Bingham, Utah, lived in a deep,

narrow canyon in the Oquirrh Mountains, and all of us—fifteen thousand bipedal moles in a massive nest—were stuffed down together, in the earth. Ramshackle wooden houses, tenements, and stores all piled on top of each other, lining both sides of the canyon walls, clear to the rim. The Kennecott Copper mine was at one end of the seven-mile-long canyon, and the only reason for Bingham's existence. The canyon itself was less than a city block wide, so every time a new house was built, it went to the end of the line like a naughty child, simply because there was no other place for it.

Father had come home for dinner that night, but he'd gone out again to play cards with his younger brother Johan, and their friends. Mama had begged him not to drink any of Johan's bootleg gin. She feared he'd go blind from the stuff, like Cotter Jones who lived two houses down from us. Father was no stranger to hooch, but he was also no Cotter Jones, who spent every waking moment of his life sucking at the teat of a dented tin flask he carried around in a hip pocket. Father was at least fully sober every Sunday, and rarely came home drunk from his card games, though his breath smelled like fermented pine from the juniper berries in the gin.

"Mama?" Agnes asked, now frightened herself. "What's wrong?"

"Everything's fine," Mama murmured, staring hard-eyed at the door, but even Agnes knew she was lying.

Until then, it had been just a normal day. Father got up for work early in the morning, same as always, at four A.M.—he worked a ten-hour shift in the copper mine, six days a week—and Mama got up, too, to make his breakfast. They spoke softly, trying not to wake my sisters and me, but they needn't have bothered. We never failed to hear everything.

"That's the last of the sugar," Mama said, pouring coffee in his thermos. "If you want more before Friday, we'll have to ask Fergus for credit."

Father was paid weekly. He gave his money to Mama and she ran the house. They bickered regularly over how little sugar she allowed him; she considered it a luxury, but Father had a sweet tooth and became irritable when none was left for his morning coffee.

"We're broke already?" His chair scraped on the wooden floor. "How come?"

Mama sighed. "Isaac needed new shoes. His toes were poking out of the old ones."

Before she became Mrs. Magnus Dahl, Mama's name was Hilda Gwozdek. Her folks and five ignorant, brooding siblings also lived in the canyon, but in the Highland Boy area with the rest of the Poles. Father always said Mama only married him to get away from her priggish mother and her short-tempered father, and there was at least a little truth to that: Mama undoubtedly loved Father for himself, but she loved him even more for not being a Gwozdek.

"That boy's growing too fast," Father said. I had my head under the covers, but I knew he was looking at me. "He needs new clothes every damn day."

"You want me to bind his feet like a Japanese girl? Make him stay small forever?"

"You betcha." Father's voice was a rumbling growl, but I didn't need to see his face to know he was smiling. "So long as there's sugar in my coffee."

"Agnes is growing out of her clothes, too, by the way."

"So? Just give her a potato sack and let her run barefoot."

Agnes could never tell when Father was joking. She huffed indignantly beside me in bed, and I elbowed her to keep her quiet; she huffed louder and elbowed me back.

"How come you get new clothes and I don't?" she hissed.

"It's a *joke*, dummy," I hissed back, rubbing my rib cage.

"Oh."

"Go to sleep, the pair of you," Mama ordered.

Father left for work and Mama returned to bed for a while, then rose again to get Agnes and me ready for school. Agnes got swatted for dawdling when Mama told her to get dressed, and she was still pouting when Mama kissed us and shoved us out the door. As usual, my best friend, Bo, was waiting on the porch, smiling as if somebody had just told him the funniest joke ever, even though his nose was running and his lips were blue from the wind.

"How many times have I told you not to stand outside in the cold, Bo Larsson?" Mama snapped. "Use the brain the good Lord gave you and come in the house next time, hear?"

"Yes, Mrs. Dahl," Bo stammered, teeth chattering.

She reached out in exasperation and roughly tugged his cap over his ears. "You're lucky you still have all your fingers and toes, child," she said. "Run along now, all of you."

We obeyed, Agnes dragging her feet as a form of protest until we were well out of Mama's sight, then she brightened and sped by us. She pretended to dislike Bo, but not even Agnes could pull off a ruse like that. Bo was by far the most handsome boy we knew—his dimpled, freckled face and big green eyes made every girl in town dote on him, including my sister—but more than that, he was also the best-natured soul on earth, and there was nobody in the canyon who didn't adore him.

"You don't need to be afraid to come in the house, Bo," I told him. "Mama won't bite."

He flushed. I couldn't blame him for being scared: Everybody was scared of my mother. She wasn't mean—far from it— but she had a tongue in her head and wasn't shy of using it. (Agnes was sounding more like her all the time, and I dreaded the day the pair of them teamed up on me, one per ear.) Still, Mama loved Bo, just like the rest of us, and I think it bothered her to know he couldn't see that.

"You have any of your Valentine's candy left?" I asked. "Agnes stole all mine."

"I didn't either!" Agnes yelled over her shoulder.

Being different genders, my sister and I weren't identical twins, of course, but we may as well have been: We both had blond hair, blue eyes, thin faces, and square chins. We also liked a lot of the same things—books, music, stories, puzzles, card games—so people were surprised that we squabbled as much as we did. Part of it was simple jealousy: I was annoyed that she was smarter than me, and she resented that most people liked me better than her. I suspect the main reason we butted heads all the time, however, was that we were so much alike, and both of us enjoyed nothing more than yanking each other's chain.

Bo dug in the pocket of his thin brown coat and gave me a Tootsie Roll. He was shorter than me by a couple of inches, but I was skinny as a fish line and he was stocky and powerful. He already had a hint of his father's massive shoulders—his daddy, Sven, worked in the mine with Father, and Father said he'd never met a stronger man—as well as the beginning of Sven's barrel chest and thick calves. Bo could carry me on his back for blocks, and if I was dumb enough to wrestle him, I'd end up facedown in the dirt and hogtied before I even knew how I got there.

Agnes drifted back, staring at the Tootsie Roll I'd just unwrapped. "Can I have half?"

"Sure." I popped the whole thing in my mouth and stuck out my tongue to show it to her.

"You're a *jackass*, Isaac," she said, running ahead again.

"You should be nicer to your sister," Bo said mildly.

"She should be nicer to me." We stepped around a drift of snow in front of Fergus's General Store and a dried horse turd hit me in the face: Agnes had deadly aim. I stumbled and fell, but Bo caught me before I hit the ground.

"Dang you, Aggie!" I sputtered. She was already twenty feet ahead, laughing her fool head off.

I wiped my face with snow, swearing. A clump of slush had wormed its way inside my coat collar, too, and was wiggling down my chest, beneath my shirt. I could tell Bo was trying not to laugh and I almost said something mean, then realized he wouldn't think of laughing if I hadn't deserved it. He helped clean my face, his mittens gentle on my cheeks and forehead.

"I'll get even with her," I muttered, glaring after Aggie.

"You sure are a slow learner," he answered.

Our schoolhouse was small because it was only for the twenty or so kids who lived in the Carr Fork area of Bingham. There were almost a dozen other schools in other parts of the canyon—Highland Boy, Lark, Dinkeyville, Frog Town, Markham, Freeman, Heaston Heights, Copper Heights, Terrace Heights—but none of them, save for the main school in Bingham proper, was much bigger than ours. Since we were mostly Swedes in Carr Fork, there was a disproportionate number of blond heads in the room when our caps and hats came off. Bo was a vivid exception to the general rule: His hair was the color of an orange peel.

We sat side by side at our desks, as always, with Agnes directly in front of us, and the only thing out of the ordinary I remember happening that entire school day was when Erik Kalberg—a hapless boy with a lazy eye and a stutter—dropped his pencil in front of Agnes's desk and bent down to fetch it, attempting to peek up her skirt. The toe of her shoe caught him squarely on the forehead, sending him sprawling at our teacher's feet. Mrs. Sundberg made them both stand with their backs to the class, in separate corners of the room; Agnes kept glowering at me over her shoulder, feeling sorely ill-used and expecting me to do something about it.

I held up my hand. "Mrs. Sundberg?"

"Yes, Isaac?"

"I think Agnes would learn her lesson a whole lot faster if you put a bag over her head."

The class's laughter and my sister's outrage were equally gratifying, but the pleasure was short-lived. I saw Bo sadly shaking his head as Mrs. Sundberg dragged me from my chair to another corner of the room.

Other random memories from that day:

Bo walking Agnes and me home after school, then leaving for his own house as soon as our feet touched the boards of our porch; my baby sister Hilda's greedy blue eyes, coveting a wooden top spinning across the kitchen table between my hands; Mama teaching Agnes and me how to make *köttbullar*—meatballs with minced beef and pork, butter and black pepper—and letting us help her knead the dough for her crusty rye bread and cut up some cabbage and onions for supper; Agnes and I doing our homework at the table as the bread baked in the oven; Father coming home from work, tired and snappish, but cheering up after eating; Mama telling Agnes to never bother with a man before his stomach was full; Mama and Father arguing about him going out again to play cards; Agnes and I reading by candlelight until Mama made us stop, fearing for our eyes; Mama heating water for our bath; Agnes and I splashing each other in the tub as Mama sang to Hilda; three or four young Poles in the street outside, yelling and clowning in their blurred, baffling language as they passed our house, their voices fading as they made their way home, no doubt to Highland Boy.

Just another day in Bingham, Utah.

The rumble in the canyon grew louder, then all-encompassing, insupportable. Mama, still clasping Hilda in one arm, yelled something I couldn't hear, then fiercely seized my shoulder with her free hand and shoved me toward the door. In a panic, I ran smack into Aggie, still standing by the tub, and accidentally knocked her into the damn thing. I tried to help her out but just fell in on top of her, bruising my thigh on one rim of the tub and banging my head against the other. We'd already drained the bathwater but the cast-iron surface was still wet. I cried out in pain as Mama leaned over us with Hilda, screaming, "Get out, get out!" But before we could regain our feet, the world ended.

A mountain of snow ripped through the walls and ceiling of our home. Mama and Hilda vanished from sight as the tub was lifted on what felt like the back of a whale; it flipped end over end, Agnes and I tumbling around inside in a mad jumble of limbs, darkness, and snow, unable to hear ourselves scream. I caught a brief glimpse of a crescent moon, far overhead, and knew we were somehow outside; the moon disappeared, reappeared, and disappeared again, all in the space of a few heartbeats. God only knows how long this horrific carnival ride lasted—in retrospect, it couldn't have been more than fifteen seconds, but it felt like an eternity—yet it ended as abruptly as it had started: one second we were spinning out of control, the next we were completely still, and on solid ground again.

Entombed in an upside-down bathtub.

The avalanche, hungry for destruction, thundered away from wherever it had left us, and only then could I hear Agnes speaking. I couldn't see her or anything else, yet I could feel her arms wrapped tightly around my ribs, so tightly I was aware of her heart beating next to mine, much as it must have when we shared Mama's womb.

"Are you hurt?" she asked, shaking me. "Isaac? Are you hurt?"

I was in shock, but her frantic voice brought me to my senses. I had blood in my mouth—I'd bitten my tongue—and from the wetness on the front of my nightshirt it seemed I'd peed myself, too, but other than that I was more or less intact.

"I'm okay," I gasped. We couldn't sit upright so we were forced to stay lying down. "What about you?"

"My ankle hurts."

For her to say anything I knew it was bad. Agnes complained about everything in life except physical pain. When she was smaller she got her hand caught in a door, snapping two fingers, and she barely even winced.

I shoved at the sides and bottom of the tub, knowing we'd never budge it. It outweighed both of us put together. I suddenly realized we were buried alive, under God only knew how many feet of snow, and my panic, on the ebb since Agnes spoke to me, returned with a vengeance.

"Mama?" My scream was deafening in the confines of our metal coffin. "Mama, WE'RE HERE!"

Agnes yelled, too, but after a couple of minutes she fell silent and made me stop as well. We listened intently for any noise aside from our own breathing but heard nothing.

"Nobody's there," Agnes said hoarsely.

"Shush. Mama will come."

She didn't argue, but I could hear her sniffle and knew what she was thinking. We'd both seen Mama and Hilda swallowed by a white monster. I began crying, too.

"What do you think happened to Father?" Agnes asked, her voice hitching.

Uncle Johan—Father's clownish, happy-go-lucky, nineteen-year-old brother—lived alone in a small shack a couple of blocks away from us, which was why his home was the usual gathering place for card games and drinking. I couldn't imagine he and Father had fared any better than us when the slide hit, but then I remembered that one side of Johan's house butted up against a ridge of rock, right in the snow's path, which might've served as a shield from the worst of the avalanche. It was a faint chance, but still something, and I told Agnes so.

"No," she said. Her voice was grim in the darkness. "It got them, too."

Her breath caught in pain. Both of us were terribly cold—our hair, still wet from our bath, had ice crystals in it, and the urine on my nightshirt was freezing as well; I couldn't keep my teeth from chattering. I pulled her close, and we listened hopelessly for signs of life outside our shell. I don't know how long we lay there, saying nothing, but my feet and hands were numb and I had drifted into a deep, nearly impenetrable sleep when I felt Agnes pinching my arm, again and again.

"Quit, Aggie," I mumbled, "that hurts." I couldn't seem to wake up.

"Someone's out there," she croaked. "Help," she called out weakly. She sounded like she had sand in her throat. "Help!"

I shook my head, trying to rouse myself, and finally heard what she had: men's shouting voices, muffled by snow and distance, but definitely there.

"We're here!" I cried, managing more volume than Agnes. "Help us, please help us!"

There was an interminable silence, then the blessed sound of shovels plunging into snow. Agnes and I, alert again but cold beyond belief, banged on the tub with our fists and kept up a rolling broadside of screaming. At last a shovel struck our tomb, tolling it like a bell, and a moment later the lip of the tub at our feet lifted, inch by inch, then the whole thing was heaved aside by a group of men, standing around in the dim glow of a kerosene lamp. I couldn't make out the faces of any of our rescuers.

"It's Magnus Dahl's twins," someone said, then raised his voice and called to another group of men half a block away. "Hey, Johan, it's your brother's kids!"

A dark, thin, familiar form lurched toward us through chest-deep snow, followed closely by someone much more thickset. "Oh, thank God!" Uncle Johan said, stumbling into the lantern light with Sven Larsson, Bo's daddy, right behind him. Johan lifted me in his arms as Sven draped a coat around Aggie. "Where's your mother? Where's Hilda? Do you know?"

I was shaking so badly I couldn't talk. I sobbed with relief as he hurried back through the narrow lane he'd created to get to us, rushing toward warmth and shelter with Sven right at his heels, carting Agnes. I tried to tell Johan what happened but nothing came out of my mouth.

"The snow got Mama and the baby," Agnes said. "She tried to get us out of the house but Isaac and I fell in the tub."

Over Johan's shoulder I saw Sven Larsson half turn without slowing; I heard his powerful voice ordering the rescue parties to hurry up and keep searching for Mama and Hilda.

"Where's Father?" I finally managed to stammer through clacking teeth.

Johan didn't answer. The heavens had burst open that night, like a piñata, spilling stars all over the sky, and I tilted back to see his face in their light. There were tears on his cheeks, and a cold hand squeezed my heart. Watching Sven Larsson carrying Agnes reminded me there was someone else I loved unaccounted for.

"Bo?" I rasped. "Where's Bo?"

Sven gave me a reassuring smile. "Bo's fine, Isaac. The slide took our house but we got out in time. He and his mother are both safe."

I must've lost consciousness then, because the next thing I remember is waking in a large room full of people, sleeping on cots. I was nestled in stiff cotton sheets with a thick wool blanket over me, and I was blessedly warm; someone had dressed me in a clean nightshirt and clean socks as well, but the sleeves of the shirt were four or five inches longer than my arms. There was a smell of stale coffee in the air, and ammonia, but I had no idea where I was, and it was too dark—in spite of candlelight coming from an adjacent room—to make out anything that might help me get my bearings.

"Aggie?" I called out softly. Aside from a handful of nights I'd spent at Bo's house, I'd never slept in a bed without my sister beside me, and I was frightened. I raised my voice as much as I dared. "Aggie, where are you?"

"I'm here," came her whispered response. She was in the cot to my right, a foot away.

I relaxed slightly. "Where's Uncle Johan?"

"Looking for Father and Mama." She paused. "He's been gone a long time."

I didn't dare ask how long.

An older woman's voice over near the door interrupted us. "Hush now, children." Whoever she was, she sounded kind, but she spoke like someone used to obedience. "Other folks is tryin' to sleep."

I subsided for a moment, but I couldn't stay still. "What about Bo?" I murmured to Aggie. "Have you seen him?"

"Hi, Isaac." It was Bo himself, somewhere to my left. "I'm here."

I started to say hi back, but the older woman by the door cleared her throat and I bit my lip to keep from antagonizing her. A moment later I was startled by the silhouette of Agnes, standing by my cot. I pulled back my blanket and made room for her, and she crawled in next to me. Her right ankle was wrapped in some sort of splint.

"I'm really scared, Isaac," she whispered. "Are you scared, too?"

I nodded into her shoulder, unable to speak. A short, stocky figure appeared on the opposite side of the cot from where Agnes had materialized; it was Bo. For the first time in his life, he was probably finding it difficult to smile, and I was glad I couldn't see his face. I lifted the blanket for him, too—Aggie and I curled up tighter to make room—and he joined us, crowding out every bit of the remaining space on the cot.

"Sorry 'bout your folks," he murmured. His breath smelled like hot cocoa. "And Hilda, too."

I started to cry, and a sob shook Agnes's whole body. Bo put his arm over us and left it there until we both quieted again. I don't know how long he stayed with us before going back to his own bed, but the last thing I remember that night was the feel of his lips, dry and moth-light, brushing my forehead.

When I woke in the morning, Agnes was still beside me, and Uncle Johan was sitting at the foot of the cot. In the light I was finally able to figure out we were in the back room of Fergus's General Store, packed in with a few dozen other people who'd lost their homes. Johan didn't have to say anything about Father, Mama, and Hilda; we could see his despair in the shadows under his eyes, and the way he kept turning away from us as he spoke. He told us other things, though: how the avalanche had killed thirty-nine people for certain, but at least that many were still missing; how the snow had dropped from a thousand feet up in the mountains before cutting a deadly swath through the canyon; how Cotter Jones, blinded by alcohol and stumbling around the street in front of his home when the slide hit, was carried on its crest for half a mile, but had nothing wrong with him save for a few bruises.

We heard later that the avalanche had tossed Father on the floor in Uncle Johan's house and crushed the life out of him. Uncle Johan was closer to the door and got out before the slide hit; he was still buried in snow but somehow managed to fight his way to the surface before suffocating. Mama and Hilda weren't so lucky; they were found together right where Aggie and I last saw them. They were both blue and frozen solid, Mama clutching Hilda to her breast.

At the time, Aggie and I weren't aware how miraculous our escape had been; the bathtub that almost became our coffin not only saved us from the mortal weight of the snow, but also allowed us to breathe until we were found.

When Agnes and I were too young for school, Mama used to sit us down at the table with graham crackers and orange juice, to keep us out of mischief whenever she needed to wash her hair in the sink. It was a weekly ritual, every Friday morning, but once we started attending school, we never saw her do it again, never saw her towel her head off, nor comb out her long, lustrous hair. I used to love watching the spill of all that yellow down her back, loved watching her tilt her head side to side to get the water from her ears, loved the sound of her humming as she cleared the crumbs from the table when Agnes and I finished our snack.

That's the clearest memory I have of my mother, and if it ever fades from my mind, I can bring it all back, simply by dunking a graham cracker in orange juice, and letting it dissolve on my tongue like a holy wafer.

Father is harder to conjure. I have no magic tricks that allow me to see him so well. No pictures survived the avalanche, and no mementos, either, aside from a cheap pocket watch and an equally cheap wedding ring. The snow took everything else save his body and the clothes he was wearing. If I try hard enough, though, I can still sometimes hear the low, half-amused, half-annoyed rumble of his voice, and every so often the smell of gin brings him back to me. Also the smell of sulfur: The copper mine reeked of sulfur, and it soaked into Father's clothes.

I hardly remember Hilda at all, because she was only a year and a half old when she died. She had blond hair, and a sweet smile, and she cried a lot. Aggie and I used to take turns holding her whenever Mama got tired of carting her around; she was fascinated with the buttons on my shirt and liked to tug at them with her chubby fingers.

Less than a month after the avalanche, Uncle Johan, Aggie, and I took a train to Oklahoma, where we had a cousin who'd agreed to take us in, in exchange for Johan's help in running a big wheat farm. All three of us were more than happy to get out of the canyon, but leaving Bo behind was nearly as painful as the death of my parents.

"Sure wish you didn't have to go," he said on the platform of the train station, right before we boarded. His eyes filled. "I'm gonna miss you something awful."

Bo was never afraid of saying exactly what he felt. I didn't want to cry in front of his folks and Johan, but my lower lip betrayed me by starting to tremble. "I wish you could come with us," I mumbled, staring at the ground.

Aggie was standing a couple of feet away, pretending to be absorbed by something on the front of her coat.

"Bye, Aggie," Bo said. "I'll miss you, too."

She looked away quickly, blinking hard. "So long, Bo. Don't be ridiculous."

I started crying in spite of myself and Bo put his arms around me. "Be nice to each other," he told both of us. Aggie started sniffling as well and edged a little closer.

"No promises," I croaked.

"Absolutely not," Aggie agreed.

Bo squeezed me tightly, then reached out and pulled Aggie into our hug. "We'll all be friends forever," he said into my neck.

"Sure we will," I said, and heard something suspiciously like a sob emerge from Aggie's throat before she broke free and darted up the train steps, not looking back. The conductor called the "All aboard," and Bo released me reluctantly and stepped away, his face wet. Johan said goodbye a final time to

Bo's folks, then took my hand and led me to our seats on the train. Aggie was by the window but I made her switch with me so I could wave to Bo on the platform. Aggie stayed seated at first, staring at her lap, but when the train began to pull out of the station, she hopped up to join me with a distressed grunt, crying as hard as I was. We pressed our faces against the glass and didn't budge a muscle until Bo disappeared from sight, his orange hair the last part of him we could make out in the distance. I was sure we'd never see him again.

Thank God I was wrong about that.

DAY TWO

May 21, 1934. Balko, Oklahoma.

I no longer believed in giants, but I believed in Hell.

I woke up when Bo sat next to me on the edge of the bed. I'd dozed off in spite of the stifling air in the house.

"I'm gonna check on Samson," he said. He blew his nose on a hanky—his snot was black, just like everybody's—then dabbed Vaseline in his nostrils before wrapping his face with an old pillowcase, leaving no skin exposed save around his eyes. "I'll be right back."

He was wearing boots, Levi's, and a light blue, long-sleeved shirt. The back of his shirt was soaked with sweat—the temperature was over a hundred that day—but he knew better than to go outdoors without covering up. Blowing dirt stung like fury on bare skin, raising welts and blisters. I was only wearing boxer trunks at the moment, but I was still boiling. All the windows and doors were closed, as they'd been for most of the past two years, and though it did little to keep the dust out, the window frames were also draped with wet sheets. Our farm was close to town, so we were lucky to have electricity for lights and a fan. Most of the people we knew used kerosene lanterns in their houses so they could see in the middle of the day.

I lifted a damp dishrag from my nose and mouth (we'd used up our weekly ration of filter masks from the Red Cross) and struggled to sit up, wanting to go with him, but the second my feet hit the floor I starting coughing again. He made me lie back down, cautiously touching my shoulder before easing me back against the pillow. We'd learned to be wary when the wind was blowing. The dry, charged air generated so much static that the jolt we got from touching somebody else at the wrong time was often potent enough to knock us down. Metal was even worse: God help the reckless soul who grasped a stove handle or a doorknob with naked fingers.

"Stay put," he ordered. "The wind's too riled up for you to go outside." He replaced the dishrag on my face. "Besides, Aggie may need something before I get back, and Johan ain't here."

"He's in town?"

He nodded. We both paused to listen to Aggie's breathing, loud and rasping, from the room across the hall. I was grateful she and I weren't still sharing a room like we had before Bo came to live with us six years before. Johan and our cousin Sam had converted a utility closet into a tiny bedroom for Aggie, so she could have privacy and Bo could bunk with me.

"Johan's nuts, and so are you," I wheezed. "Nobody should be outside today."

He shook his head stubbornly. "It's just a mite frisky. It ain't a full-on black roller." Black rollers were towering walls of blowing dirt and sand, hundreds and even thousands of feet high. "I need to make sure Samson's okay."

Samson was our horse, and the last surviving animal on the farm. He wouldn't last long; the dust storms were killing him, just as they'd killed all our other livestock. Bo was determined not to put the poor beast down, though, until there was no other choice. We all loved Samson, but he was crazy about him. Barring a miracle, however, nothing would save him. The dust got into everything, no matter how many doors we taped shut or cracks in the walls we crammed with newspaper. Animals we'd cut open after they'd died were stuffed with sand, and even Samson—once a fine, strong, beautiful, chestnut draft pony, now just a pitiful sack of bones—couldn't keep on going forever with a bellyful of Oklahoma's finest red prairie dirt. I didn't like to think it, but I assumed Aggie's and my insides weren't much better off than Samson's, judging from all the black crud that kept coming out of us whenever we had a coughing fit.

"Did Uncle Johan say when he'd be back?" I asked, knowing there was no point in talking about the horse.

"Before dinner. He said he was gonna bring us meat tonight for sure."

I snorted. "That's what he always says."

"Yeah, well, maybe this time we'll get lucky."

I knew he was smiling behind the cloth on his face. He didn't smile as much as when we were little, but he was still a lot more cheerful than any sane person had a right to be. I told him the heavy clothes he was wearing were roasting his brain, and I was only half joking; in this heat none of us ever wore a stitch beyond what was strictly necessary for decency, and just looking at him all bundled up made me squirm with sympathy. He laughed and told me to get some rest and I listened as he walked down the hall, the heels of his boots rapping out a light cadence on the wooden floor. When he opened the front door, the wind rose to a screech that would've put an Apache war cry to shame; he closed the door behind him, muting the scream.

"You okay, Aggie?" I called across the hall, knowing she was awake.

"Never better," she called back, hacking up her lungs like a ninety-year-old, three-pack-a-day smoker instead of a willowy sixteen-year-old girl. "Don't ask ridiculous questions."

When Agnes, Uncle Johan, and I left Bingham Canyon and moved to Balko, Oklahoma, life treated us well for a while. True, our cousins Sam and Sally Becklus—devout, childless Lutherans—were humorless souls, yet they were also decent and generous, taking us in with no conditions save one, best expressed by what Sally said to Aggie and me on the first morning she came to wake us.

"Time to get up, y'all, and earn your keep."

It was a fair bargain on the face of it, and not even Aggie grumbled. We were grateful for the roof over our heads, far away from the lowering, deadly mountains of Utah. We also soon grew to love Oklahoma for itself. The vast, stark openness of the prairie under a full moon was like nothing we'd ever experienced, and when the wheat in Sam's fields was nearly grown but not yet harvested, the flat, somewhat barren world around us was transformed by the summer sun into a sea of gold from horizon to horizon, capped by a sky so clear and blue it made my heart ache.

According to Uncle Johan, he and Father had grown up together with Sam Becklus in Sweden. (He also told us Sam used to be a whole lot more fun before he married Sally.) The young couple had seen a newspaper advertisement saying there was cheap farmland for sale in the United States, in out-of-the-way places like Oklahoma and Texas, but Father and Johan, coming through Ellis Island a year after Sam and Sally, opted for the mines of Utah instead.

Anyway, when our parents were killed in the avalanche, Johan was determined to get Aggie and me out of Bingham and start a better life elsewhere, preferably in a mountain-free corner of creation. He wrote to Sam to ask if he could use help running his wheat farm, and Sam told him we'd be more than welcome, especially since his spread was doing so well, he couldn't keep up with all the work. He also mentioned Sally might ask every now and then for "a helpin' hand from the little 'uns," and Aggie and I assured Johan we'd be happy to pitch in.

It turned out, however, that "a helpin' hand" meant something a bit different to Sally than what we had in mind.

Sally was a thin, leathery woman with wispy brown hair and an incomprehensible accent, half-Swedish singsong and half-Oklahoma drawl. She was not overly fond of any of the seven deadly sins, but sloth was her chief bugaboo, so Aggie and I were subjected to an endless litany of cleaning, gardening, canning, mowing, painting, and animal husbandry. School was the only respite we ever got from physical labor, and Sally begrudged every second we spent away from the house.

Johan was tall and bony like Father, and he sounded like him, too, with his low voice and quiet way of talking. We used to catch him standing outside in all kinds of weather, staring up at a bird in the sky, or at some rodent or insect on the ground, and when we'd ask him what he was doing he'd say, "Betcha that falcon's gonna fly clean 'round the sun someday," or "S'pose that there rabbit likes oatmeal?" No matter how worn out he was in the evenings, he always came to our room to say good night, ruffling my hair and kissing Aggie on the cheek. I knew he didn't much care for the chore regimen Sally made us do, but he told us she meant no harm. He said she'd been raised by a family who thought work was the only thing on earth that mattered, and leisure was reserved solely for the kingdom of God.

"But don't y'all worry," he reassured us in a whisper, every night for the first few months we lived in Balko. "We'll get our own little corner of heaven soon as I squirrel away a good-sized nest egg."

Unfortunately, Johan's nest egg never came close to hatching, and he eventually stopped making promises. The farm was prosperous enough to see us all clothed and fed—and even for Sam to share a small percentage of the profits with Johan—but Johan could no more save money than a chipmunk could do calculus. Aggie and I didn't know it back then, but we eventually learned there was a house of "ill repute" on a run-down ranch a few miles away, and Johan went there at least once a week to see a lady friend. All he told any of us at the time was that he was courting a "sweet ol' country gal" and could he please borrow Sam's truck to go visit her. I'm pretty sure Sam had an inkling of what was going on, but Sally certainly didn't. If she had, she would've chased Johan out of the county and salted every inch of earth he'd ever defiled with his libidinous feet.

Anyway, this bucolic pastime of Johan's must've been costly, because he never had a penny to spare. Sam gave Johan his wages every Saturday morning, and by Saturday night his wallet was empty. Not even Aggie could find it in her heart to condemn him, though, after we discovered where his money went. He was an odd, randy duck, true enough, but he was also unfailingly gentle, uncomplaining, and openhearted. Nor did he ever truly lie about his "sweet ol' country gal." He simply failed to mention he was paying for her company. And though I never met her, I suspected her appeal wasn't all about sex. Johan must've been desperate for a reminder that not all women were like Sally, whose sour disposition would've induced Don Juan to self-castrate. Every time Sam told Johan it was time for him to settle down and get a wife like Sally, a look came over Johan's face that could only be interpreted as mortal terror. Aggie's secret nickname for Sally was "Sally Saltpeter," and the first time Johan heard Aggie call her that, he laughed so hard he bruised a rib.

Almost two years to the day after we moved to Balko, my best friend back in Utah, Bo Larsson, became an orphan, too.

His folks were killed in a grisly accident, their horse-drawn wagon plunging off a mountain bridge. Having no living relatives, Bo was taken in by a minister until other arrangements could be made. Bo didn't much care for the idea of waiting around for a foster family, so he snuck on a freight train headed east, getting off again two days later, a few miles from Balko. Aggie and I pretended to be as shocked as everybody else when he appeared on our doorstep, but I was the one who'd told him to come.

I'd missed Bo almost as much I'd missed Father and Mama. Ever since we'd been separated, we'd kept tabs on each other with weekly postcards. His handwriting left a lot to be desired, but puzzling out his scrawls was always worth the effort.

"Howdy, Isaac," said the first postcard he sent, a few days after we'd left Utah and got to Balko. "Remember me? It's Bo, your buddy with red hair."

I wrote him back at once and told him not to be ridiculous: His hair was orange, not red, and of course I remembered him. He responded right away and said I sounded like Aggie: Her love of the word *ridiculous* was rubbing off on me.

"Howdy, Isaac," said another postcard six weeks later. "How tall are you now? I'm 4'5" and weigh 107 lbs." He kept me current on the important events in Bingham Canyon: who got in trouble at school, whose daddy got maimed in the mine, what Ellie Cederstrom did with Tim Olvin behind the post office when they thought nobody could see them. "Howdy, Isaac," he wrote. "Today Peader Gylling threw a rock at a rabbit. I made him promise not to do it again."

That one really startled me. Peader Gylling was a toadish, thick-skulled bully—four years older than Bo and a lot bigger—and the only way Bo could've made him promise anything was to beat him up. Bo getting mad enough to fight anybody was completely out of character. Then again, he had a serious soft spot for animals and couldn't bear to see one mistreated, so I guess I shouldn't have been surprised. Nor, when I thought about it, should I have been surprised at the outcome: Peader had likely found himself bloody and beaten in record time. Pound for pound, nobody on the planet was stronger than Bo Larsson, nor less afraid of other boys.

Girls, however, were another matter.

"Howdy, Isaac," he wrote. "I miss you and Aggie a lot, but don't tell Aggie."

I didn't say a word to my sister, but I didn't have to. She read everything Bo wrote, since one of her chores was to go to the post office every day and get the mail. She pretended not to be interested in anything he had to say and would toss his post-cards at me with a disdainful flick of her wrist, muttering something like "Bo gets more bizarre every day," but she'd always be hiding a smile when she said it.

"Howdy, Isaac," Bo wrote, in the final hurried postcard he sent, telling me how his parents had been killed, and how he was staying with the minister of the Lutheran church; he said he was waiting to hear about a foster home. "Minister Huss says I can't come live with you and Aggie, but I want to. Can I?"

I asked Johan right away, who asked Sam and Sally. Sam wasn't opposed, but Sally balked. Family was one thing, she said, but taking in a strange child was another, so eventually Sam and Johan were forced to say no to me, just to keep peace in the house. I promptly wrote a postcard to Bo, care of the Lutheran minister: "Hey, Bo. You bet you can live with us." It never occurred to me to worry about how a penniless ten-year-old boy would manage to travel several hundred miles on his own. "When can you get here?"

I gave Aggie the postcard and swore her to secrecy, and she mailed it the next day. Bo said later that Minister Huss told him he couldn't just let him leave on my say-so; he'd need to talk things over with the authorities. Bo ran away that night and made his way east, slipping onto one freight train after another like a seasoned hobo until he at last reached the Oklahoma Panhandle.

He showed up on our porch on a cold Saturday morning in mid-March, exhausted, dirty, half-frozen, and starving. Sally was the one who opened the door, so his initial welcome was perhaps less than what he might've hoped for. Yet when Aggie and I saw him standing on our porch—taller and more sunken-eyed than we'd last seen him, but still with the same perpetual, happy smile—we virtually trampled Sally in our haste to get to him, both of us bawling like a pair of mooncalves. Sally's eyes were oddly misty when we finally let Bo go, and I knew then it was only a matter of time before she changed her mind about letting him stay.

Not even Sally Saltpeter was immune to Bo Larsson.

Six years after Bo came to live with us, our farm was in ruins, just like everybody else's. We were on the eastern edge of what the whole country had started calling "No Man's Land." Dust took to the sky every time the wind kicked up and dumped oceans of black, stinging, choking sand all over creation, burying those of us who were too poor, stubborn, or stupid to leave the Panhandle. The only money we had to live on was a small check the government sent us, in exchange for signing a contract to not plant wheat for a while. Uncle Johan signed the contract—forging Sally's signature—to get the money; Sam Becklus was two years dead of melanoma by then, and Sally, broken by grief, had retired to her bedroom.

She barely spoke anymore, or ate more than a few mouthfuls of whatever food we took her. Were it not for the creeping, merciless invasion of her home by her old nemesis, dirt, she might've eventually gotten over losing Sam, but the combined strain was too much for her. When the storms blotted out the sky, we'd end up with bucketfuls of the stuff in our house, and her beautiful white walls and shining floors turned black and gritty. After fighting a losing battle for months on end, she finally figured out there was nothing she could do to make her world look nice again, and the fight went out of her.

The government money kept us alive for a time, but it wasn't enough to get us out of Oklahoma. It might've done so initially, but after Johan's "sweet ol' country gal" at the brothel ended up stealing more than half of it from his wallet and skedaddled to Atlanta, we had little choice but to wait out the storms.

Uncle Johan was back from town when I woke again. The wind had died down and he and Bo were talking in the kitchen, horsing around as usual—Johan always called Bo "Little Bo Peep," and made rhymes of his name ("Hey there, Bo, want a cuppa joe?"), and Bo would respond with "Wow, Johan, you're really giving old Longfellow a run for his money." I knew better than to hope for anything for dinner besides beans and cornbread, but just hearing Johan bang pots around made me long for more substantial fare. Ever since Sally withdrew from the world, Johan had done the cooking, and each day he went into town, trying to scrounge meat. Now and then he'd find somebody who'd give him a rabbit or a squirrel in exchange for a hoarded can of condensed milk or peaches, but most days we lived on beans, cornbread, and scraps of this or that.

I managed to get out of bed without having a coughing fit and shuffled across the hall to Aggie's cramped room. She was sitting in bed reading the school library's copy of *All Quiet on the Western Front*. The day before, it was *The Great Gatsby;* the day after would be something else. She always had a book in her hand, even when she fell asleep at night. So did I, for that matter; we both loved books, but she read them ten times faster.

"Hey," I said, stretching across the foot of her mattress. "I was still reading that."

"Hey yourself," she said, not bothering to move her feet out of my way or lift her nose from the story. "You can have it back in a couple of hours."

She was dressed in one of Johan's old sleeveless T-shirts and a pair of my boxer trunks; she said underpants for girls weren't half as comfortable. In the old days, Sally kept a sharp, critical eye on us and would've been scandalized by such a breach of decorum; by this point she wouldn't have noticed if we'd daubed ourselves with blood and sacrificed a virgin on a stone altar in the living room.

I flicked Aggie's ankle. "Ask next time before stealing books off my nightstand."

She glanced at me over the top of the book. Her face was drawn and pale but her eyes were just as bright as ever. "Sorry. You were sleeping and I didn't want to wake you."

Both of us sounded hoarse, but at least since the wind had subsided, we didn't need hankies on our faces and could talk without coughing. I lay on my back and stared at the rough plywood boards of her ceiling. The house had a crawlspace attic, thinly insulated and completely useless for keeping out the dust that snuck in through the roof.

"Think we'll be able to go to school tomorrow?" Aggie asked.

Our school was closed more often than not. Our teacher, Miss Hyatt—Balko's own personal canary in a coal mine—was the first to get sick every time the wind blew. Aggie and I usually recovered quickly once the dust from the storms settled, but Miss Hyatt took weeks to get back on her feet. She'd managed to open the school a few times in early May, but we hadn't had classes since the last huge storm tore through town two weeks ago.

"I doubt it." I wiped sweat from my eyes and wondered if we dared open a window. Aggie had an electric fan—the only one we owned—pointed straight at her bed, but all it did was blow hot air. "Besides, we've only got a week before summer vacation."

"Oh, yeah, vacation." She gave me a rare, wry smile. "Let's sail to Greece this year, shall we? I don't know about you, but I'm sick to death of Paris."

In our entire lives, we'd only been two places: Bingham, Utah, and Balko, Oklahoma. We were bored senseless with the sameness of our everyday lives and desperate to go somewhere new, having long since figured out that the ravening curiosity we shared for the outside world wasn't exactly a common trait in Balko. We'd been daydreaming for years about exotic places we'd read about in books—places with people who didn't look, speak, or dress like anybody we knew; places with cultural histories stretching back millennia instead of just a century or two; places with intriguing things like koala bears, or houseboats, or glaciers, or symphony orchestras, or baklava—anything, really, so long as we'd never seen, heard, felt, tasted, or smelled it before.

"Nah, not Greece," I said. "How about we go someplace colder this time? *Lots* colder, like Antarctica."

She nodded wearily, grin fading, and wiped her face with the hem of her T-shirt. Her hair, long and blond just like our mother's, was wet and oily, just like mine. "That works for me."

"Hallelujah," said Bo from the doorway, startling us. "You're both still alive."

He'd stripped out of the work clothes he'd had on earlier and was only wearing gray cotton drawers. He'd lost weight in the past couple of years—we all had—but he was still more muscular than me by far, with his dad's thick shoulders and forearms. Before the dust storms turned our world into a desert, he'd been a lot more modest around Aggie, but modesty was long gone, like green grass, baths, and farm ponds.

I rose up on my elbows. "Hey, Bo, whattaya know?"

He grinned. "Don't you start, too. Johan's rhymes are bad enough."

"What's for supper?" Aggie asked. "Fried chicken and gravy? Buttermilk biscuits?"

"Nah," I said. "Ham and sweet potatoes."

"Sorry, y'all." Bo's grin faltered; he was worried about us not getting enough to eat. "All we got is beans, but at least Johan snagged some butter tonight to go with them."

Bo blamed the lack of variety in our diet for Aggie's and my chronic lethargy—and it was certainly a contributing factor—but the toxic air quality was the real culprit; our lungs just weren't as hardy as Bo's, and for the past two years we'd felt like we were slowly suffocating to death. The days when the storms hit were exponentially worse, and it was all we could do to get out of bed.

"Really? What did he have to trade for butter?" Aggie asked. She made the mistake of setting my book where I could snatch it from her, and she got huffy. "Please, *please* tell me he traded Isaac."

"No such luck." Bo stepped over to the bed and we made room for him to stretch out between us. "He promised to share some propane with Mrs. Hill next winter."

We didn't have much propane left to share: We hadn't been able to afford to refill our tanks for months. Still, I wasn't too worried about what would happen when it was gone. Butter in our beans was well worth whatever it cost.

"Think we can open a window tonight?" I asked. "Aggie stinks something awful."

We all stank to high heaven, but Aggie was the only one who cared anymore. What little water we were able to get from our well by hand was strictly for drinking and cooking; our windmill was useless for pumping water because when a storm blew through it could rip the blades clean off, like a vicious little boy plucking off a grasshopper's wings. I'd grown so used to the reek of our unwashed bodies I barely noticed it, save for when I went outside and then came back into the caveman fug in our house.

Bo shook his head as Aggie launched a kick at me over his stomach. "Nah, better keep everything shut tight. The wind's calmed down, but I'd hate to get the pair of you coughing again."

"Dinner's ready," Uncle Johan said from the doorway. "Y'all havin' a party in here?"

Every time I saw Johan it saddened me. The past few years had aged him immeasurably; he was only twenty-six, but all the worry and hardship had taken a huge toll and he looked fifty. He'd always been lanky, but now he was skeletal, with a thick beard that was more white than blond. He was dressed like Aggie, in a sleeveless T-shirt and faded boxer trunks.

"Hey, Johan," I said. "Welcome to the Dahl family sweat lodge."

He grinned, then glanced down the hall toward Sally's room and called out, telling her dinner was ready. He did this every night, of course, but she never responded.

"Guess it's my turn for Sally duty," he said, sighing. We all traded off feeding Sally in her room—and cleaning up after her, as necessary.

"I'll do it, Johan," Bo said. "I don't mind."

"It'll be bad today," I reminded him. Due to the dust storm earlier, Sally wouldn't have gotten to the outhouse, and she wasn't always overly fastidious when she was forced to use her chamber pot. It was hard to believe she was the same woman who used to run us ragged to keep her house spotless.

"Isaac's right, Bo Peep," Johan said. "I'll tend her tonight. Too much falls on you, with Isaac and Aggie feelin' so poorly."

I felt my face flush, though I knew neither Johan nor Bo blamed us for being so useless much of the time. Johan was right, however; Bo was having to take up all the slack of whatever needed doing around the place, since Aggie and I were more or less deadweight if the wind was blowing, and the wind was almost always blowing. When the dust storms first started, we'd still been able to pull our weight, more or less, but the truth was we were getting weaker, day by day, and I'd recently begun having nightmares about my lungs filling with sand like the bottom half of an hourglass, until there was no room for a single grain more.

And then my rib cage would burst apart and I'd just blow away.

That night I told Bo I was sorry for being sick all the time. He had his back to me in our bed and didn't answer at first; I wondered if he'd fallen asleep, but then he yawned and rolled over. We'd shared a bed for years and weren't at all shy of each other—we often spooned as we slept—but in the present heat we were sleeping as far apart on the mattress as we could get.

"I don't mind," he said, sounding groggy. There was a full moon tonight, allowing me to see his serene, sleepy face. "I just wish you felt better."

"Me, too. I'm sick of being sick."

We'd finally opened all the windows in the house, but it made no difference. There was no wind outside—the only reason we could have the windows open—and the last few days had been just as hot out as in. Even in the middle of the night, the thermostat we kept by the kitchen window rarely registered less than ninety degrees.

"I wish we could move away," I told him.

"Where would we go?"

He was right, of course. Lots of people we knew had moved away—most drifting west—but from what we'd read in the newspapers or heard on the radio, there were precious few jobs elsewhere, either, and what little work there was didn't pay enough to live on.

"I don't know," I told him. "But someplace with water would be nice."

"It'll get better real soon, you'll see." He reached out and rested his hand lightly on my neck. "Just give it time."

He yawned again and closed his eyes; one second they were

pale and blinking in the moonlight, the next they vanished behind his eyelids. His breathing changed as he fell asleep—he always went to sleep all at once, just like that—but his hand
didn't move. His fingers were hot on my throat, but I didn't
mind.

Far from it.

I was in love with him, of course. I had been for years. I
knew I wasn't supposed to feel that way about another boy—in
Balko, Oklahoma, anyone suspected of "deviant tendencies"
was a complete pariah—but I couldn't help it. Unfortunately, it
wasn't quite the same for Bo. In the past year we'd messed
around sexually now and then, touching each other and even
jerking off together, but the last time we'd done it a couple of
months ago he'd asked if we could stop because it didn't feel
right to him. He told me he loved me but he wasn't really attracted to other guys; he said he wasn't comfortable with where
things were heading and didn't want to risk our friendship by
continuing. It hurt to hear him say this, of course, but if I was
being honest with myself, I knew what he meant: As we'd been
messing around, part of me could tell he was mostly just doing
it to make me happy. For himself, all he really wanted was the
steady, abiding, easy companionship we'd always had.

And while I still wished things were otherwise—and would
keep on wishing for a long time—I wasn't even that unhappy
about the situation, truly, once I got used to it. He was still as
affectionate as ever, maybe even more so, and he never made
me feel like there was anything wrong with me for liking boys.
And though we'd stopped doing the overtly sexual stuff, he still
slept with his arm across my chest all the time, or with his feet
intertwined with mine. The intimacy wasn't always easy—I
loved how close we were, but sometimes it made me horny almost past bearing, and frustrated as hell since I could never
have everything I wanted—yet most days I felt lucky for having so much.

*   *   *

"No school today," Aggie said, hanging up the kitchen phone.

Our phone service was scheduled to be cut off at the end of the month. We'd been able to hold on to a phone and electricity a bit longer than most—before the clouds dried up, our farm was one of the most lucrative in all of Beaver County—but now we, too, were being pushed back to the Stone Age. We'd set aside enough to keep our lights on for the next few months, but the time was coming all too soon when we'd be using candles and kerosene lamps again, just as we had in Utah.

Uncle Johan added a bit of milk and the last of the butter he'd gotten yesterday to the leftover cornbread, then mashed it up and divvied out the mixture amongst five bowls. "Okay, y'all, come and get it."

Bo picked up two of the bowls, one for himself and one for Sally, but I took Sally's from him and told him it was my turn. He asked if I was sure I was up to it and I said yes. For once the wind wasn't going full tilt and I felt fine. I was still a little weak, but at least I was able to breathe again, and I'd be damned if I was going to just sit around when I could finally help.

Sally was awake in bed, staring up at a picture near her dresser of a bearded, somewhat Swedish-looking Jesus, dolled up in outlandish green and purple robes, standing in a garden of pink and yellow flowers. The other walls of her room were dingy and bare.

"Morning, Sally." I sat beside her on the mattress. "The wind's not so bad today."

She didn't answer, of course, though her gray eyes did meet mine for a moment—a rare occurrence. I cradled both bowls of what Johan facetiously called "cornbread chowder" against my chest and took turns spooning the slop first into my mouth and then hers. She opened her mouth automatically and swallowed without pleasure, but at least she didn't spit it back up.

The window on the wall across from Jesus was still open—a

temporary miracle—but the room nevertheless reeked of urine and sweat. We tried our best to keep things clean, but it was impossible; even apart from the chamber pot in the corner of her room, there was no way to combat the general filth in the house, especially when Sally herself no longer gave a hoot. There was a heavy layer of dust on everything, from the wooden chair by her bedside to the dishes in the kitchen cupboards, but that was the least of the battle. If it weren't for us, she wouldn't have brushed her teeth or changed her sheets for the past year or more, and if it weren't for Aggie, she would've been wearing the same off-white nightie for the rest of eternity.

"No school today," I said. "Miss Hyatt's sick again."

"What day is it, Isaac?" Her husky whisper caught me by surprise; the spoon in my hand froze in midair.

"Monday," I said as casually as I could. She hadn't spoken in a month or more.

"Was there services yesterday?" she asked.

It figured the first thing she'd want to talk about after such a long silence would be religion. Until Sam died and the storms came, she'd never missed a single service at the Lutheran church, nor allowed the rest of us to miss one, either.

"No, ma'am. The wind was too bad, so Reverend Paul told everyone to stay home."

Her eyes flickered over my face then traveled back to Jesus. "Are ya still sayin' your prayers, Isaac?"

I hesitated. "No, ma'am."

She didn't even blink; in the past, such an admission from me would've earned a rap on the head from her knobby knuckles. "Well," she said, "guess I don't blame ya."

I didn't know how to respond. In the eight years we'd lived in Sally's home, I'd never heard her say anything remotely like this. Back when she used to speak, our conversations had been mainly limited to two things: what needed doing around the house, and all the ways Aggie and I (Bo was exempt from her tongue lashings) weren't living up to God's expectations.

"You feeling okay, Sally?" I asked.

She shrugged. "I been better."

"Why don't you come out to the kitchen this morning? It might perk you up a bit to have some company."

"Thank you, no." She shook her head, refusing another spoonful of the soppy cornbread. "I believe I'll stay put."

I ate the rest of my portion; what she'd left uneaten of hers I'd share with the others. I looked at her again when I finished and was startled to find her looking me up and down like she hadn't done in forever, and I suddenly felt self-conscious. Two years before, no matter how hot a day it was, I never would've dreamed of walking around the house in my underwear; she would've dragged me down the hall by the ear and stuffed me into clothes faster than I could blink.

"When'd you start gettin' so tall and handsome?" she asked. "You look just like your father. Some lucky girl's gonna snatch you up any day now."

I felt my face get warm and changed the subject quickly; I asked her if she ever missed her home in Sweden.

"I surely do." She turned her head when a fly buzzed against the screen of her window, trying to escape. "I'd go there right this second if I could. Sam and me never, *never* shoulda come to this terrible place."

It was hard to argue with her. I knew the whole world was in a bad way, not just Oklahoma, but at least Sweden didn't have dust storms.

"I keep askin' myself what I done so wrong, the Lord saw fit to punish me," Sally said. "I just ain't got no sense a'what I done that was so bad."

I almost laughed. Leave it to Sally to think she alone should've been spared God's wrath, while everybody else in the American Southwest was being held to account.

"How about one more bite?" I asked her. "You need to get your strength back."

She looked down at her hands. "Bein' strong don't make a bit of difference, boy."

Bo spoke my name from Sally's doorway. I glanced at him and was shocked to see tears in his eyes; he didn't even seem to notice Sally looking up again and watching him, too.

"What is it, Bo?" I asked, frightened. "What's wrong?"

Tears spilled down his cheeks. "Samson's dead. I just went to the barn and found him."

Without a word, Sally took the bowls from me and nudged me to get up. She knew as well as the rest of us what the horse had meant to him, and there was pity on her worn and defeated face. I went to Bo and put my arms around him, and he cried into my shoulder. I'd never heard him cry like this, not even when he talked about his parents, or when Sam Becklus died, or when our soil turned to ash.

"Like I said," Sally murmured from her bed. "Bein' strong don't make no difference."

DAY THREE

February 27, 1942. The USS Houston, *Java Sea.*

"There's only eight or nine of them," Alan said. "Good odds, right?"

I nodded, not trusting my voice. Alan and the rest of the *Houston*'s crew—most of the men were on deck, crowding the rails—were excited to finally find the fight they'd been seeking, but I had bile in my throat. Thus far I could only make out a few vague, ghostly outlines of the ships to the north of us, but I took no comfort from the distance.

"Take it easy, Isaac," Alan said more quietly, so only I could hear him. "We can handle these guys."

The *Houston* was sailing in the company of thirteen other ships, one a heavy cruiser like herself, as well as three light cruisers and nine destroyers. When we'd first joined the international, Dutch-led squadron a few days past, I'd felt confident, thinking we'd surely be a match for anything headed our way.

I wished I still believed that.

"Oops, there's another one," Alan amended, "but still no big deal. Things may get a little hairy, but—"

He fell silent, squinting at the distant flotilla. It was late afternoon and the air was hazy in the heat. I waited for him to say more, but he remained still, as did the rest of the men around us. Ten minutes passed, and then twenty, and Japanese ships kept popping up on the horizon. God only knew how many more were coming, but by my count there were already sixteen.

"Uh, Alan?" I breathed. My hands, grasping the rail, were trembling.

Alan's normally ruddy face was pale as he turned toward me. "Well, hell," he said, trying to grin but failing. "Looks like you'll really have something to write about for the newspapers."

When I'd boarded the *Houston* two weeks before, I was carrying two letters in my duffel bag. One of them—a bit pawed over by the military censors—was from Bo, who'd shipped somewhere with the 34th Infantry at the end of January, and the other was from Aggie, back in Des Moines. My nominal address was a cheap boardinghouse in Kansas City, but as I'd been traveling nonstop since the first of the year, it was pure luck their letters found me before I flew to Australia.

> *Dear Isaac,* Bo wrote.

> *Holy smoke, my best buddy's a reporter for the
> United Press! I can't stop bragging about you.
> You've really made it to the big time buddy but
> I'm not surprised. Nobody deserves it more. Guess
> I'm also worried to tell the truth. I was hoping
> you'd stay out of this thing but I should've known
> better. I sure hope they send you somewhere safe.*

*The censors won't let me tell you where we are
but I love the way folks talk hereabouts. I can't
understand half of what they say but they don't
understand me neither so I guess we're even.
Weird story, but there's an ex-Okie kid in my unit,
from over by Dalhart, who grew up like us right
smack in the good old scenic rectum of our very
own Dust Bowl. Both me and him can't believe
we ended up together on the other side of the
world. The Army gave us all a pamphlet on how
to make nice with the natives. We're not supposed
to say bad things about their customs or politicians
or anything we don't like, or complain about their
crappy coffee because that would be "impolite."
No kidding. Do they think we were born in a
barn? Well, on second thought a few fellows in my
unit might have farm animals for kin because
what they say they've done in the sack with girls
ain't possible for folks with no hooves or horns.
There's a whole bunch more to tell but I'm tuck-
ered out so I best stop. Aggie sent me a picture of
you and the kids. I miss you all so much I can't
stand it. Okay, love, Bo.*

    Dear Isaac, Aggie wrote in her letter. *You're
being absolutely ridiculous. I was recently hired
by a wealthy family in Windsor Heights to tutor
their sizable litter of overprivileged, beetle-
browed, inarticulate, pimply children, and Johan
now has a job sacking groceries at B&Bs. I don't
know what you were thinking when you snuck
that money into my purse before you left, but you
certainly can't afford such largesse. Karen, Ty, and*

> *Johan say to give you their love, and for what it's*
> *worth you have mine as well, but stop babying us.*
> *We're FINE.*

I assumed her letters to Bo were chattier.

After our cousin Sally passed away in Oklahoma, Johan inherited her farm, but it was worthless. The land was stone dead
and the beams of the house were caving in from the sand we
couldn't keep off the roof, so we couldn't even give the place
away.

Fortunately, when Aggie, Bo, and I graduated from high
school, Aggie and I took the advice of a teacher with connections at Drake University, in Des Moines, and we applied for
admission. I don't know why I was so surprised when we were
both offered full scholarships: Aggie was the smartest person I
knew—if also the most irritating—and all the two of us ever
did was read and study. I guess it just never occurred to me
good things could happen, too, since so much of our lives
hadn't gone all that smoothly. Nonetheless, we still didn't
think we'd be able to go, since the idea of leaving Bo and Uncle
Johan behind in hopeless poverty was unacceptable.

Bo had no interest in college himself but was ecstatic for
Aggie and me. He said he'd be damned if he'd let us stay in Oklahoma for his sake when "y'all finally got a way outta this
godforsaken shithole," and Johan agreed. The deadlock was
broken when Aggie wrote to Drake's head of admissions and
explained the situation; he somehow arranged a temporary job
in construction for Bo and Johan. It wasn't much of a job, but
at least it would get the four of us to Des Moines in the fall and
put a roof over our heads for a month or two.

"But what happens when there's no more work?" Aggie
asked Bo and Johan. "Isaac and I can stay in the dorms, but the
two of you won't have that option."

"Don't be a wet blanket," Bo said. "Something will turn up once we're there."

He was right, as always: As soon as Aggie and I started college, he and Johan found a better job, helping build a new bridge across the Raccoon River. The foreman who hired them was a gruff, brooding man named Billy Tyburn, who soon became Aggie's husband, as well as the father of her twins, Karen and Ty. Those two kids were the only things Billy and Aggie ever did right together, but I can only dream of doing anything half so fine.

I volunteered for military service the day after the Japanese bombed Pearl Harbor, but I was rejected for flat feet—a trait common to all Dahl men, according to Uncle Johan, who was turned down, too. Bo's feet were fine; he'd already been welcomed in the Army eight months before I failed to follow in his regulation 9-D footsteps. Certain the United States was going to get pulled into the war eventually, he enlisted early, not wanting to wait until the enemy was beating down our gate.

Anyway, I was determined not to be entirely useless while my best friend was overseas risking his life (or as Aggie put it, "gallivanting around Europe smiling sweetly at all the nice Nazis shooting at him"), so I begged the Army to let me join as a noncombatant. The recruiter I spoke to asked what skills I possessed, and when he found out I was a reporter for the *Des Moines Tribune*, he said he could maybe get me work as a clerk. I told him the offer was hardly appealing—being chained to a desk churning out memos in triplicate was not the kind of contribution I was hoping to make to the war effort—but he only shrugged and said take it or leave it.

I left it, thankfully, and applied to the United Press as a war correspondent.

My interview for the job was in Kansas City. I was only twenty-four years old and had no experience covering anything save local news, but my timing was ideal, as several veteran UP reporters had just been promoted to bureau positions. When I was hired, I asked to be sent overseas right away, but my new editor—Ben Oakes, a manic, obscene, die-hard Republican with unbelievably fetid breath and a 1939 Pulitzer Prize hanging on his office wall—insisted I do several stateside stories first, to prove myself.

Fortunately, I didn't have to stay stateside for long.

Oakes was a Texas boy, born and raised, with an obsession for his hometown's naval namesake, the USS *Houston*, a heavy cruiser in the U.S. Asiatic Fleet. Most of the country's attention leading up to Pearl Harbor was on Europe, but Oakes was fixated on the Dutch East Indies, where his beloved *Houston,* famous for hosting FDR on occasion, was keeping an eye on the Japanese. When things in the Pacific got heated to a rolling boil, Oakes somehow obtained permission from the Navy—even over the objection of the *Houston*'s captain—to send a reporter to do an in-depth story about life aboard the cruiser. The reporter initially slated to do the piece got hit by a jeep, so I found myself with a one-way ticket to Australia in my hands, and the inspirational advice of Ben Oakes still ringing in my ears: "Stay away from the whorehouse by the naval base, buddy, unless you're partial to the clap."

I told him gonorrhea was the least of my worries.

Sailing in shark-infested waters with only a few inches of metal between me and oblivion would've made me uneasy, even in peacetime, but to be put to sea in the middle of a war was terrifying. The *Houston*'s captain and crew had a stellar reputation, yet I could still imagine all too easily what one unlucky hit from an enemy torpedo or aerial bomb could do. The evidence of such a thing was right on the *Houston* herself: A week and a half before I boarded her, a Japanese bomb had plummeted from the sky and pulverized the ship's after turret, killing forty-six men and reducing a massive, triple-barreled, eight-inch gun mount into an unrecognizable scrap heap of blackened, useless steel. The crew told me horror stories of the explosion: how men in the crew quarters near the blast looked as if they'd been run through a cheese grater; how that night on deck their corpses jerked like puppets as rigor mortis tightened their limbs.

I met up with the *Houston* in Darwin, Australia, on a brutally hot Valentine's Day. The new captain, Albert Rooks, allowed me to board but I only saw him across the deck. He sent a curt note via Alan Weintraub—the chatty, amiable sailor appointed to keep an eye on me—saying he had no time for the press. Captain Rooks was not the only one who considered me a nuisance; I'd been foisted on the crew at the worst moment possible. They were playing a murderous game of cat and mouse with an enemy who had already drawn serious blood, and I was worse than useless. Luckily, Alan Weintraub didn't seem to share his shipmates' opinion; he welcomed me aboard warmly, shaking my hand and relieving me of my duffel bag.

Compared to a battleship or an ocean liner, the *Houston* wasn't particularly large, but to me she was a brooding, belligerent, six-hundred-foot-long monstrosity; the conning tower alone dwarfed most of the buildings I'd known as a kid. She was also a sleek, bustling, self-sufficient village; her deck bristled with guns and blinded the eye with brass. There was even a swing band aboard to keep up morale. As I wandered around my first day, gawping at everything like a half-wit, the band came on deck and played "Don't Get Around Much Anymore," and "Ain't She Sweet."

Dear Bo, I wrote that night, from the cramped bunk I'd been assigned in one of the crew berths. *Boy, did I miss you today. I'm supposed to write a story that will—in the immortal words of my potty-mouthed cliché of an editor, Ben Oakes—"capture the heroic fucking flavor of the* Houston." *He also told me I should strive to make every able-bodied man in America run out and join the U.S. Navy, and "every gooey-eyed schoolgirl hot and horny" for the* Houston's *crew.*

I was in so far over my head I feared I'd never see daylight again.

The last article I'd submitted to the *Tribune* back in Iowa was a human-interest piece about a sweet old snowplow sales-man at a Sears store. I'd written slightly higher-profile things since joining the UP, but I was criminally underprepared for an assignment like this. Oakes had been in such a rush to get me down to Java, I'd had no time to do research about the *Houston* or her crew of over a thousand men; I didn't know the first thing about naval warfare, or the Dutch East Indies, or a mil-lion other things I should've been familiar with before ever stepping onboard.

Alan Weintraub stopped by my bunk, checking to see if I needed anything, just as I was finishing my whining to Bo that first night. I thanked him and told him no, then read over what I'd written before lights out. I knew most of my letter would never get past the censors, but I didn't care; I simply needed to pretend Bo might someday read my words and know I'd been thinking of him. I soon fell asleep and dreamed about drowning.

Dear Bo. The Japanese found us today.

It was my third night aboard the *Houston.* I'd continued writing my letter to Bo each night before bed. I needed sleep badly, but I was too wound up to close my eyes. I'd already told him that the *Houston* had been ordered to gather and lead a convoy to an island called Timor, home to a vital airbase be-tween Java and Australia. When we'd left Darwin the previous night, we were in the company of a destroyer called the USS *Peary*, along with four troop ships and two Australian escort sloops. All were stuffed to the gills with Aussie and American soldiers when the Japanese appeared in the sky.

They had three dozen twin-engine bombers and nine of those

*flying boats the Navy calls Mavises. Have you seen those damn
things? The Mavises, I mean. They look like ugly silver canoes
with wings. Anyway, when I saw them coming, I almost pissed
my pants, but I was too scared to accomplish even that much.
They showed up all at once, and when they started diving at us,
I had to cover my mouth to keep from screaming.*

"Stay put!" Alan had yelled at me, stuffing me in the relative
safety of an open hatch and scampering off to assist the gun
crews.

I should've obeyed but I couldn't stand not seeing what was
going on. I crept on the afterdeck and latched on to a handrail
just as the first wave of planes strafed us, shooting and bombing
everything in sight. The wail of the planes' engines as they
passed overhead was appalling, but the roar of the *Houston*'s
big guns completely drowned them out; I was nearly driven to
my knees by the noise.

"Jesus Christ!" A passing ensign cartwheeled across the white
teakwood deck, bellowing in panic when the ship swerved violently, churning up so much ocean it felt as if we were in the
middle of a tidal wave. A bomb had missed her bow by inches
and detonated, sending up a geyser of water that crashed down
on the ship, drenching the forward gun crews.

"Get below, Isaac, goddammit!" Alan roared, reappearing
briefly as he ran by, grabbing the bicep of the man who'd fallen
and yanking him to his feet. "You're not safe up here!"

"I'm not safe anywhere!" I yelled back.

He said something else I couldn't hear because our guns
were all banging away, throwing up so much flak, the whole
world seemed on fire. The sky was orange and red, and the
ship's deck was crawling with flames and black, oily smoke; all
I could do was gape at everything in terror. Alan shook his
head and gestured imperatively at a hatch, then charged off
again, joining a group of men with fire hoses and extinguishers.
Another bomb narrowly missed our stern—Captain Rooks

seemed able to read the enemy pilots' minds, ordering course corrections with uncanny speed and precision—but for one heart-stopping second the ship lurched so far over to one side, that I was standing in two feet of water, along with half the crew on deck.

"Fuck me!" gasped a marine thrown against my side at the rail. We clung to each other helplessly until the ship righted itself again; he grinned like a lunatic and sprinted off, his pants soaked to the knees.

It soon became clear Rooks wasn't only trying to save his own ship; he was also doing his damnedest to protect the troopships, darting around and between them to keep the full force of the attack on us. It was working, too; from what I could see, the planes didn't have time to go after the other ships because they were too busy doing their level best to bomb the *Houston* back to creation. A feral cheer burst out amidships as one of the Mavises burst into flames and plunged into the ocean; I found myself whooping along with everybody else. One of the gunners who'd brought down the plane pumped his fists in the air and gave the finger to another Mavis that turned tail and fled out of range. "Eat shit, asshole!" the gunner screamed to general applause.

I found out later the attack only lasted forty-five minutes, but it seemed like days. Some of the men at the guns passed out from heat exhaustion, and there wasn't a soul aboard who wasn't going full tilt the whole time. I lost track of how many planes the gunners knocked out of the sky (I heard afterward it was seven) but I saw the last one that got hit go up in a fireball, and a few seconds later the rest finally peeled off. Unbelievably, our convoy only had one casualty—a soldier on one of the transports caught a piece of shrapnel in the neck and bled to death.

I told Bo in my letter how the day ended. Not long after the attack we were ordered to turn around because Timor, the island we'd been headed for, had already fallen to the Japanese. The *Houston*'s crew was devastated; the men and supplies we were escorting could've made all the difference in the world if we'd gotten there first. I was on deck with Alan when we started passing by the other ships to lead the convoy back to Australia. Almost the whole crew was topside because of the heat below. They were filthy with oil and sweat, and staggering from fatigue. Everybody was staring off into space or down at their feet, as if they couldn't bear to look at each other, and not even Alan, usually irrepressible, knew what to say.

And that's when the troops on all the ships we were escorting started yelling their fool heads off, praising the *Houston* for saving their lives.

My God, Bo, you should've heard the fuss they made. The cheering went on and on; they climbed the rails of their ships and waved their arms and caps like they'd all gone crazy. When the men near me figured out what was going on, they started lifting their heads and standing up a little straighter. Some of them had these lopsided, boyish grins on their faces, and a good few of them were bawling.

I bawled, too, but Bo would know that without me telling him.

The *Houston*'s crew warmed up to me as they got used to having me along for the ride. By my fifth night aboard I was starting to make headway on my story. Having Alan at my side helped, of course, since everyone on the ship liked him, but I still wasn't allowed to talk to anybody on duty. Tensions were running too high, and Alan said the captain didn't want his men distracted. Unfortunately, this meant I could only interview them when they were eating or getting ready to hit the rack, and no one ever wanted to talk for long because they were bone-weary. They'd been at general quarters so often that most of them just ate and slept at their posts. Tokyo Rose, that infernally chipper harlot of a radio propagandist for the Japanese, had more than once claimed in her daily broadcasts that the *Houston* had been sunk—inspiring the *Houston*'s crew to nickname their ship "The Galloping Ghost of the Java Coast"—but I for one didn't find it amusing that the vessel I was counting on to keep me alive had been singled out by the enemy.

"Hey, Mr. Newsman, you gonna write about me?" asked a marine I found smoking on deck late at night. The all-clear siren had finally sounded a while ago, and the crew was taking advantage of this rare chance to relax a little. Word was we were headed to join an Allied strike force somewhere near Surabaya.

"Sure thing," I said, joining him at the rail. We introduced ourselves; his name was Paulie Morse. I told him I couldn't use his real name in my story, since anonymity for enlisted men was official Navy policy.

"No shit?" He spoke quietly, trying not to disturb the officer on duty a few feet away. His face was briefly visible in the darkness as he lit another cigarette; in the flare of his match I glimpsed a pug nose, freckles, and thick red eyebrows. "Guess that figures."

"What should I write about you?" I asked.

Alan Weintraub, my ever-present shadow, showed up at my other side. The only time he wasn't near me was when he had to visit the head. Lanky and handsome, with a long nose and sharp cheekbones, he looked nothing like Bo, but reminded me of him, anyway, sharing a gift for putting people at ease.

"Hey, Paulie," Alan said, reaching across me to bum a cigarette. "How about you tell all the folks back home about the time that dog in Slapjack started humping your leg?"

Paulie's teeth glittered in the moonlight. "No, Weintraub, I don't believe I will." He wiped sweat from his forehead with his shirtsleeve and snorted. "And P.S., go screw yourself, okay?"

"Where's Slapjack?" I asked.

"Oh, Christ," Paulie groaned. "Please don't write about that goddamn dog."

I promised Paulie his secret was safe with me as Alan leaked smoke through his nose like a dragon. He explained that Slapjack was a nickname for Tjilatjap, where we'd refuel in a couple of days.

"What kind of a messed-up language have they all got down here anyway?" Paulie wondered. "Does it make any damn sense to either of you?"

"Nope," Alan said, "but what else is new?"

Given what we all knew was out there waiting in the darkness—the Japanese net was tightening more every hour—I was struck by how casual they sounded. Just that day the port of Darwin, where we'd refueled the day before, had been almost annihilated. Two of the ships lost in the devastation—the destroyer *Peary*, and the troop ship *Mauna Loa*—had been with us in the convoy to Timor. I asked if it was normal for sailors to make ordinary conversation when they were facing imminent danger.

Alan tilted his head at me. "Who says we're in danger?" he asked, deadpan.

I sighed, knowing it was the only answer I'd ever get. Alan would talk my ear off about anything else, but he was a superstitious soul when it came to discussing the *Houston*'s odds for survival. I turned to Paulie and asked where he was from.

"The great metropolis of Fall River, Massachusetts." He offered me a cigarette, but I declined; the damage to my lungs from the dust in the Panhandle had ruined my ability to enjoy a smoke.

"Proud home of Lizzie Borden," Alan murmured.

"Ah, shut your hole, wiseass," Paulie said, laughing.

Lieutenant Hamlin walked by and Alan and Paulie saluted; Hamlin greeted them both by name before disappearing down the hatch that led to the officers' quarters. The three of us fell silent and stared down at the black surface of the ocean, listening to the low, reassuring hum of the *Houston*'s engines. I asked Paulie if he was going back home after the war, and he nodded in the darkness.

"You betcha, first chance I get." He paused. "Just hope I get that chance."

"Don't say that, Paulie," Alan snapped, for once not kidding around. He flicked his cigarette butt over the rail. "It's bad luck."

Aggie's five-year-old twins, Ty and Karen, looked just like Aggie and me at their age: blue-eyed, towheaded, and thin and wiry as snakes. But unlike their mother and me, they were the best of friends. Their closeness had nothing to do with their father, either. Billy Tyburn was a hard man, quick to anger and slow to forgive, and his arguments with Aggie were loud and acrimonious. Thank God for Bo and Johan; at least the kids had two adults in their lives who knew how to play well with others.

The evening before I left for Kansas City to apply for the job at the UP, Ty and Karen came to stand in my doorway while I packed my suitcase. I expected to be back soon, but they were convinced I was leaving forever. Until Bo left for the Army, the kids had never known a world without three uncles—Johan, Bo, and myself—sharing the house with them. I didn't flatter myself that the prospect of me leaving was as upsetting as Bo's departure: I was their flesh-and-blood uncle, true enough, but Bo was Bo.

"You better hurry up, Uncle Isaac," Karen said. She had a vocabulary well beyond her years, and her voice had an odd, disconcerting huskiness to it: The combination made her sound more like a worldly teenager than a little girl. "Momma says if you don't come play Monopoly right now, she'll pour your beer down the toilet."

Karen was far sweeter than her mother, but she delighted in relaying Aggie's threats.

"Is that a fact?" I said. "Well, if she touches my beer I'll pee in her Coke."

Ty chortled. He was as bright as Karen, but he was also very much a five-year-old boy. "You're supposed to say *urinate*, Isaac," he said. Ty never called me Uncle Isaac; I was always plain Isaac to him. "Momma says people who say *pee* are vulgar." He clambered on my bed and inspected my open suitcase. "You have a lot of underwear."

"Unlike some people I know, I occasionally change mine."

He blushed. "I only forgot that once."

"Well, I'm glad to hear it. I'd hate to have a nephew who smelled like the wrong end of a dead duck."

Ty considered his answer for a moment. "You smell like a dead duck's *fart*, Isaac."

"Oh, yeah?" I tossed him on the bed, squealing, and tickled him. "Who raised you to be such a wise guy?"

"You, of course," Aggie said, from the doorway. "You're a terrible influence."

My sister was thinner and paler than before she divorced Billy, yet she was still inordinately beautiful—her long blond hair would've made a Viking goddess jealous, and her skin was flawless, like silk. I knew I was causing her pain by interviewing for a job elsewhere, and the sadness in her face moved me. She, too, like the kids, believed I'd get hired by UP, no matter how many times I told them I wasn't qualified.

"I never taught him to sass his elders," I said, raising my voice to carry to the living room. "That's Johan's fault."

"Bullcrap!" Johan bellowed back. "I'm the only reason those mouthy little pygmies got any manners at all!"

"Come play a game with the children, Isaac," Aggie said. "I'll help you pack later."

"I can pack my own suitcase, thanks."

"Uh-huh." She glanced in my suitcase. "You forgot your tie."

"No, I didn't," I lied. "I was just going to grab it."

"And don't wear that green shirt to your interview, whatever you do. You'll look like a depraved Swedish elf."

Karen fingered the green shirt with distaste. "Momma's right, Uncle Isaac. This shirt is *ugly*. Wear your white one."

"No," Ty said. "The white one makes him look like a deras—what's that word again?"

"Depraved," Karen said.

"Yeah, like a depraved Swedish *ghost*."

Aggie beamed with pride. "Thank God you both take after me, instead of Isaac."

"Everybody says I look like Isaac," Ty said.

"Sadly, that's true, you poor homely child, but at least you have my brains."

"Ty and Uncle Isaac aren't homely, Momma," Karen said. "And you always say Uncle Isaac is super smart."

"I was only teasing about the homely part," Aggie said. "But your uncle is clearly *not* intelligent, or he wouldn't be in such a rush to see a war firsthand." She got my tie out of the closet and folded it. "He'd also realize war correspondents get killed and mutilated just like soldiers and—"

"Who wants to play Monopoly?" I interrupted loudly, but it was too late; both kids were gaping at her in horror.

"For pity's sake," Aggie muttered, gathering them to her as they started to blubber. She glared at me as if her big mouth was my fault. "It's all right, sweeties. Don't worry. Isaac will be fine, and so will Bo."

"Nice job," I mouthed at her over the kids' heads.

"Go to hell," she mouthed back.

Before I put the kids to bed later that evening, Ty gave me a talisman: a polished turquoise stone on a rawhide cord he'd worn around his neck for two years, ever since I'd bought it for him at a rock museum. Not to be outdone, Karen presented me with a hideous rabbit's foot she'd won at a carnival; it was dyed cotton-candy pink, and was bald in spots. When I hugged and kissed the twins good night, they clung to me like barnacles. Uncle Johan shook my hand and told me to come home as soon as I could; his eyes were dry, but his voice faltered. Aggie took me to the bus station before dawn. We argued all the way there—about what, I can't remember—but she kissed me on the cheek and cried when I boarded the bus.

From that day forward I wore Ty's stone around my neck, under my shirt, and I kept Karen's rabbit's foot in my pants pocket. I liked knowing the smooth stone of Ty's necklace had once rested on his small, warm sternum just as it did on mine, and I often found myself clutching Karen's rabbit's foot almost without being aware of it.

Leaving home when I didn't have to was the stupidest thing I've ever done.

What I remember most about my last day aboard the *Houston* is the stench. Piss and gun grease, puke and smoke, scorching hot metal, unwashed bodies slick with fear-and-adrenaline-infused sweat. The smell was especially sickening belowdecks where it was like a furnace and the munitions were handled during the battle; the men down there had to relieve themselves right on the spot because there was no time to do otherwise. The first marathon stretch of fighting lasted nearly four hours and only ended when we lost the Japanese in darkness and vast curtains of smoke. The heat was so bad below—nearly one hundred and fifty degrees, somebody said later—that more than a dozen members of the crew lost consciousness and had to be dragged from harm's way. The engineers were staggering like drunks. During the worst of the action I asked Alan if there was any-thing I could do to help, and he thrust a jug of water and a wet strip of cloth into my hands and told me to revive the men who'd fainted. I briefly passed out myself and woke on the floor a few minutes later, soaked to the skin and stinking like a sewer.

Nothing in my life had ever prepared me for such chaos. The

Japanese had more ships, more munitions, more air cover, more everything; the fight was grossly unequal. Early in the battle, the *Houston* was hit by two warheads but miraculously both were duds. At one point I saw three torpedoes, one right after another, passing within inches of our hull, and the noise from our own guns and all the other ships was relentless and ear-shattering. The enemy didn't escape completely unharmed—I heard later two of their cruisers were badly damaged and had to flee—but if any of their ships went down, we didn't see it.

It was the first time I witnessed the wholesale slaughter of men firsthand, and if I'd known then how familiar I'd become with such things, I'm not sure I could've borne it.

The detonation from the torpedo that hit the Dutch destroyer *Kortenaer* an hour or so into the fight ripped her in two. She was nearby; the torpedo had been intended for the *Houston,* but Captain Rooks evaded it. The *Kortenaer* wasn't as lucky. She went down so fast, it was as if a vast sea creature seized her hull amidships and yanked her under; her bow and stern each jutted up in the air briefly before she slid implacably beneath the surface of the water. The surviving members of her crew were left dog-paddling in the ocean with no rescue possible; no ship in our squadron could linger to help. While we were still reeling from that horror, the British destroyer *Electra* got hit by three separate shells that pounded her into fiery oblivion as well. Her crew joined the survivors of the *Kortenaer* in the Java Sea, thrashing around as their ship burned to the waterline and sharks began to feed. We all watched in shock as the men who had been injured and maimed in the blasts sank from sight, one after another.

"Oh Jesus, oh Jesus," I heard a man sob as he ran past me on the deck; it was Paulie Morse, the tough young marine from Fall River.

When our squadron finally lost track of the Japanese at nightfall, I was naive enough to hope the worst was over. Our numbers were pitifully reduced. In addition to the loss of the *Kortenaer* and the *Electra*, four of our destroyers, almost out of fuel, were forced to return to port. Another went back for survivors of the two destroyed ships, and the other heavy cruiser, the HMS *Exeter*—badly mauled during the earlier carnage—had withdrawn at sunset for safe harbor, guarded by one of the two remaining destroyers. The sole destroyer left, the *Jupiter*, wasn't in our company long, either; she struck a mine an hour after full dark, and the blast lit up the night sky like the noonday sun.

So there were only four of us remaining when the Japanese reappeared.

De Ruyter and *Java* got hit at virtually the same instant. The two light cruisers went down in tandem with nightmarish speed. For a moment both ships were flaming in the night like Olympic torches, then they winked out and disappeared. The sight of hundreds of dead and dying men in the water—not to mention the smell of burning flesh wafting over the waves—stunned the entire crew of the *Houston* into a grim silence.

The only other surviving ship was *Perth*, equally mute in our wake.

Somehow the enemy fleet lost us again in smoke, darkness, and rain. One moment they were everywhere, the next, nowhere. I found Alan standing at the rail amidships with half a dozen other men. They made room for me and we all stared out, hardly breathing, into the eerily quiet night. Nearly every man aboard seemed to be doing the same thing; the rails of the deck, both fore and aft, were jammed with grave, silent watchers.

"What happened?" Alan whispered. "Where are they?"

The *Perth* was following us closely. In a brief patch of moonlight I could see her Aussie crew lining their own rails, as frazzled and bewildered as we were. Excruciatingly tense minutes passed, but when the quiet of the night remained unbroken, we began to breathe again; after an hour, word came from the *Houston*'s officers that we were on our way to Batavia and would arrive early tomorrow afternoon. Belowdecks was a rank, festering sauna no one cared to brave, so men stretched out to sleep on the deck wherever they could.

I fell asleep sometime around three in the morning, seated upright with my back against the base of the conning tower, and Alan woke me at sunrise with a cup of coffee. The *Houston* and the *Perth* had the ocean to ourselves; the Japanese had vanished. Alan and I stood together—he smelled as badly as I did; we'd managed to find clean clothes but we were still filthy—and looked around with the rest of the crew, all of us amazed to be alive. The *Houston* had suffered no fatalities; it seemed we'd been blessed by a guardian angel.

We limped back to Batavia, and that's where Captain Rooks finally ordered me off the ship, sending a quickly scribbled note with Alan that the British Naval Liaison Office had room for me aboard a plane of theirs, bound for Sydney. Rooks' message to me was blunt but not unkind: *"Son, get the hell out of here while you still can."*

Alan escorted me to the ramp leading to the dock. There were shadows under his eyes, but his ready smile was back. He shook my hand and told me not to worry about him or his crew mates. "Don't worry, buddy. We'll be fine," he said. "We've made it this far, right?"

I nodded, hiding my doubt. "Keep your head down, Alan. I'd like to buy you a beer someday, when this is over."

"I'll hold you to that. Write something good about me in your story, okay?"

I told him I would. He squeezed my hand again, then released me. To this day, I can still feel the grip of his fingers on my own; I can still feel the ship's deck, solid and reassuring under my feet.

The guardian angel who watched over the *Houston* when I

was aboard must've been too worn out to show up the next day. During the Battle of Sunda Strait, *Houston* and *Perth*, surrounded and ludicrously outgunned, went down together in blood and flames. Until the end of the war three years later, no one knew for sure that there were both American and Australian survivors of the battle; it would be a long, ugly ordeal for them as prisoners of the Japanese. Paulie Morse, the marine from Fall River, was one of these men, and he contacted me after the war to tell me their story.

Alan Weintraub went down with the *Houston*, as did Captain Rooks and nearly a thousand other men from both ships.

DAY FOUR

February 15, 1950. Des Moines, Iowa.

"I still can't believe you dragged me to this abomination," Aggie muttered. "How can you be so cruel to your own sister?"

"For God's sake," I said, paying for the movie tickets for *Cinderella*. Aggie had been bellyaching ever since we left the house, and I was two seconds away from stuffing a sock—or better yet, my entire foot—into her big, pretty mouth. "Can you please just shut up for once and not spoil the evening for the kids?"

"In case you hadn't noticed, they're not exactly thrilled to be here, either," she said as we followed Ty and Karen to get popcorn. "They're too old for cartoons."

At thirteen, Ty and Karen were nearly as tall as their mother and me. Their height made them easy to keep an eye on in the crowd, as did the bright, striped hats they were wearing over their blond hair. Ty's hat was green and red, Karen's red and white, and both were recent Christmas gifts from Bo's wife,

Janet, who knitted them herself—no doubt grudgingly, martyring herself with every flick of the needles. Bo and his family were supposed to meet us here. If I knew Janet, she'd already have her husband and son corralled in the exact center of the theater, scrubbed, groomed, and impeccably dressed, with four empty seats next to them, reserved for us. Janet always arrived early to everything and commandeered the best seats in the house.

"Since when did you become a snob about fairy tales?" I asked, studying wall posters of coming attractions. *Father of the Bride* and *The Third Man* were the only ones I was interested in seeing. "You used to love them."

"I still do." She pinched the bridge of her nose, fighting a sinus headache that was making her even crankier than usual. "But I guarantee this movie will have nothing to do with the original story. American audiences simply can't stomach anything as unsettling as an undiluted fairy tale. All they want to do is sidle up to the communal entertainment trough and gorge themselves on sickly-sweet pap."

"Just because the movie may not be as grim and bloody as the original story doesn't mean it won't be good." Playing devil's advocate to Aggie was so ingrained, I couldn't stop arguing, even when I feared she was right. "Besides, haven't you had your fill lately of depressing stories?"

"There's some truth to that, I suppose." Her eyes darkened as she ran her hand along the red felt rope separating the popcorn line from the rest of the lobby. "What with McCarthy spouting his vicious, idiotic accusations, it's a wonder there's not a lynch mob on every—"

I shushed her before she could get worked up. The couple behind us in line—a pudgy, fussy-looking bald man and a cadaverous, nervous woman with a permanent frown etched in the corners of her mouth—were already eyeing Aggie with disfavor. As a highly vocal member of the tiny, fledgling Socialist

Party of Iowa, my sister was viewed as the next thing to the devil by almost everyone we knew. The last thing I wanted was for the kids to have to deal with seeing their mother in another ugly public confrontation.

"Don't you dare muzzle me, Isaac!" she snapped. "I'll say whatever I please."

According to Aggie, anyone who didn't speak their mind every second of every day was a coward.

"Fine," I said. "Foam at the mouth to your heart's content. Ty and Karen absolutely *love* it when you get on your soapbox in front of complete strangers."

The kids were several feet ahead in the line; she glanced at them somewhat guiltily and lowered her voice. "They're not even paying attention."

She was wrong. From the set of Ty's thin shoulders and the way Karen was avoiding our eyes, I knew they were both listening. They were used to their mother's rants, of course—and sadly, also more than a little accustomed to the two of us squabbling—but they'd recently begun to cringe in mortification whenever Aggie lost her temper. She'd been worse ever since Uncle Johan died the previous autumn; his mildness and easy humor had often reigned in her worst impulses.

Lord, how I missed that man. The leukemia that took him from us was so advanced by the time it got diagnosed that he only lasted seven weeks after learning of it. We were all still reeling from how quickly we'd lost him. I kept finding myself standing in the doorway of his empty bedroom, half expecting to find him puttering around in there, humming to himself. I suspected the shock would eventually pass, but I feared the ache of losing him was there to stay.

"Of course they're paying attention," I said. "And unless showing off your dubious proletariat credentials matters more than the well-being of your offspring, you might consider sparing them another round of humiliation."

She started to retort, stung, but just then Elias Larsson, Bo's freckled, extraordinarily handsome seven-year-old son appeared, running up to Ty and Karen in the line. He was wearing a white button-down shirt with long sleeves—freshly starched, of course—under a checkered red vest; a narrow black tie was cinched as tightly around his neck as a dog collar.

"I knew you guys were already here!" he crowed. "Mother said you'd be late, but I said you were getting popcorn. Daddy told me I could come see."

"Aunt Janet let you come out here by yourself?" Ty asked, raising his eyebrows. He mussed the younger boy's neatly combed hair and loosened Elias's tie; he could never resist undoing Janet's careful mothering even though it aggravated the poor woman to distraction. "Is she on her deathbed or something?"

Elias gave a very Bo-like shrug. "She wanted to come, but Daddy said no."

"Uh-oh," I murmured to Aggie. "Bo will be in big trouble for that."

"No kidding," she murmured back. "Janet's probably attaching electrodes to his penis as we speak."

Bo had met Janet in Belfast, Ireland, early in the war, where he'd been stationed for a while with the 34th Infantry—the Red Bull Division—before being shipped to Africa. In the few months they were together, he'd accidentally gotten her pregnant, married her to appease her family, then after the Army released him at the end of the war, he'd gone back for her and Elias and brought them home to Iowa. Neither Aggie nor I particularly cared for Janet; she henpecked Bo and was openly jealous of his friendship with us. She did have redeeming qualities—she was pretty, for one thing: freckled and redheaded just like Bo, with a round, cherubic face, vivid green eyes, and a remarkable, if rare, smile. She also had an achingly sweet alto voice that could bring tears to my eyes whenever Bo could persuade her to sing something for us.

"Hello, Uncle Isaac," Elias said, breaking free from Ty and

shaking my hand. Janet insisted on his being formal with his elders, but considering how often we saw him and his parents—their house was two blocks from ours and a week never passed without all of us getting together for some kind of outing—the stiffness of his ritual hello was endearingly absurd. He released me and moved on to Aggie, offering his small hand to her as well.

"Hello, Aunt Agnes," he said.

"Hello, Elias," she said, stooping to embrace him. He blushed crimson, but when she let him go again he was beaming, just as his father used to as a child.

"Daddy says this movie will make you mad," he told her. "He says you might even go bald from pulling your hair out."

Aggie snorted, amused in spite of herself. "Yes, well, I'll try not to disappoint."

We bought our popcorn and drinks, and on our way into the theater I found myself walking beside my niece. Aside from the barest vestige of teenaged gangliness still in her stride, Karen's resemblance to her mother at that age—self-possessed, elegant, and willowy—was almost eerie.

"Thanks," she said quietly.

"For what?"

"For not letting Mom get up to full steam back in the line."

I grinned. "I told her you guys were listening."

She smiled back. "Of course we were. Neither of us could take another scene like last week."

Aggie had caused a commotion in front of the grocery store a few days before. I wasn't there myself, thank God, but Ty and Karen told me that while they were inside getting milk, Aggie was in the parking lot, soliciting signatures for a petition to ban the hydrogen bomb. When a college boy showing off for friends made the mistake of baiting her—he even went so far as to call her a "traitor"—Aggie lost her temper, and by the time Ty and Karen emerged from the store, the unwise young man was in a defensive crouch, squealing from an onslaught of corrective slaps to the head. The kids had to drag their mother back to the car before the police got involved.

"Don't worry," I told Karen, dropping my voice. "I went through her purse and stole all her pens and paper before we left the house."

"Oh, God," Karen said, her blue eyes widening. "She'll kill you if she finds out."

"I'll just blame it on you and Ty."

"Ha ha, very funny."

We spotted Bo and Janet and made our way to them. Janet attempted to orchestrate how we all entered the row—she wanted Aggie and me on one side of the children with herself and Bo on the other side, but Aggie rebelled.

"Don't herd us, Janet. We're not cows," she said, waving the kids back to the aisle and propelling me down the row first. She followed close behind and shoved me into the seat to Bo's left.

"Moo, fellow cow," Bo murmured, tugging his indignant wife back into the seat to his right before things could escalate. Janet glared at him as Aggie sank into the seat on my left and Elias, Ty, and Karen filed down the row to join us.

"I wouldn't want to be you tonight," I whispered in Bo's ear. Janet was forever accusing him of taking Aggie's side during arguments.

"Yeah, I'm a dead man," he whispered back, helping himself to my popcorn since his was already gone. He had a voracious appetite and claimed it came from our years of deprivation in Oklahoma; it was a wonder he was still as thin as when we were kids. "How was the trip to Illinois?"

"Great. We just got back a couple hours ago."

Ty and I had driven to Chicago the day before, staying overnight at a hotel so we could rise early and spend the morning at the Art Institute's Van Gogh exhibit. (I'd given up my position at the United Press and now freelanced for various news organizations, covering everything from geopolitics to cultural events. My income as a freelancer was much less stable, but I loved being able to cherry-pick the stories I was writing.) Ty was a talented young artist, so he'd begged his mother to let him skip school and tag along with me.

"You should've seen Ty in the museum," I said, shrugging off my coat. "He didn't blink for three hours straight."

"I bet," Bo said, sounding wistful. He was a manager at Kurtz Hardware and could seldom find time for lunch, let alone a trip out of town. "He must've been in hog heaven."

Hoping Janet had cooled down by now, I leaned across Bo to say hello.

"Isaac," she said, forcing a smile as I kissed her lightly on the cheek. "It's a bloody *miracle* you survived all these years with that sister of yours. She's a right fierce pain in the arse." Her Irish brogue was always more pronounced when she was riled.

I lowered my voice. "How about we go halfsies and hire an assassin?"

Her smile became a little less strained. "Yes, thanks, that would be lovely."

"Juveniles," Aggie sniffed, eavesdropping as I'd known she would be. "If I weren't already numb from the impending horror of this movie, I'd be terribly offended."

Janet scowled. "Well, Agnes, maybe if you weren't so hoity-toity about everything we lesser mortals enjoy—"

The screen flared to life and the theater darkened, blessedly cutting short the rest of Janet's rejoinder. Bo and I both sighed in relief and settled back in our chairs; he stole more popcorn and tilted his head to speak quietly in my ear.

"I found one of Johan's little ladies today when I was going through my desk at the store," he said. "I had to step out in the alley so no one would catch me crying."

Johan had taken to wood carving in the last few years before he died. He'd started off with things like whistles and tops, but then progressed to figurines of people and animals. Toward the end he got good, often carving nudes of women that were somehow both delicate and sensuous without being pornographic. He called them his "little ladies," and gave them away as gifts. I owned half a dozen or more, along with a veritable Noah's Ark of wooden animals—everything from mice to elephants. Seeing his creations now was a painful reminder of both his sweetness and his abiding calm; he used to sit for hours at a time, unruffled by whatever was happening around him, his hands perpetually busy with a knife and a block of wood. Even when the cancer ravaged his body and left him little more than a skeleton, he would sit and carve, pausing only to nap or talk.

"I've been thinking about him today, too," I told Bo, as Bugs Bunny tormented Elmer Fudd in the cartoon before the movie. "Every time I turn around, I keep hoping to see him."

"Shush, you two," Janet admonished. "You're bothering people."

Bo and I were barely talking loudly enough to hear ourselves, but we fell silent anyway, knowing Janet was mostly irritated because she couldn't hear what we were saying. In some ways I couldn't blame her for resenting our friendship, yet her possessiveness of Bo made me less than sympathetic. When Aggie and I first met her, we'd done our best to make her see that our closeness with Bo was no threat, but it soon became obvious Janet would be far happier if the two of us—as well as Ty and Karen—fell in a hole and were never heard from again.

Aggie leaned in from my other side. "Did you talk to Ty while you were in Chicago?"

She'd asked me to have a birds-and-bees chat with Ty on our trip. She'd seen him walking with a girl from his class recently, holding hands, and wanted to make sure they weren't getting too serious for their age.

"Yes, we talked," I told her, my eyes watering as a cloud of cigarette smoke descended on us; at least half the people in the audience were smoking. "And you can relax. He's not an idiot. He knows how girls get pregnant."

Bo had leaned in closer, too, to listen to us. "Our godson has a girlfriend?"

"Not according to him," I said. "He claims they're just friends."

"Of course he's going to say that," Aggie said. "He's thirteen."

"Shush!" Janet hissed.

I glanced down the row at the kids. Elias was next to Aggie, and Ty was between Elias and Karen. I was sure they couldn't hear us, but it didn't surprise me to find Ty gazing back at me, anyway. I smiled and waved; he scowled and returned his attention to the movie screen.

"He knows we're talking about him," Bo said. "I swear that kid is psychic." He stole more of my popcorn, so I gave him the carton and helped myself to Aggie's.

"Good grief, Isaac," she complained. "You just ate an entire chicken *and* a quart of potato salad an hour ago. Don't you ever get full?"

Like Bo, I also blamed my appetite on Oklahoma. "Are you going to drink your Coke?" I asked her.

"Will the three of you *please* shut up?" Janet huffed. "Whatever you're talking about surely can wait until *after* the movie."

Bo grinned at Aggie and me and settled back in his seat, turning to Janet and whispering something to mollify her.

"Oh, dear, Janet's upset again," Aggie murmured. "I'm beside myself with remorse."

The movie began at last, eventually introducing a sleeping Cinderella being serenaded by birds and mice. Aggie groaned and I shushed her.

"What's wrong, Aunt Aggie?" Elias asked, leaning in from her other side.

"Nothing, sweetie." Aggie put her arm around him, and he rested his head on her shoulder.

I could hear Janet whispering invective in Bo's ear, and my heart went out to him. She finally reached the end of her homily and released him to mull over his sins. He grinned at me, looking tired but otherwise unfazed, and his grin grew wider as he glanced at Aggie and Elias. Elias was the only one these days who consistently brought out Aggie's gentler side. Ty and Karen, though affectionate by nature, were growing somewhat gun-shy of their mother's mood swings, and no longer sought her out the way they used to. It made me sad because I wasn't sure she even noticed.

When Aggie met Billy Tyburn, we were in our freshman year at Drake University. Bo was working with Johan in construction, and Billy Tyburn was the foreman on their job. He was in his mid-twenties and a native Iowan. He had pale blue eyes, sparse blond hair, and a two-pack-a-day cigarette habit; he was terse, self-assured, and built like a pit bull. He fell for Aggie and set about wooing her, though in reality it didn't take much effort. For all Aggie's brains, bravado, and natural grace, she was still a young girl from rural Oklahoma, who had previously been on only one date in her life, to our senior prom. Billy Tyburn was smart, unpredictable, and at least occasionally funny—he once said Eleanor Roosevelt, whom he admired, was "ugly as sin, but I'll be goddamned if she ain't twice the man I'll ever be"—and at first glance he also appeared to be generous and decent, if a bit rough around the edges.

A few glances later, though—after their whirlwind romance had culminated in an equally hasty marriage, their own apartment, and twin babies in Aggie's womb—they began to fight about everything: his chauvinism, her adamant refusal to change her last name to his; his time spent on barstools, her time spent on lost causes; his roving eye for other women, her disdain for his cultural ignorance; his temper, her decidedly worse temper; his inability to forgive her for being cruel, her inability to forgive him for not being as smart as she was. The birth of the twins worsened matters; Billy and babies were a terrible combination.

When we graduated from Drake, Aggie predictably finished at the top of our class, with a double major in English and math, as well as four minors in psychology, philosophy, history, and political science. She did all this while raising Ty and Karen with little help from Billy, who was intimidated by her success, and openly resented it, so much so that even after they'd divorced and she'd moved back in with us, he still came over to fight with her, usually on the front lawn, sometime between midnight and three in the morning. He finally found another woman to torment, and relocated to Montana when the kids were six (Aggie immediately changed their last names from Tyburn to Dahl), and none of us had seen him since.

Anyway, Aggie buried herself in politics and volunteered for every organization that opposed social injustice; she read endless newspapers and manifestos, stuffing her brain with facts and statistics to use as ammo in her battles with all who disagreed with her. She wrote monthly letters to the editors of *Time*, *Newsweek*, and *The New Yorker*, and scrawled diatribes to local media. She dated quite a few men after her divorce, but as she never found anybody half as much fun to fight with as Billy, she quickly discarded them. She adored Ty and Karen and did her best to be a good mother, but as they grew older, she neglected them until something they said or did surprised her, then she fretted about them unduly for days. Johan, Bo, and I tried to take up the parental slack when she was unavailable, but now with Johan gone and Bo busy with his own family, the kids were turning more and more to me. I was grateful for their love, yet I often feared I was supplanting their mother. It was Aggie's own fault, I told myself, for relying on me as a surrogate parent; I certainly wasn't to blame for her political zealotry, nor for her lack of sensitivity toward her children's needs.

About most things my sister was a genius, but when it came to her own son and daughter she was a moron.

"Did you and Ty see Paulie while you were in Chicago?" Bo asked quietly, after a few minutes of watching *Cinderella* and listening to Aggie grouse. I'd elbowed her several times to shut her up, but she was determined not to enjoy the silly sweetness of the movie.

Bo was referring to Paulie Morse, the coarse, friendly young marine I'd met aboard the *Houston* during the war. Paulie somehow survived both the sinking of his ship and the deaths of hundreds of his shipmates; he also managed—though God knows how—to endure two horrific years as a Japanese POW in Singapore. We reconnected after the war and he now lived in Chicago. I'd visited him often over the past five years, but hadn't gotten together with him on the trip I'd just taken with Ty.

"There wasn't enough time," I said. Bo raised his eyebrows and I looked away. "Fine, don't believe me."

"You always see Paulie when you go to Chicago. Didn't he want to meet Ty?"

I sighed. "I thought it would be awkward."

On the screen, Cinderella's fairy godmother had just introduced herself and was now trying to find her lost wand. Aggie leaned in from my other side. "If Giambattista Basile ever saw this imbecilic incarnation of his fairy godmother—"

"Who the hell is Giambattista Basile?" I demanded.

"The author of the first European version of the Cinderella story," she said. "There are, of course, much older Greek and Egyptian antecedents. Anyway, as I was saying, if Basile ever saw this vile rendering of his fairy godmother, he'd probably take the fatuous old busybody's wand and stick it right up Walt Disney's—"

"Shush," I hissed. "Elias is trying to watch the movie."

The fairy godmother began to sing "Bibbidi-Bobbidi-Boo"

and Aggie put her face in her hands. "Oh, God, I'm in hell," she moaned.

Bo leaned in again. "Nothing's gonna change how much Ty loves you," he murmured, his lips by my ear to ensure no one else could hear him. "Same goes for Karen. You don't have to worry about them meeting Paulie, buddy."

Bo and Aggie were the only ones who knew Paulie and I were more than friends. Our relationship wasn't something I could trust sharing with anyone besides them since neither Paulie nor I were prepared to be professionally blacklisted and/or socially shunned if the nature of our attachment became public knowledge.

Bo, of course, had known I was attracted to men since we were teenagers messing around with each other in bed, and as adults we'd always been perfectly candid with each other about the people we were attracted to. Aggie had officially been let in on the secret during our junior year in college, when she accidentally interrupted me and my first real lover—an awkward, gap-toothed, and rather sweet journalism major named Joe Thierry—mere seconds after I'd lost my virginity. Once Aggie got over the shock of seeing Joe tumble naked off my mattress, pull on his pants, and skedaddle down the hallway, she said she wasn't overly surprised; she told me she should've figured it out years before, having watched me moon over Bo in high school and several of my college classmates since. For my part, I don't know why I'd never told her before; I should've realized she'd be no more judgmental about my sex life than Bo. All she said was "Just be careful, brother. This country is terribly cruel to people who don't fit in neat little boxes."

Elias was squirming in his chair and Karen leaned over to ask him something; he nodded, and they both stood up and made their way to the aisle.

"I told him not to drink so much Coke before the movie," Bo said. "He'll be upset he missed part of it."

"Go with them, Bo!" Janet said, clutching Bo's arm in panic. "Karen can't take him in the men's restroom, and he shouldn't be alone in there."

Aggie leaned across me. "Can you lower your voice a bit, Janet dear?" she asked politely. "Some of us are trying to watch the movie."

Janet began spluttering, and Bo put a hand on her knee to calm her. "Elias will be fine," he said. "Karen will be right outside the door."

An usher in the aisle startled us with a bright flashlight beam in our faces and a hiss for silence. I waved a hand in apology, and the light blinked out again.

"Blinding us was uncalled for," Aggie muttered. "I think I should demand to speak to the manager, don't you?"

"Nice try," I said, knowing she'd like nothing better than to make a scene. "Just sit there and suffer in silence for once in your life, would you please?

The swift transition from friendly acquaintances to lovers took both Paulie and me by surprise. After the war ended, the Japanese finally freed the 289 surviving members of the *Houston's* crew. I eventually saw Paulie's name on the list of released POWs and tracked him down for an interview, wanting to learn more about the *Houston*'s last day and what had happened to the survivors. When I found him, he'd just moved from his hometown in Massachusetts to Chicago, where he'd found work as an electrician.

The interview was hard because he was still traumatized from his experiences: On the *Houston*, the young man I'd known had been stocky, cheerful, and energetic, but during his two years in Singapore as a prisoner, he'd been tortured, starved, and worked nearly to death. I barely recognized him when we met for drinks at a bar on Michigan Avenue: I knew he was in his early twenties, but he could've passed for forty. I tried to hide my shock but failed.

"If you think I look bad now," he said with the ghost of a smile, "you shoulda seen me when I first got out."

He told me that before his capture he'd weighed 163 pounds, but when the doctors examined him upon his release, he was down to eighty-nine and could barely stand without help. He'd spent over a month in a naval hospital and gradually gained back about half of his lost weight, but he was still ridiculously thin and frail.

"They keep telling me I'll get back to normal soon, but I'm pretty sure that's a load of shit." He was still a smoker, even though it made him cough his lungs up.

We spoke for hours about the harrowing last battle in Sunda Strait and the death of so many of his friends, but he didn't want to talk about his time as a prisoner. The Japanese had fished 368 survivors of the *Houston* from the ocean that night, but seventy-nine died in the camps and he couldn't bear to speak of any of them.

Because he still weighed so little, he was seriously impaired after four beers; I was concerned he couldn't get home on his own, so I called a taxi and rode with him to his place. He lived on the third floor of a five-story apartment building with no elevator, so I helped him up the stairs, his arm over my shoulder, my arm around his waist. I was a little tipsy myself, and both of us were weaving and giggling as we climbed. It took a long time to reach his door. He fumbled with the lock—we banged heads retrieving his keys from the floor—and once we were inside the apartment I half carried, half dragged him to his bed, helped him strip down to his underwear, and pulled a blanket over his emaciated body.

He caught my hand as I was turning to go and pulled me back to sit on the bed. We hadn't turned on the lights when we came in, but the blinds were open and there was enough illumination coming from the street below for me to make out a small, single-room apartment with a hot plate, counter, and fridge in one corner and a toilet, sink, and tub in another. The room was sparsely furnished, with no visible clutter save for a half-full ashtray on the nightstand beside the bed.

"I like you, Isaac," he said, still holding my hand. "You're a hell of a good guy."

I squeezed his fingers; his hands were smaller than mine. "I like you, too, Paulie."

"Can you keep a secret, Mr. Reporter?" he asked.

"Sure. You're officially off the record."

"Lean over close and I'll whisper it to you."

I obeyed, and his lips lightly brushed my earlobe as he spoke. "I think you're like I am, but I'm not sure. Are you?"

The warmth of his breath made my heart speed up, and I pulled back a little to look at him. He was partly in shadows, but I could still make out the earnest, nervous expression on his face.

I leaned in close again. "How do you mean?" I murmured back.

His free hand traveled down my spine, pausing briefly when it reached my belt. "Like this," he said, tugging my shirttail out of my pants. His fingers tickled my lower back before slipping beneath the waistband of my boxers.

"Oh," I gasped. "Like that."

Since sweet, gap-toothed Joe Thierry relieved me of my virginity in college eight years before, I'd only had two other lovers—a grad student in mathematics I met when I was a senior at Drake, and a British reporter I crossed paths with a few times during the war—but neither of them was in my life for long. The math guy got a job in New Mexico a couple of weeks after we started seeing each other, and the reporter and I only shared a few pleasant nights here and there, wherever we happened to be covering the same story. Unsatisfyingly brief as these relationships were, I counted myself lucky to have had even that much romantic experience, as virtually every gay person in the world at that time was closeted, and letting another man know you were interested in him could literally destroy your life. The only places where I could be certain I was among my own kind were clubs that frequently got raided by the police.

Suffice it to say, I was delighted to discover Paulie liked me as much as I liked him.

We didn't fall asleep until dawn, and when we woke around ten in the morning, we were a little shy of each other at first, not knowing if what we'd done was just a drunken aberration, or something else. I was especially suspicious of my own motives, because I couldn't help noticing that Paulie was a redhead with a lot of freckles—like Bo. Was I only drawn to him because he resembled my dearest friend and was available to me in a way that Bo would never be?

But after another few hours in bed, I stopped asking myself those kinds of questions. I liked Paulie, and he liked me, and we both knew we were lucky to find each other, whether or not we ever got together again. Right then I honestly doubted we would, but there was something about him that at least made me think it was feasible. After all, he'd survived the sinking of his ship and two-plus years as a POW. Whatever else might be true, I was unlikely to scare him off.

Then again, few things on earth are more frightening than the possibility of love.

Fifteen months after VE Day, Bo stepped off the bus with Janet and their baby. The Army had finally released Bo from duty, but he'd needed to retrieve Janet and Elias in Ireland, prior to coming back to the States. The three of them took a boat from Limerick to New York, where they caught a bus to Des Moines. It was late afternoon and we were all slick with sweat; my light cotton shirt was plastered to my torso, and Aggie had her long hair tied up in a bun. Ty and Karen stampeded Bo the instant he appeared, with Aggie, Johan, and me right behind them. He grabbed each of us in turn for a ferocious bear hug, saving me for last. We hadn't seen each other for four years.

"Damned if you ain't even taller than you used to be," he said into my neck, squeezing me so tightly I could barely breathe. "Big shot reporters like you must eat a lot of raw meat."

It was so good to see him again, I was fighting tears. I'd feared the war might've roughened him as it had so many other soldiers I'd known, but if the strength of his grip and the love in his voice were any kind of reliable yardstick, he was the same old Bo.

"Welcome back, Lieutenant," I rasped. "I wasn't sure you still knew the way home."

Bo spent most of the war as a sergeant, but shortly before the end he'd gotten a promotion. He didn't tell me how he'd earned it, of course; all I knew from the self-effacing letter he'd sent was that his gain in rank had also come with a generous helping of shrapnel in his legs and lower back, in Bologna.

"I wasn't sure, either," he said, finally releasing me. "But I'm here now, and I ain't leaving again." He turned and pulled Janet forward with their baby. "Don't be shy, sweetie. No one here bites." He grinned at Aggie. "Except Aggie, sometimes."

Janet had been watching our reunion with a somewhat uncertain expression; she now favored us with a pretty, reserved smile, and said hello.

"Hello," Aggie said. "I'm Agnes. Don't believe anything Bo says about me."

I nudged my sister aside. "I bet you're exhausted, Janet. Let's get you home, shall we?"

"That would be nice," Janet said. "I am a wee bit tired."

"Can I hold the baby?" Johan asked.

Her smile faltered. "Elias doesn't do very well with strangers."

Bo snorted. "Since when?"

Janet reluctantly handed Elias to Johan; the baby burbled happily as Johan held him up for inspection. "Lord have mercy, but you're a dead ringer for your daddy, ain't you just?"

We crowded into our station wagon—Bo, Janet, and Elias were staying with us until they could get their own place—and once we arrived home, it was so stifling inside that we changed clothes and fled into the backyard, where at least there was shade and a breeze. In swimsuits, Ty and Karen ran through the lawn sprinkler while the rest of us drank vodka tonics and talked. It was surreal to be with Bo again after so much time apart. The conversation never lagged, but part of me didn't believe he was any more real than a desert mirage. He was keen to hear about everything he'd missed, and since I'd only returned to the States myself a short time ago, Johan and Aggie did most of the talking. Janet made no attempt to join the conversation, content to rock Elias in a baby swing while fanning him.

"For God's sake, it's *Iowa*, Bo," Aggie said at last, fending off another question from him. "Nothing really changes here, as you well know, and we want to hear about *you*. Your letters were criminally uninformative." She gave me a pointed glance. "I've given up on Isaac ever sharing anything, so I hope you're not as stingy with details."

I sighed. "Oh, good, here we go again."

"It's the truth. You never say a word about the war. I'm beginning to suspect someone else wrote your articles while you were taking a long nap, like Rip Van Winkle."

Bo's eyes met mine for a moment before he resumed watching Ty and Karen dart in and out of the water, their tanned, wiry little bodies glistening in the sun. "Let Isaac be, Aggie," he said. "He told us all plenty in the papers."

My heart hurt with how much I'd missed him. As a war correspondent I'd seen more than my share of horrors, but it was a safe bet Bo had seen worse. His division, the Red Bull, had logged more time on the front lines than any other in the

Army, and had suffered terrible casualties. The list of atrocities I'd cataloged for the UP was long and bloody—and included Bergen-Belsen and Nagasaki—yet if the war had taught me anything, it was that barbarism was universal.

"Fine," Aggie told me grudgingly, "keep your secrets." She was thrown by Bo's quiet admonition, and she studied him with a plaintive expression. "Are you *really* going to be as closemouthed as my ridiculous twin?"

"You know me," Bo said, grinning. "I'm an open book."

She told him that she and Johan had been wildly frustrated by the lack of news in his letters, due to the censors. "We didn't even know until a few months ago that you'd been to Ireland and Africa, let alone Italy. It still makes me furious that no one in authority would tell me *anything*."

"There's an Army fella in Public Relations who got a purple heart just for talkin' to her," Johan said. "The hollerin' made his ears bleed."

"Shush, Johan," Aggie said, smiling at him before turning back to Bo. She was happier than I'd seen her in years. "The most insufferable part was knowing that Isaac almost certainly knew where you were but wouldn't share the information with us in his letters."

I rolled my eyes; she knew perfectly well the censors would never have allowed me to say where Bo's division was deployed. "Aggie thinks I should've committed treason to keep her better informed," I told him.

"You knew where I was?" Bo asked. "How'd you manage that?"

"I had a source in the commander corps who tracked your division, but he always warned me not to trust his info. He said you guys in the Red Bull were pretty hard to keep tabs on."

"That's a fact," Bo said, laughing. "Half the damn time we was lost."

He told us about people he'd met in the Italian countryside, and various oddities he'd seen in and around Rome, but he barely mentioned the war, as if he'd been a tourist instead of a battle-hardened soldier trudging from one bloodbath to another. The sun chased away the shade above his chair and he excused himself, stripping off his shirt and running over to the sprinkler to play with the kids. I flinched when I saw that the left side of his lower back was now a network of white, ugly scars. His body was still slim and powerfully muscled, but the scars were a desecration, like a patch of graffiti on a marble statue.

"I couldn't stop crying when I saw what they'd done to him," Janet murmured, surprising me as I watched Bo. "His hip is even worse."

Bo came back toting Ty under one arm and Karen under the other, squirming and giggling. When he sat down, they fought over who got to sit on his lap; he scooped them both up, his lawn chair creaking. The kids, worn out from playing in the hot sun, quieted almost at once against his chest. Aggie asked if he still had pain from his injuries.

He shrugged. "Not much. I was luckier than most."

"You don't look so lucky to me," Johan said. "If I'd got chewed up like that, I'd still be screamin' my damn head off."

"You wouldn't either, you old liar," Bo said. "I saw a horse the size of a goddamn dinosaur stomp on your foot once, and you didn't even blink."

"I remember that, too," Aggie said. "It was an impressive display of manly stoicism."

Johan grinned at her. "It sure impressed the hell outta me."

"How come I don't remember that?" I asked. The only horses we'd ever had were back in Oklahoma. "Where was I?"

"You were in dutch with Sally for being mouthy," Bo said. "She made you mop floors while Aggie and I went to town with Johan and Sam."

"It was about time she punished you instead of me," Aggie said. "I usually caught the brunt of her tyranny."

"Sally wasn't no tyrant," Johan said mildly. "If you two hadn't sassed her so much, she woulda been sweet as pie."

"Aggie was way worse than I was," I protested. "I was too terrified of Sally to give her any grief."

Aggie snorted. "Is that why you always mimicked her so mercilessly?" She turned to Ty and Karen: "Whenever Sally asked us to do something, your uncle Isaac would say something like '*Yah, yah, Sally, we're wery hoppy to geef the floer a nice goot scroobing.*'"

Her uncanny imitation of Sally's singsong Swedish accent made Bo, Johan, and me laugh; Ty and Karen joined in, delighted by the rare sight of their mother enjoying herself.

"Did you really make fun of the way she talked, Uncle Isaac?" Karen asked.

"Of course not," I said. "I was such an angel that people often mistook me for Jesus."

Bo slid the kids off his lap and sprang to his feet. "I believe it's time to drag Jesus through the lawn sprinkler." My family cheered as he seized me under the armpits and dumped me unceremoniously on the ground.

"You're going to wake the baby," Janet complained.

"They had no right to throw us out of the movie," Aggie clucked, buttoning her coat in front of the Varsity Theater. The marquee above our heads announced WALT DISNEY'S *CINDER-ELLA* in bold red letters, but the letters were quickly being obscured by enormous wet flakes of snow.

"Stop looking so pleased with yourself," I said. After the usher's first warning, it had taken Aggie only five minutes to shoot off her mouth again. "In case you didn't notice what just happened in there, Ty and Karen were humiliated."

In exchange for removing Aggie from the theater, I'd persuaded the exasperated usher to let the kids stay for the rest of the movie with Bo and Janet; Ty and Karen hadn't even looked at us as we were marched out the door.

"All I did was ask you to consider the likelihood of foot fungus in Cinderella's pretty little glass slipper," Aggie said. "Every woman in the kingdom tried it on, for Pete's sake."

"That's not all you said, and you know it." I brushed snow from my eyelashes. "You were being unforgivably obnoxious."

"Then why were you laughing so hard?"

I stooped down and pretended to tie my shoe. "You caught me at a weak moment."

"I see." She sighed. "Well, regardless, it's a shame we were expelled. I was *so* looking forward to yet another grisly, jejune, overorchestrated ditty featuring singing mice. I may be a pacifist, but if I ever meet the sadist who composed those insipid little jingles, I'll snap his neck with a clean conscience. Just what do you think you're doing, Isaac? Don't you dare come closer or I'll—"

"Oh, my," I said, surveying the handful of snow I'd just plastered to the crown of her head. "That's very pretty."

Thank God I could still outrun her.

DAY FIVE

July 22, 1958. Wotho Atoll, the Marshall Islands.

"They'd just arrest you if you got any closer," Karen reminded me. "You'd be caught the second you stepped foot off this island."

I nodded, kicking at the sand on the beach as I gazed north. There was nothing to see but a serene, empty blue sky and the restless blue ocean fretting at the shore.

She took my hand. "They're likely irradiating everybody they catch, too, just for fun." Aside from Bo, Karen was the sweetest soul I knew, and the uncharacteristic edge in her voice was jarring. "I wonder how many reporters have ended up as guinea pigs in their experiments."

I suddenly felt guilty for bringing her and Ty along on this assignment. "Goats, not guinea pigs." My own bitterness spilled out. "Our military is overly fond of goats."

We'd arrived earlier that day on Wotho Atoll, 111 miles from Bikini, and from this distance we'd likely never see the explosion, maybe not even the telltale mushroom cloud. I'd found a pilot from Kwajalein to bring us this far via his battered, creaky flying boat, but he'd refused to go farther, even though I'd offered him more money than he could make in a month and only asked to view the blast from well outside the perimeter of the test area, completely safe from radiation fallout. I was frustrated at being balked, but I couldn't truly blame him: Only an idiot would risk running afoul of the Coast Guard and Navy patrols guarding the perimeter.

I kicked at the sand again and bit my lip to keep from screaming.

It made little sense, even to me, why I felt I needed to witness firsthand one of the tests. In Nagasaki, I'd already seen how much damage an atom bomb could do, I had no wish to stir up memories I'd spent thirteen years repressing. Yet if my information was correct, the boys at the Pentagon were playing with some brand-new toys—the kind of toys they only felt comfortable sharing with foreign VIPs, or homegrown politicians with top secret security clearance. It made my skin crawl to contemplate what was being unleashed in this remote corner of the world, away from prying journalistic eyes like mine.

Boys will be boys, after all.

"You did all you could, Uncle Isaac," Karen said, squeezing my hand. "You're a big part of all the protests going on."

She meant well, but I was too aware of my own uselessness to believe her. What I'd written about the devastating effects of America's nuclear testing program—the brunt of which were being borne by anyone unlucky enough to live in what was blithely referred to as the "Pacific Proving Ground"—may have added impetus to the push for an international test ban, but Eisenhower's consideration of a moratorium had thus far only incentivized every paranoid politician in the nuclear-armed world to drop as many bombs as possible before it went into effect.

I glanced at my watch: it was almost 4:00. The schedule that a source of mine had leaked to me last week in Honolulu said today's test—code-named "Juniper"—was set for 4:20, launching off a barge on the south side of Bikini Island. It would be a relatively small explosion, just sixty-five kilotons.

Three times more powerful than the bomb that leveled Nagasaki.

The U.S. had been detonating nuclear weapons on, above, below, and next door to Bikini Atoll for a dozen years, and many of them had been so monstrous they defied comprehension. The bomb used four years before, in the Castle Bravo test—affectionately nicknamed "Shrimp" by its oh-so-droll creators—was, all by itself, a *thousand* times more powerful than the Nagasaki explosion, vaporizing three islands, and God only knew what else in the blink of an eye. Next to that scale of destruction, poor little Juniper would seem cute and cuddly, like a radioactive bunny in a bonnet.

"Another twenty minutes," I said.

We heard Ty's voice from down the beach and turned to see him and Edward, our Marshallese translator, walking toward us, shoes and shirts dangling from their fingers. They'd gone for a swim in the lagoon and were still dripping wet, Ty in cut-off shorts and Edward in white cotton pants. The two young men looked so different from one other, it was almost comical. Each was handsome in his own way, but Ty was long-limbed and lanky, with pale, lightly sunburned skin, and hair the color of bleached straw; Edward was squat, black-haired, and brown-skinned. The height difference between them was at least ten inches, yet even more striking was the difference in their footprints in the sand. Ty's steps wandered from side to side as his attention drifted from one thing to another—he was always so interested in the world around him, he couldn't be bothered to focus on anything so confining as a destination—but Edward kept to a measured, somber line, setting one small brown foot in front of the other, like a tightrope walker.

"I wonder if that's a cultural thing, or just an Edward versus Ty thing," Karen said.

"What do you mean?"

"How they walk," she said, smiling. "It's what you were thinking about, right?"

I made the sign of the cross. "Get out of my head, she-devil."

Not even Aggie and Bo could read me like my niece and nephew could. I was capable of maintaining a decent poker face with the rest of the world, but Karen and Ty were ridiculously perceptive.

"You guys really should go for a swim," Ty said as he and Edward came up to join us. "I feel almost human again."

The water was theoretically free of radiation this far from Bikini, but I still had an irrational fear of going in the ocean anywhere in the same hemisphere. I'd tried to talk Ty out of swimming, even though Edward had assured me Wotho's lagoon was perfectly safe (aside from the occasional shark). If anyone knew where *not* to swim around here, it was him: He'd grown up on Bikini and had been shuffled from one place to another for years, along with the rest of his village, ever since the U.S. military turned their home into a plutonium playground.

"I'll go in if you will," Karen said to me. "I wouldn't mind feeling clean again."

None of us had showered in forever. The various islands and atolls we'd visited since arriving in Kwajalein eight days ago were stunningly beautiful, but notably lacking in basic plumbing.

"Maybe later," I said. "When the test is done."

"No use to wait," Edward said. His English was easy to understand but often blunt. "Can't see nothing much from here. Bomb's too small."

I grimaced. "I know, but I'm hoping we'll still hear it, at least. Sound travels pretty far across the water, doesn't it?"

"Won't hear nothing much, either."

"Ed's right, Isaac," Ty said. "Go for a swim." He gave me a distinctly Bo-like grin. "Or are you having too much fun glaring at the horizon like a gargoyle?"

"What's a gargoyle?" Ed asked.

"Come on, Uncle Isaac," Karen said. "Let's swim." She called over her shoulder to her brother as she tugged me toward the lagoon. "You guys mind setting up camp?"

"Sure," Ty said. "As long as you don't mind us starting happy hour before you get back."

Our pilot had gone back to Kwajalein for the night; we'd brought along a few necessities to survive until his return in the morning. Ed had told us the Wotho natives would likely offer to feed us—the Marshallese people we'd met were highly generous, in spite of the paucity of their own diet—but we didn't feel right about imposing on their hospitality. In addition to a mountain of cheese, fruit, bread, and cured meats in my backpack, I also had a full bottle of rum, and I knew Ty and Karen were similarly provisioned. We didn't mind roughing it when it came to sleeping on the ground and not having access to a toilet, but going hungry or thirsty was against the Dahl family creed.

I glanced out at the ocean to the north again, toward Bikini Atoll.

"Hands off my rum," I warned Ty.

Ben Oakes, my longtime editor at the United Press, was a seventy-four-year-old grandfather who, with each passing day, looked more and more like Mahatma Gandhi. The resemblance, sadly, was purely physical, given how he was becoming more salacious and profane with each passing year. He'd asked me earlier that spring to freelance for him, covering an antinuclear protest march in England. I'd just returned to Iowa when he called again, asking me to do an in-depth story about the ongoing series of atom bomb tests in the Marshall Islands.

"Isaac," he'd barked, not bothering to identify himself. "That shit-licking Hungarian prick is up to his old tricks."

I was used to this sort of greeting from Ben. "Can you be more specific?" I asked.

"Sure, happy to. Edward Fucking Teller is once again corn-holing the natives of Bikini Island, while the generals and admirals sit back and jack off with their pet lapdogs from Los Alamos." He paused to yawn; he suffered from chronic insomnia. "What really pisses me off is they're not allowing the press to join in their degenerate orgy this time."

Staunch Republican or not, Ben was deeply suspicious of America's nuclear program. He'd been present for the Castle Bravo test in '54, and the enormity of the blast scared the bejesus out of him. What dismayed him far more, however, was the arrogance of the men responsible for it. He'd seen what had been done to Bikini, and he couldn't abide Edward Teller, the physicist who was the main instigator of the Marshall Islands tests. When a Japanese fishing boat got caught in a cloud of lethal fallout, contaminating the crew, Teller was heard to comment, "It's unreasonable to make such a big deal over the death of a fisherman," and from that point on, Oakes always referred to Teller as "that shit-licking Hungarian prick."

Anyway, Ty and Karen were on summer vacation from college, and when Ben hired me, I'd invited them along, mainly because I knew that after a month with Aggie they were climbing the walls. Aggie had wanted to come as well, but I'd threatened to shoot her if she got near the plane. The last thing I needed while conducting a semicovert investigation was the presence of my volatile, radical, socialist sister who couldn't read the words *atom bomb* in a newspaper without screaming. After three days of argument, she finally conceded I might have a point, but on the morning of our flight she woke in a petty mood.

"Admit it, Isaac, you've become timid in your reporting," she'd said, pouting as we loaded our suitcases into the back of Bo's station wagon. "The only reason you don't want me to come is because I'd make you ask all the questions you're afraid to ask."

I rolled my eyes. "It's called journalism, Aggie. I'm a reporter, not a gossip columnist."

"As if there's a difference." She was barefoot and wearing a pair of my jeans; her white T-shirt was stained with red wine, and her long blond hair was tied up in a sloppy bun on top of her head. She was forty years old but looked twenty-five. "You need to rediscover your testicles."

"Leave him be, Aggie," Bo said, climbing into the driver's seat. "Believe it or not, not everything wrong with the world is Isaac's fault." He grinned at me as Ty and Karen said their goodbyes to their mother and got in the back seat. I kissed Aggie on her cheek, and she briefly rested her forehead against mine before pulling away.

"Keep out of my room while I'm gone," I warned her. My bedroom was her favorite place to read, ever since I'd constructed a cozy nook in one corner with an overstuffed chair and a wall of books within reach. "I'm tired of cleaning up coffee spills on everything I own."

She bent down to ruffle Ty's hair through his open window. "Be careful," she said, blowing a kiss at Karen as I slid into the front passenger seat. "Please don't let your uncle Isaac's kowtowing to authority rub off on you."

Bo started the car. "I'll send Elias over to see you when I get back home," he said to Aggie. "He needs to apologize for this morning."

"He has nothing to apologize for," Aggie said.

I'd always believed that Bo's sweet-natured son, now fifteen, had inherited little of his mother's moodiness, but Elias had been very Janet-like that morning. He and Bo had joined us for breakfast—Janet had declined our invitation due to a recent feud with Aggie—and Elias sulked through the entire meal, rising from the table the instant he was done eating and brusquely telling Bo he was walking home. He fled the house before Bo could respond, and we'd all been taken aback.

"When your god has forsaken you," Karen said, "two weeks is an eternity."

I glanced over my shoulder in time to see Ty frowning at his sister. "What are you talking about?" he asked.

"You, of course," Karen said. "Elias is hurt because you decided to come with us for two whole weeks of his summer vacation, instead of staying here with him."

"That's stupid," Ty protested. "He must've been mad about something else."

"Karen's right," Aggie said, still leaning through Ty's window to be part of the conversation. "Elias hates sharing you with anybody, Ty. He has a crush on you."

"He has a *what*?"

"There's some hero worship mixed in, too," Karen said.

"You're both nuts," Ty said, "but especially you, Mom. Elias and I talk about girls all the time. He likes them as much as I do."

Bo fiddled with his key chain in the ignition. "I'm not so sure that's true," he said. "Janet and I have had a few doubts on that front lately."

"Oh, good, you and Aunt Janet have gone insane, too," Ty said. "Maybe I shouldn't tell you this, Bo, but Elias has a stash of *Playboy* magazines in his closet. He showed them to me at your Fourth of July party."

"That only proves he's a teenager," Aggie said. "Haven't you noticed how red-faced and tongue-tied he gets every time you walk in the room? He reminds me a lot of Isaac at that age."

I reached over the seat to shove her head out of the car, but she evaded me.

Bo met my eyes, looking uncomfortable. "Do you think Elias is like you, Isaac?"

His disquiet startled me, because he'd never had an issue with my sexuality, and I knew he remembered as well as I did what we'd sometimes done in bed together when we were Elias's age.

He saw my surprise and squeezed my shoulder. "I'm just worried about Elias, buddy," he said. "I don't want what happened to Paulie to happen to him, too."

Nor did I, of course.

Paulie Morse and I had broken off our relationship several years before—the long-distance thing wasn't working for us—but had remained in touch until he was arrested last winter in Chicago for soliciting an undercover cop. He'd avoided prison, but the scandal had cost him his job and reputation. He'd since moved to a small town in Oregon, severing ties with everyone he knew, including me.

"I don't know for sure," I said, turning back to Ty. "But I think Aggie may be right."

Ty's face fell. "Oh, God, Isaac, are you serious? Elias is like my little brother. How can he have a crush on me?"

I glanced sideways at Bo. "Stranger things have happened."

Karen and I had a quiet corner of Wotho's lagoon to ourselves for our swim. A single fisherman—an old man with a toothless smile and a pronounced limp—was tinkering with his boat nearby on the beach, but the rest of the island's seventy or so permanent residents were nowhere to be seen, their village hidden by coconut trees and dense vegetation. White faces like ours were still an oddity here; our arrival had caused quite a stir. Once the village chief learned I was a journalist, however, he became worried I might draw too much attention to his small island, bringing down the wrath of those who had the power to obliterate it with the flick of a finger. He shooed his people away, telling them not to bother me. His anxiety was misplaced and unreasonable, but I couldn't blame him, any more than I blamed the pilot for not getting me closer to Bikini.

Anyway, by the time Karen and I finished swimming and returned to where Ty and Edward had set up camp, the Juniper test over Bikini Island was presumably over and done with—aside from the fallout no doubt wafting around Bikini like snow—and as Edward had predicted, I hadn't seen or heard anything. It was a hot day and sunset was hours away, so the young men hadn't bothered to build a fire; they'd simply piled a mountain of bread, cheese, fruit, and beef jerky in the middle of a large blanket and were sitting on each side of the blanket, sharing a fifth of Jack Daniel's. Ty was still in his cutoff shorts, but Edward was primly buttoned up in a short-sleeved, white cotton shirt, and blue pants. Ty offered me the bottle of whiskey—already half-empty—as I squatted beside him.

"Cheers," he said. "Ed wanted to drink your rum, but I wouldn't let him."

"Ty is a big liar," Edward informed me amiably. "He says open your rum, but I say no."

Physical and cultural dissimilarities aside, the two had become fast friends. From the moment we'd hired the laconic, soft-spoken Edward as our guide in Kwajalein, Ty had peppered him with questions about everything from Marshallese customs to local gossip, and within an hour they'd begun ribbing each other like old frat buddies.

I took a swig of Jack and passed the bottle to Edward. "Thank you for having more honor than my nephew," I said. "He and his mother steal my booze all the time."

"Only when we can find it," Ty said, grinning. "You've gotten good at hiding your stash."

Karen, dressed in a halter top and shorts, knelt next to Edward and dug a comb from her backpack. She took a swallow of whiskey as it passed by, then started untangling the knots in her long hair. When her hair was wet, it was dark gold; when dry, it was so blond it was nearly white. Edward was trying to be a gentleman and not gawk, but his eyes kept drifting over her as she ran the comb through her hair. Karen had inherited all of Aggie's long-legged, fine-boned beauty, but to her credit I don't believe she noticed the effect she was having on Edward. She was accustomed to being stared at and never seemed to give it much thought.

"The bread's stale, but the cheese and jerky are good," Ty told me. He waved a mosquito from my bare shoulder; I was still wet from swimming and in no hurry to dress, either.

Three youngsters—a girl and two boys—appeared from the trees farther down the beach and eyeballed us for a minute before ambling our way, their curiosity trumping their chief's admonition to avoid us. The kids were walnut-skinned like Edward; they wore bright orange shirts and white shorts. One of the boys was shod in sneakers, but the girl and the other boy were barefoot. The boy in sneakers called out as they got closer.

"He asks if you are surfers," Edward translated. "He saw magazine picture of boy surfer with same yellow hair."

Karen laughed. "Tell him the Dahl family is too clumsy to surf." She turned to Ty with a grin. "Can you imagine anything more pathetic than Uncle Isaac on a surfboard?"

"Don't be cruel," I said. "If I didn't have two left feet, I'd be a wonderful athlete."

"What's wrong with feet?" Edward asked, staring at mine.

"It's a joke, buddy," Ty explained. "Balance isn't really Isaac's strong suit."

"*Yokwe*," Karen greeted the kids in Marshallese as they came up to stand beside our picnic blanket.

They answered her shyly. I guessed them to be in their early teens. All three were short and very thin—Edward had told us food was often scarce for the islanders, and consisted of mostly fish, pandanus, and coconuts. The barefoot girl and boy had the same round chins, small ears, and delicate hands, so I guessed they were brother and sister. The boy in sneakers was almost preternaturally beautiful, with a wide, happy smile and large brown eyes that darted from Ty to Karen to me, as if he couldn't get enough of us. We were just as curious about the three of them; I couldn't imagine growing up on a tiny atoll like this, so separate from the rest of the world. I asked Edward to introduce us, and as he told the kids our names I offered an apple to the girl. The boys eyed her jealously as she bit into it.

"Are you hungry?" I asked through Edward, gesturing at the indecent amount of food on our blanket. "There's plenty for everybody."

They gaped at Edward as if they couldn't believe he'd translated correctly; then they nodded enthusiastically and stepped forward. The girl was Dilini, her brother was Henry, and the boy in sneakers was Jobel. Ty scooted over to make room for Jobel to sit between us; Dilini and Henry squatted between Karen and Edward. We encouraged them to help themselves to the food, but they seemed unsure of the protocol until Karen stuffed a huge chunk of cheese in her mouth, putting them at ease. Jobel, through Edward, asked what we were drinking, and Ty told him he'd be far wiser to stick with coconut milk. The boy asked why we were drinking something bad for us.

"Great question," Karen said. "Stop hogging that poison, Ty, and let me have some."

Wotho's white beaches and coconut trees were lovely, but I felt oddly claustrophobic surrounded by so much water. It suddenly occurred to me that Marshallese kids this age were the first in their culture to have no memory of the world without American bombs raining down on them. I asked what they knew about all the nuclear testing going on at Bikini and Eniwetok, and Jobel answered, saying the U.S. military used to notify them when the tests were being conducted on the other islands, but no longer deemed it necessary to do so, as Wotho had been declared safe from the radiation.

"Did you hear anything about the *Golden Rule,* or the *Phoenix*?" Ty asked them.

Two separate sailboat crews had recently attempted sailing to Bikini to protest the bombs. The *Golden Rule* was detained the instant they left Hawaii; its crew tried again shortly thereafter, defying a judge's order, and was imprisoned. The *Phoenix of Hiroshima,* manned by an American family and a Japanese sailor, actually made it into the test area in early July, but was then boarded by the Coast Guard. The father of the family was still in jail, and likely to remain there for some time. All three of our dinner guests began to jabber excitedly after Ty's question, but Dilini, the girl, outtalked the boys.

"*Phoenix* came to Wotho before Bikini," Edward relayed. "They stay in Wotho lagoon and eat supper here in village. Dilini like boy on boat. Name was Ted."

"Ted," repeated Dilini, nodding and smiling.

Jobel seemed annoyed, either by losing his position as spokesperson or perhaps by less-than-fond memories of Ted. I asked if they'd heard what happened to the crew of the *Phoenix*. Dilini's face fell when I shared the bad news, but she recovered quickly after Karen reassured her Ted was fine. Henry reached up as Karen was talking, touching her hair with wonder. Karen rewarded the boy with a sweet smile that would likely wreak havoc in his dreams.

Jobel asked, around a mouthful of beef jerky, why we were on Wotho. I sighed, unwilling to dwell on how I'd dragged my nephew and niece on a fool's errand.

"Because, Jobel," Ty answered, glancing slyly at me, "Isaac is a reporter, and he can't stand giving up on a story, even when it's perfectly clear he's reached a dead end and is in danger of giving himself an aneurysm because he's so pissed off. You see, Isaac doesn't seem to realize that any second now his head is going to explode if he doesn't relax, and—"

"Okay, okay," I interrupted. "Point taken."

Edward frowned at Ty. "You say too much to translate."

Karen reached over Henry and Dilini and patted Edward's wrist. "Just tell them Isaac is trying to stop the bombs."

Edward passed this on to the kids, or at least I assumed that's what he was doing, but as he spoke, he was blushing, clearly thrown by Karen's touch. Ty leaned over and dropped his voice so only Jobel and I could hear him. "I think Ed's in love."

I nodded. "And Karen's utterly clueless."

Jobel, not understanding a word of English, watched our faces as we spoke, cocking his head. I glanced at Karen again, laughing at Henry as the boy jammed so much bread into his mouth he couldn't chew. Edward laughed, too, but his gaze never left Karen's face. She caught me looking at her and raised her eyebrows.

"Something wrong?" she asked.

"Not a thing," I said. "Pass the whiskey, would you?"

After dark we built a fire on the beach. The mosquitos were vicious, so Ty, Karen, and I pulled on pants and long-sleeved shirts in spite of the hot night air. Dilini and Henry's mother, Lomina, came to retrieve her offspring just as we were introducing them to their first graham cracker sandwiches. Lomina declined our invitation to join us and insisted Dilini and Henry follow her home. Their protests merged with the cry of a solitary seagull in the sky, and they returned to the village in tears, fingers sticky with marshmallows and melted chocolate. Jobel stayed put, however, and the toothless old fisherman that Karen and I had seen earlier came to sit with us, too. His name was Junior, and he was Jobel's grandfather. Jobel's father had been killed by a shark when Jobel was an infant. Jobel's mother refused food and water afterward, and was found facedown in the surf a week later. Junior—who was alarmingly fond of my rum—had picked up a handful of English phrases from his years around sailors and fishermen. I don't think he really knew what most of them meant, but his favorites seemed to be: "Pleased as punch to meetya," and "No skin off my goddamn nose."

I rose late in the evening, somewhat unsteadily, to take a walk on the beach. I found myself accompanied by Jobel, who seemed to think I needed a chaperone in the darkness. In truth, I could see just fine. The stars were glorious, crowding the sky and sparkling like rock salt on black velvet, and the crescent moon was drawing a wide, shimmering line of light on the ocean, hundreds of miles long. In spite of our inability to communicate, Jobel was easy company, cheerful and quiet, with a playful streak. He'd abandoned his sneakers by the fire, and he scampered ahead of me, barefoot and fast. I watched him dig in the sand at the water's edge and then sprint back, holding something out to me, glittering in the moonlight. It was a type of shell I'd never seen, with two sharp, tented edges and several short, wartlike prongs jutting from its middle; the vertical aperture was smooth and graceful.

"Thanks, Jobel, it's beautiful," I said. "What kind of creature calls this home?"

He seemed to understand my question; he took my free hand and drew a spiral on my palm with his index finger.

"A snail?" I asked.

He said something that sounded like "*jinenpokpok*," and when I repeated it, he nodded and smiled, releasing my hand. We walked a little farther in silence. I listened to the sound of the surf, rolling in again and again, and found myself wondering what would happen to this boy by the time he was forty, like me. Even assuming the radiation from Bikini and Eniwetok never made it this far, I feared his life was destined to worsen very soon. The world was growing smaller by the second, and I doubted Wotho would escape the ravages of civilization. On the plus side, Jobel and his people might acquire indoor plumbing, televisions, and a more reliable diet; on the minus side they'd likely follow Hawaii's destiny and become so westernized that their elders would no longer recognize their own children.

Jobel wandered to the tree line to urinate, and I did the same nearby, listening to the steady soughing of the ocean behind us, lapping at the shore. About half a mile back the way we'd come, I could see our fire, surrounded by Ty, Karen, Edward, and Junior. I heard their laughter on the breeze and was grateful Ty and Karen had come with me on this trip. I wished Bo and Aggie could have seen this place, too, even though my disgruntled sister's presence would have been a mixed blessing.

Jobel and I wandered ankle-deep in the surf and gazed at the ocean, hypnotic as ever in its immensity and beauty. Jobel seemed content to stay with me as long as I wanted to stand there. I was transfixed by the night and wished time might stop; I tilted my head back to gaze at the stars. I didn't recognize the constellations, save for the Southern Cross. The last time I'd been in that part of the world and could see the sky this well was when I was aboard the *Houston*, in '42. It occurred to me that the men who'd made it off the ship when she sank had seen the same sky overhead, before they either drowned or were captured, and I wondered if they'd found any comfort in its unearthly peace.

"You're lucky, Jobel, to live here," I murmured. "Don't ever leave home and go to war."

He cocked his head, and the moon was so bright that I could see him smile uncertainly. "*Eañ?*" He was standing right at my elbow, and the top of his head only came up to my shoulder. He pointed at a bright star directly overhead and said an unpronounceable word I assumed was the star's name.

"Yeah?" I asked. "I'll have to take your word for it." Maybe it was only the booze, but I was feeling terribly sad. Dwelling on the dead from the *Houston* had been a mistake, because now their ghosts were with me, milling about on the beach.

"Ah, Jobel, I'm sick of writing epitaphs for lost souls and lost causes," I breathed. "That's why I'm here, by the way. I'm an artist with last words." I glanced down at the boy. "Got any headstones you want me to inscribe? Corpses I can commemorate?"

Lord, I was drunk.

"Even if I could make the bombs stop falling, buddy, would it matter?" I rubbed my temples. "What's the big deal about an island or two in the middle of nowhere? A tidal wave could come along tomorrow and wipe you all off the face of the earth, so what does it matter if Edward Teller gets here first with his nukes?" I was surprised to find Jobel's small arms around my waist; he must've heard the pain in my voice. "You may say I've had too much to drink," I muttered, resting my chin on his head, "but sometimes that's the only sane response to human stupidity."

A familiar voice crowed from behind us, making us both jump. "Ha, I was right!"

Jobel and I turned to find Karen a few feet away, her feet in the ocean and her long hair tied in a ponytail.

"Ty and I made a bet," she said. "He said you'd be passed out on the beach, but I said it was far more likely that you were talking Jobel to death. You just won me twenty dollars."

Seeing her lessened the tightness in my chest. "For your information," I said, pulling her into a tight embrace with Jobel and me, "Jobel was just holding forth—and most eloquently, too, I might add—about Mother Nature and Edward Teller, who are clearly in cahoots to end the human race."

"I see," she said drily. "Jobel must be quite intoxicated to talk like that."

"Hush, now, and look up at that sky, would you? Look at that moon. Have you ever seen anything so gorgeous? Who in his right goddamn mind would drop a bomb on a place like this?" I snorted in her hair. "Your mom's vegetable garden should be ground zero, for God's sake. It's an abomination— she force-feeds dog excrement to her poor tomato plants, to make them grow. Anyway, when I'm done exposing Teller- and-Company's latest outbreak of insanity, all will be right with the universe, just you wait and see. Everything may *seem* utterly pointless to those who lack faith, but never fear! My mighty pen will stave off Armageddon."

"You need sleep, Uncle Isaac," she said, taking my hand. "How about we go back to the fire for a nightcap? Junior drank all your rum, but I saved you a little of my brandy."

"That's my girl," I said, letting her and Jobel gently guide me home.

DAY SIX

September 12, 1966. Grenada, Mississippi.

"Jesus, it's like a field hospital in here," Stephen muttered.

I nodded bleakly as I watched a silent, grim woman bind Elias's torso with a strip of cloth torn from a bedsheet. Elias bit his lip to keep from crying out. The skin on his right side, from waist to armpit, had already turned an ugly, yellowish black. His left eye was also swollen shut, and two fingers on his right hand—the pinky and ring finger—were broken. His shirt was in tatters beside him on the pew; he'd been dragged down a gravel alley and beaten by five men before we were able to rescue him.

Stephen asked if I needed anything and I shook my head, so he went to work snapping photos of all the wounded sprawled on the pews and the floors of the Bell Flower Baptist Church. There were dozens of casualties from the morning's march, maybe as many as a hundred, maybe more. Most were black children, some as young as six years old. The church smelled of sweat, rubbing alcohol, vomit, and urine. Some of the smallest kids had lost control of their bladders when the mob came after them.

The woman tending to Elias finished wrapping his ribs, securing the cloth with duct tape. She'd set up a crude triage area near the altar of the church. Those with the most serious injuries had already been shipped to the hospital in the bed of a pickup. I'd learned she'd attended nursing school at Tuskegee for almost two years when she was younger but hadn't finished her education because she'd been needed at home.

"You best go along with Roy to the hospital, when he comes back with the truck," she told Elias, rising from the pew with a sigh after checking her handiwork a final time, her brown fingers tugging gently at the white cloth bandage to make sure it was snug. "You likely got some busted ribs, but you're breathing fine, so leastwise you ain't got to worry about your lungs."

He thanked her, wincing with pain, and she gave him a tired smile.

"What can I do to help?" I asked her.

She eyed me skeptically. "Know anything about first aid?"

I shook my head. "Not much, I'm afraid."

"Well, some of the kids there by the door ain't hurt too bad." She handed me iodine and a carton of cotton before turning to a teenaged boy with a badly swollen face, missing teeth, and a broken arm. "Clean 'em up as best you can, and try to keep 'em calm till I get to 'em."

I glanced down at Elias and he nodded. "Go ahead, Uncle Isaac. I'll be fine."

"I'm so, *so* sorry for this," I told him, squeezing his shoulder. His skin was sticky with blood and sweat.

He took my hand. "I'm the reason you're here, not the other way around. Remember?"

"Yeah, but your mom and dad are still going to kill me."

The grin he gave me was so much like Bo's it hurt my heart. "Mom thinks I'm in Iowa, and Dad's smart enough to know this is my own fault." He squeezed my fingers tightly and his grin evaporated. "I'd be a whole lot worse off if it weren't for you and Stephen."

My terror rose up again like it had when I saw him hauled off the street. If Stephen hadn't been there, God only knows what would've happened. Together, we'd barreled into the thugs beating Elias; Stephen was a big man and had sent them all sprawling, tripping over their own feet. They'd recovered quickly, however, and chased the three of us for blocks, screaming obscenities and throwing rocks when they couldn't catch us. Elias was somehow still able to run on his own steam, and they finally gave up, turning around and returning to the march to seek slower, easier prey.

Prey, like the little black kids crying and bleeding all over the church.

It was the first day of school in Grenada, Mississippi, and a frenzied mob was doing everything in its power to keep black kids out of white schools. The local police and state troopers were turning a blind eye to the mayhem, as was the governor of Mississippi. The mob wasn't well-organized, but what they lacked in brains and basic human decency they more than made up for in spittle-spraying savagery. It wasn't only men, either, who were guilty of the violence; there were women and children among them, equally vicious.

Elias had come here to join in a series of protest marches to confront the rampant racism in Mississippi's educational system. At twenty-three, he seemed intent on becoming a full-time activist; he'd joined every protest march he could find since graduating college, and had already been arrested four times for disturbing the peace. This was his first venture into the Deep South, though, and for all his passion I doubted very much he'd really known what he was getting into. Middle-class white boys from Iowa seldom got bloodied for their beliefs.

I was ostensibly on hand as a reporter—with Stephen Waters, a photographer and close friend I'd been working with for several months—but the real reason we'd come was to keep an eye on Elias. Bo was worried sick about his son's safety but couldn't get away from his work to accompany him; Stephen and I were on a hiatus from our current assignment in Vietnam, and not due back for another two weeks, so we'd volunteered to come in Bo's place. Having been on the far side of the globe for some time, we'd missed much of the ugliness happening in our own country. I'd known things were bad, but seeing such malice against schoolchildren was still shocking. As I made my way down a long row of kids lined up against the church wall— their eyes huge and disbelieving from what had just happened to them, most of them injured and some still visibly trembling—I found myself wondering how on earth any of them would ever get past a morning like this one.

"Hi, I'm Isaac," I told a little boy who only came up to my waist. "What's your name?" I bent down to examine him, and he stared at me, wide-eyed and mute. "Can I clean that cut on your head? It looks like it hurts."

He didn't answer; he just watched me tip iodine on a cotton ball. I told him it was going to sting, but he barely flinched as I cleaned the wound. When I applied a bandage, though, he began to cry, silently, his eyes flooding all at once. My own throat tightened as I hugged him; I could feel his heart beating against mine. I gave his back a final pat and told him I needed to help the next person. He released me without a fuss, drying his nose on his sleeve.

"Hello there," I said to a young girl with a torn pink dress and a terrible welt on the left side of her neck. "My name is Isaac."

"I'm Mary," she whispered. The wound on her neck was a horror of puffy, violated skin, with a vivid red stripe running through the middle that could only have come from a whip. I asked her if she knew who'd hurt her and she nodded. "Mr. Pernod," she said, gasping as I dabbed her cut with iodine. "From the hardware store."

She told me about a friend of hers named Jade Winningham, who'd marched beside her. Jade had a bad knee and couldn't run. Mary said she saw three Klansmen fling Jade to the ground and stick a gun to her head, telling her they'd kill her if she went to the white school. A local policemen watched it happen and was laughing along with the Klansmen, as if it were the funniest thing he'd ever seen. "They hurt Jade bad," Mary said. "She couldn't walk no more after they was done."

"Isaac?"

Stephen had joined me while Mary was talking. His pale, bearded face looked as placid as ever—people often made the mistake of thinking him slow-witted, because his habitual expression was one of almost bovine contentment—but I knew better. Beneath that calm exterior was a sharp mind and a fierce temper, and unless I missed my guess, he was nearing his boiling point.

"Hey," I said, "take it easy, okay?"

He nodded curtly and drew a slow, ragged breath before speaking. "Roy just got back with the pickup. He's taking Elias and some of the others to the hospital."

I glanced over and found Elias, now on his feet by the altar, his tattered shirt draped over his shoulders. He looked awfully young and vulnerable with the bandage wrapped around his chest like a corset. His normally handsome face, marred by pain and a black eye, was pale and drawn. "I better go along," I said, handing Stephen the iodine and cotton. "You staying here?"

"Yeah. I need more pictures."

I nodded and told him I'd be back as soon as I got Elias squared away. I didn't have to tell him to be careful while I was gone: We both knew the Klan was targeting journalists along with black activists and children.

"Elias won't let you come back without him," he said.

I nodded, grimacing. "I'm hoping the doctor will talk some

sense into him. His ribs can't take another beating like that. He'll start coughing up bone shards."

"He's tougher than he looks. I still can't believe he was able to run so fast after those assholes worked him over."

"I still can't believe *we* were able to run that fast, either," I said. "I almost had a heart attack." I took a last look around the church. Everywhere I turned there was somebody bleeding, or with a broken limb, or swathed in bandages. Everybody was moving slowly, like residents in a nursing home; some of the young men and women looked crushed by exhaustion and despair. A few, though, had a pent-up, smoldering fury in their eyes that I found oddly comforting, though it also frightened me.

This fight was far from over.

"I'm starting to think it would've been smarter to stay in Vietnam," Stephen said quietly.

I fed coins into the phone, grateful the hospital provided a wooden booth for privacy in the hall outside the waiting room. Aggie answered at once, as I'd known she would. She seldom left the house anymore because she didn't have to. She'd quit working as a tutor and had become a copy editor for a university press; her expertise in multiple fields made her invaluable. She spent most of her days—and nights—poring over manuscripts at our kitchen table, swilling strong black coffee by the potful and chain-smoking Winston cigarettes.

"Don't start yelling, please," I said. "I couldn't get to a phone until now."

"Isaac, thank God!" The relief in her voice was palpable. "I've been worrying myself sick, listening to the radio. Bo is climbing the walls, too. He keeps calling from the store to see if I've heard anything."

"I'll have Elias call him."

"Tell him he'd also better call Janet. The silly cow is threatening to fly back to America if she doesn't hear from him right away."

Janet and Bo had divorced the year before and she'd returned home to Ireland immediately after Elias graduated from college. I told Aggie that Elias didn't think Janet even knew where he was.

"No, but she's figured out he's in trouble," Aggie said. "She tried to get the details out of me this morning, but I played dumb until she lost her temper and hung up." Aggie's tone changed when I didn't respond. "What aren't you telling me, Isaac? Are you hurt?"

"I'm fine, but Elias wasn't so lucky." I shared the events of the morning, and it was her turn to be silent. Our connection was clear enough for me to hear her striking a match as she lit another cigarette.

"I knew I should've come with you," she muttered. Her voice skirled out of control. "Goddamn redneck *assholes*!"

I'd known she'd be livid, which was why I'd put off calling until I was sure Elias was going to be okay. Three of his ribs were indeed cracked, but his lungs were fine. The doctor who'd rebound his torso and splinted his broken fingers had told him he'd been extremely lucky, but had also warned him that any further damage to his rib cage would puree his insides like a blender.

"How did things get so out of hand?" Aggie demanded. "Where were the police when those poor children were running the gauntlet and Elias was being beaten half to death? Where was the goddamn National Guard?"

"The police were there, but apparently they had better things to do with their time." The tremor in my voice surprised me; I hadn't realized until that moment how raw I still felt about the atrocities I'd witnessed that morning. "Things like clubbing little black kids senseless with their nightsticks, for instance."

"Christ, Isaac, if President Johnson had any spine at all, he'd order the army into that miserable hellhole and geld every Klansman they find."

I smiled in spite of myself. "I thought you disapproved of presidents siccing the military on civilians."

"Not when the civilians are barbarians." She took a long, shaky drag on her cigarette. "Barbarians with tiny little brains, and even tinier little penises."

I told her I had to go. Elias and I were getting ready to return to the church, and Elias still needed to call Bo. Classes at the school were being released at noon, and the mob would be waiting outside for the black kids who'd managed to elude them that morning.

"You're letting Elias go back there?" Aggie asked in disbelief. "He'll get himself killed, Isaac!"

"I know, but he won't listen."

"Put him on the phone this instant."

I opened the door of the booth and beckoned to Elias. He was sitting across the hall, chatting with a young black man who'd also been injured. Elias rose in obvious discomfort and shuffled over to join me. Somebody had given him a white T-shirt to replace his ruined one, but it was several sizes too large and made him look like a young boy.

"Aggie wants to talk to you," I said, handing him the receiver. He took it warily.

"Hi, Aunt Aggie." His expression turned obstinate as he listened to whatever Aggie was saying. "Uncle Isaac was exaggerating. I'm fine."

"No, you're not," I told him. "You look like hell."

"If you were here with us," he said to Aggie, ignoring me, "you'd be the first one trying to protect those kids. Don't even try to pretend otherwise."

That was true enough, as far as it went. Aggie was as much of a firebrand as she'd ever been, but a year or so before she'd finally listened when I told her she was far more useful on paper than in person. She'd gained notoriety as a writer of brilliant, inflammatory essays for progressive magazines, but whenever she ventured out in the world, she was a liability to her allies, provoking ugly confrontations in situations that might otherwise have remained peaceful. When her last outing resulted in a free-for-all that put three of her friends in the hospital, I was at last able to convince her that she was doing more harm than good by attending demonstrations.

"I promise I'll be more careful, okay?" Elias said, attempting to shut her up. It didn't work, of course; he glanced at me helplessly as she continued to harangue him. "I have to go now, Aunt Aggie. Here's Uncle Isaac again. Bye, love you!"

He thrust the phone back in my hands and retreated.

"Coward," I mouthed at him, cupping the receiver.

"—not done talking to you yet, young man," Aggie snapped, unaware of her change in audience. "Being careful isn't enough. I know you grew up listening to Isaac's stories, and you think if you're smart like him, nothing bad will happen to you. What you don't understand, however, is that Isaac's good fortune has absolutely nothing to do with brains. He's just absurdly *lucky*. That sweet fool of a man could douse his head in gasoline and walk into a burning building without suffering more than a fever blister. But you're not him, Elias, and—"

"Yes, indeedy," I broke in, "my life has been nothing but pure bliss. Well, I guess there was that little avalanche in Utah, and near-starvation in the Dust Bowl, and a ruptured appendix in Guam, and malaria in the Philippines, and frostbite in Korea, and typhoid in Cambodia—"

"—all of which just goes to prove my point," she retorted, unfazed. "It's only by the grace of God you're still breathing, Isaac Dahl, and I'm scared to death Elias won't survive being around you. Chain him to a hospital bed if you must, but don't you dare let him go back to that school."

"He doesn't need my permission, Aggie. He's a grown man." I sighed at her dissatisfied snort. "I have to hang up now. He needs to call his dad."

"Bo won't have any luck talking to him, either. Karen or Ty might make him listen, but God knows how impossible it is to get hold of those two."

Karen was living in Germany and working as a translator for the U.S. Mission to Berlin (she'd majored in German in college, mastering it with absurd ease); Ty was in Queens, barely eking out a living as a painter. They were both notoriously difficult to reach. Karen was almost never at her apartment, and Ty didn't own a phone. They each wrote to us on a regular basis, but neither Aggie nor I had spoken to either of them in months.

"I'll call you again when all this is over," I said.

"How very comforting."

The leader of the mob at the school was a man named Virgil Jordan. He was stocky and square-jawed, with a cauliflower ear and a crewcut. As he paced at the forefront of the jeering, sweating rabble arrayed against us, he was smoking a cigarette and drinking a Coke. Were it not for the predatory expression on his face and a leech-shaped mole on his Adam's apple, I would've called him handsome. In addition to being a town councilman, he was almost certainly a key figure in the Klan— maybe even Mississippi's very own Grand Dragon, though I hadn't been able to confirm that. Whatever the source of his authority, watching him pace was mesmerizing, like watching a wolf prowl at the edge of a campfire. His followers kept glancing at him after shouting something particularly vile, seeking his approval.

Seeking his approval or waiting for a signal.

"Best get ready," Stephen murmured. He, too, was uneasily eyeing Jordan. "The Grand Poobah's getting restless."

"Grand Dragon," I corrected.

"Whatever."

I was short of breath from the chaos of the past few minutes. Soon after Elias and I rejoined Stephen at the church, we'd found ourselves among sixty or seventy grimly determined men and women, all hustling back to the school to shepherd the black kids to safety when they emerged from their classes at noon. Aside from a handful of activists like Elias and a few journalists like Stephen and me, the people we were with were all black, and the white mob waiting in the school parking lot needed no other incentive to fall on us the instant we approached. We would've been forced to retreat if it weren't for Lucien Averol—a wiry, grizzled organizer from the Southern Christian Leadership Conference—who shouted out to lock arms and push ahead; we'd miraculously gotten through the initial onslaught and staked out a small patch of asphalt near the main doors of the school, but many of us were badly battered and bruised, and in no condition for much else. My heart was pounding and I had bile in my throat.

"Hey," Stephen said, "do you think Jordan would give me a sip of Coke if I ask nicely?"

"Sure." I managed a grin, knowing he was as frightened as I was. "I hear he's a sweetheart."

"Uh-huh." He wiped sweat from his forehead. "Christ, I fucking hate the South."

While he still could, he snapped a few last pictures of the mob. He was using his backup camera because his good Nikon had been torn from his hands earlier that day and smashed on the sidewalk. I still had my notebook and pen in my back pocket, but I'd given up any pretense of being an impartial observer. My only real interest at the moment was our survival. We all knew that Virgil Jordan and his army of jeering thugs would overrun us the second the kids were released from the building, and the dozen local policemen standing by had no intention of interfering.

I turned to Elias, who was pale but composed. "Stick close, okay?" I said quietly. "I can't bear to tell your dad if you get hurt again."

His lips twitched, reminding me of Bo. "I'd be more scared of telling Aunt Aggie."

I winced—he was right, of course—but there was no time for anything else. The doors of the school were opening, hinges screeching, and Virgil Jordan had his hand raised above his head.

"Aw, shit," Stephen breathed.

"Heads up, boys and girls!" Jordan's surprisingly high-pitched voice cut through the clamor. "Y'all ready for a good old-fashioned coon hunt?"

The crowd roared on cue as the first kids emerged from the school, faces haggard with fear. Several were weeping, and one little girl with a white skirt and bright yellow blouse had already wet herself. Several of the men and women in our group called out to the kids, urging them to join us quickly so we could leave, but as they hurried toward us Jordan kept his hand in the air, clearly relishing the moment.

"Form a circle around the children and lock your arms!" Lucien Averol yelled. "As soon as we've got them all we'll—"

Jordan dropped his hand, almost casually.

"Aw, *SHIT*!" Stephen cried.

The mob, hundreds strong and shouting, surged toward the children. A red-faced, doughy, middle-aged man with thinning blond hair and a paunch was the first to plow into our line, flailing a bicycle chain and striking a young woman on the forearm as he tried to get past her. She fell to her knees, wailing, and Elias darted to her side, taking her position.

"What the hell is *wrong* with you, mister?" he yelled at the man with the chain. "They're only kids!"

The man swung the chain again; it missed Elias's chin by a couple of inches, but he still went down, tripping over the fallen woman. A small man with skin as black as a Kalamata olive—his first name was Oscar, but that was all I knew about him—helped me yank Elias upright before he got trampled. As the swarm began to tear our line apart, Lucien barked a frantic reminder to not fight back: he and the rest of the organizers of the demonstration had been emphatic about remaining peaceful, no matter the cost.

"We can't hold them," Oscar panted.

White boys had come out of the school with the black boys and girls, but I saw no white girls; they'd apparently been kept inside. The mob parted to allow the white boys passage but closed in at once around the black kids, trapping them. I saw one white boy look over his shoulder with dismay as a black girl who'd been a few feet behind him was clubbed to the ground, but several other white boys, hooting and laughing, joined the mob and turned with brutish glee on their black classmates.

Forced to abandon his idea of forming a protective circle, Lucien Averol bellowed at us to get moving and lead as many children as we could away from the school. We jostled to stay together as Lucien ducked a rock hurled at his head; a young woman beside him got punched in her stomach and dropped to her knees, retching. I looked over my shoulder to see if we could retreat into the school, but the doors were already closed behind us, barring any escape.

"Goddamn niggers don't belong here!"

"What the fuck d'ya think you're doin', coon?"

A truncheon caught Oscar on the collarbone and he cried out and fell into me. He immediately righted himself, though, and staggered over to a young girl curled up on the pavement, her face a mask of blood. "Get up, sweetie!" he begged her. "You got to get up!"

Someone struck the side of my head as I stooped to help with the girl, and the world spun wildly.

"Goddamn nigger lover!"

I heard Elias yell my name as my eyesight cleared. He was trying to save a black boy from being beaten by two huge men. Oscar somehow had the injured girl on her feet again, so I lurched over to Elias's side and reflexively dodged a punch from one of the men confronting him; the other man grabbed my shirtfront and head-butted me in the bridge of my nose. I fell down, dazed by the pain and tasting blood in my mouth.

Stephen was suddenly there, bellowing incoherently and shaking the guy who'd struck me as if he were a rag doll.

"Don't fight back!" Lucien Averol commanded from behind us. "Get the kids to safety, but don't fight back!"

"I'm all right!" I yelled. "Let him go, Stephen!"

With contempt, Stephen tossed away the man he was terrorizing. The boy that Elias had been trying to help—he was no more than ten years old—was unconscious; Elias lifted him in his arms and stumbled forward as Stephen used his bulk to force an opening in the sea of angry, howling faces. Lucien and Oscar were supporting two kids each as the mob closed in on us. A woman with a red bandanna on her head and a resolute look on her face was now beside me, clutching two little girls by the wrists; I lifted one of them in my arms just as somebody threw a rock that struck her left ear. She shrieked in terror as I cradled her against my chest.

"Keep going forward!" Lucien cried. "Keep moving!"

The mob pressed in on all sides and I fought to stay on my feet as I was shoved and kicked. I saw Stephen take a brutal kidney punch as he was clearing a path for us; he staggered but kept pushing ahead. Elias was close behind, followed by Lucien and Oscar, then the red bandanna woman, then me, all carrying or supporting kids. I got occasional glimpses of others from our original group in the seething tangle of bodies, but none were making much headway. A big black man about twenty feet away got pulled to the ground and battered without mercy; nearby, an older woman cried out in fury and despair as the child she was guarding was torn from her arms and vanished in the confusion. Fending off a screeching, bird-thin woman intent on gouging out my eyes, I saw a man with a raised baseball bat loom up behind Elias.

"Elias!" I howled.

Either my shout or some animal instinct saved him: He ducked down as the bat whipped through the air where his head had been an instant before. Stephen turned around and tore the bat from the man's fingers, sending him sprawling with a shove to the chest.

"OKAY, PLAYTIME'S OVER, ASSHOLES!" Stephen yelled, swinging the bat around his head with lethal force. "WHO WANTS TO DIE FIRST?"

The mob parted as if by magic. I gripped the girl I was holding and stumbled after the woman with the red bandanna as she drew even with Elias and the two black men. Stephen held his ground until we all caught up to him; then he began to lead us slowly out of the danger zone, wagging the bat in warning at anybody who came within reach even as Lucien pleaded with him to not hurt anybody. Virgil Jordan suddenly materialized out of nowhere and flung a rock at Stephen's chest, but Stephen sidestepped and gamely smacked the hell out of it with the bat. It rocketed back at Jordan, and he and about a dozen of his cronies all dove out of the way in a panic. Stephen yelled for us to keep following him and he pushed ahead, cleaving his way through the crowd and glancing back every few seconds to make sure we were still on his heels. I stayed as near to Elias as I could. From the agonized grimace on his face and the way he was gasping, I feared his broken ribs were slicing up his lungs. As we drew near the town square, we finally broke free of the worst of the violence and the noise, and people from our original group—nearly all bloodied and limping—fought their way clear as well, merging with us. Following Lucien's hasty instructions, the adults who could still make it on their own handed off the kids they were warding and turned around to return for stragglers. Pausing briefly, Lucien ordered our small group to proceed to the church without him.

"No way, Lucien," Elias wheezed, passing the child he was carrying to an older man. "I'm coming with you."

"Like hell you are!" I snapped. "You can hardly walk."

We started to argue, but Lucien took one look at Elias and intervened. "Sorry, son," he said, "but the last thing we need right now is another body to carry." His eyes caught mine before returning to Elias. "Besides that, your uncle Isaac's got a job to do, and he can't get it done if he's chasing after you."

I promised I'd call in my story to as soon as I could, and he nodded his thanks and left us. Elias stared after him, crestfallen, and refused to budge until I took him by the hand and pulled him after me, weeping and swearing in frustration. I let him blow off steam, knowing he'd soon forgive me. He was no better at holding a grudge than his father. The little girl I was carrying—she'd told me her name was Candace—gradually calmed, and as we caught up to Stephen, I lifted her on my shoulders to give my aching arms a rest. Stephen still had the baseball bat but looked as if he would never again have the strength to swing it. Whatever superhuman force had taken over his body back at the school had departed, leaving him with the uncertain gait of an old man.

"Hey there, Babe Ruth," I said. "You still alive?"

"Damned if I know." He glanced at me wearily and his eyes widened. "Wow. You look like shit, Isaac."

I grinned. His nose was swollen and he had an ugly bruise on his left cheek; there was matted blood in his mustache and beard, and a deep, jagged scratch running from one side of his forehead to the other. He looked positively savage.

"Not to burst your bubble or anything," I said, "but you're not exactly the prettiest girl at the prom, either." I hesitated, sobering. "Thanks for getting us out of there, Stephen. You were amazing."

He flushed a little. "All I did was lose my temper." He spat blood on the ground. "Jesus, have you ever seen such a bunch of inbred, bucktoothed sons of bitches?"

Oscar overheard him and grunted in sour amusement, in spite of nursing what was likely a broken collarbone. "Welcome to the great sovereign state of Mississippi."

The sudden sound of running footsteps in the street behind

us made us all jump. We spun around to find four policeman bearing down on us, guns drawn.

"Drop the bat, *motherfucker*!" one of the men yelled, aiming his pistol at Stephen.

A young custodian with a pimpled chin and a shy smile was mopping the hallway floor near the nurses' station at the hospital and whistling snatches of "I Can't Help Myself" by the Four Tops. Something about watching his mop swish across the checkered floor in time to the song was soothing; it was one of the few harmless things I'd seen all day.

It was nearly midnight. Elias and I were in the hall, waiting for a nurse to bring me the final tally of the day's injuries. We'd only been seated for a few minutes, but Elias was already fast asleep, snoring softly, his head lolling on the back of his chair, his bruised face turned toward me. I'd called in my story hours before, but I was still tracking down loose ends. The town mayor had agreed to see me in the morning, and I wanted to have all my facts straight before we met. He'd been lying to journalists all day about the carnage in his town, and I intended to hold him accountable. Elias, fearing for my safety on the streets without Stephen, had insisted on coming along until I was done for the night, even though I'd reminded him that in his current condition he'd be useless as a bodyguard. I wasn't in much better shape myself, but thankfully this was our last stop before we could head back to our hotel.

From what I'd already learned, at least three of the children who'd come out of the school at noon had been hospitalized for broken bones, and one had a fractured skull. God only knew how many others had been hurt in the madness before school began that morning, and the butcher's bill for the adult victims—parents, activists, journalists—was likely also sky-high. It was no exaggeration to say that the streets of Grenada were awash in blood: My sneakers and shirt were tacky with the stuff—some of it mine, most not.

Elias, miraculously, was not as badly off as I'd feared. The same exasperated doctor who'd examined him earlier in the day had reexamined him that afternoon and assured me his lungs were still intact; the labored breathing that had so frightened me was "only to be expected" when every breath he took was aggravating severely inflamed muscle tissue. Pain or no, however, he wasn't likely to have much trouble sleeping that night. Between the medication he'd been given and his exhaustion, I wasn't even sure I'd be able to wake him when it was time to go back to the hotel. He'd originally intended to stay the night at the church, but when I'd insisted he take Stephen's bed instead, he didn't argue.

Stephen had no need for his bed, of course, as he was in jail.

The police were holding him without bail, on a bogus charge of assaulting an "innocent bystander" at the school. The ACLU had hired a defense attorney from Biloxi who was supposed to arrive in time for the hearing in the morning, but I doubted it would matter if he showed up or not. Given what was going on around us, I was worried Stephen might actually end up serving prison time, though he'd hurt no one, and there were dozens of witnesses to gainsay the charge against him.

"Mr. Dahl?"

I looked up, startled to find the night nurse looking down at me. She was a small, stern-looking woman with bags under her eyes and a raspy voice. It clearly hadn't been an easy day for her, either. She handed over a sheet of yellow legal paper. "That's the best I can do," she said. "I'm not allowed to give you any names, so it's strictly a list of the injuries we treated."

I thanked her and scanned the list. She'd grouped the injuries into categories, running the gamut from open head traumas to severe lacerations; it was a long list and made for grim reading, the more so because many people who'd been hurt at the school hadn't come to the hospital for treatment. "This is a good start," I said, "but—"

"I'll lose my job if I give you anything else." She looked away, biting her lip. "This town has gone stark raving mad."

I realized there was no point in pushing her for more information, but was unable to resist asking if she'd heard about the town council meeting earlier that evening, where the city manager had been fired.

"McEachin?" She waited for my nod. "I should hope so. He never should've allowed things to get so far out of hand."

"From what I understand, he was fired for not going far *enough*."

Her face seemed to age on the spot, and I felt guilty for giving her a hard time. Obviously not every white person in Grenada was a monster; it wasn't her fault that the hyenas had taken over the zoo. "We're not all like that," she said quietly, echoing my thoughts.

Elias stirred and opened his good eye—the other was still swollen shut—as the nurse said good night and returned to her work. For a moment I could tell he didn't even know where he was. He came around slowly, sitting up with a groan when he saw the paper in my hands. "How bad is it?" he asked.

"Bad enough." I gave him the list and watched his face whiten as he glanced over the entries. He handed it back to me, avoiding my eyes.

"I think I need to go to bed now, Uncle Isaac," he said quietly. "Wake me in a couple of centuries, will you?"

DAY SEVEN

June 8, 1974. Saint-Rémy-de-Provence, France.

"You look very intelligent in your new glasses," Aggie said, smiling. "It's rather misleading. Every time I look at you I experience cognitive dissonance."

"Nice." I poured myself more wine. "Shut up and pass the olives, will you?"

It was the last week of our monthlong family vacation, and the fact that Aggie and I were still getting along after so much time together was a miracle. The two of us, Bo, and the kids (Ty, Karen, and Elias were all in their thirties, but remained "kids" to me) had rented a two-hundred-year-old farmhouse in the south of France, just outside of Saint-Rémy.

"I know you hate wearing glasses, Uncle Isaac," Karen said, reaching across the table for a slice of baguette, smeared with foie gras. "But truly, you look quite distinguished."

I grunted, unconvinced.

It was happy hour and we were sitting on the farmhouse's graveled patio, enjoying our third bottle of wine and gazing out at an expansive, elegant front lawn; an overhead grape arbor provided welcome shade from the hot sun. The house and grounds were bordered by pine trees and a high stone wall, and a few feet from our table was a dirt path leading to a pair of stately cypress trees and a fountain. The path was lined by flowers—red and white roses, orange nasturtiums, yellow daisies, pink lilies, blue and gold irises, and thick purple patches of Provence's signature lavender—as well as thyme and rosemary bushes, growing wild and scenting the air like a hearty stew. The farmhouse had once served as both stable and bakery for a nobleman's estate. Its stone walls were nearly two feet thick, and its doors were solid oak, ponderous, and imposing; I'd never stayed in a place that felt so impregnable. Half a mile away and hidden from our view by the pine trees was the long-dead nobleman's mansion, now a pricey hotel, complete with turrets, gatehouse, and a cobblestone courtyard.

"This recent vanity of yours is appalling," Aggie told me. "You never used to give a damn about your looks, but you spent ten full minutes preening in front of the mirror this morning."

"I wasn't preening, I was in shock." I swirled my wine, admiring how it sparkled in the sunlight filtering through the grape vines. "Some old guy with glasses, gray hair, and a paunch was looking back at me, and I had no idea who he was."

"Wow," Bo said, grinning. "Did you say hello to the old fart?"

I grinned back. "I would've, but I assumed his hearing was as bad as his eyesight."

Ty snorted. "You've only got a few gray hairs, Isaac, and you haven't gained a pound for thirty years. You're just feeling old because of Glanum."

A little south of Saint-Rémy were the Roman ruins of Glanum—once a thriving town nestled in high, rocky hills, with a spectacular view of the surrounding countryside. The six

of us had gone wandering among its enormous stones, founda-
tions, wells, sewers, and shrines, and something about the place
had, as Ty said, unnerved me.

"Was it that obvious?" I asked him.

Karen patted my arm. "Only to each and every one of us."
She smiled at Aggie. "Excluding Mom, of course. She was too
busy making those kids cry."

Aggie flushed. "Those boys were too fragile for their own
good."

A group of summer school students from Marseille had also
been at Glanum, and three of them had started roughhousing
near Aggie. She lost her patience, rendering the boys contrite
and speechless, and I knew she felt badly about it. I still had no
idea what she said to them—her French was far better than
mine.

"You've always been so good with the young," I told her.

"Shush," she muttered.

"I'm not surprised Glanum did a number on you, Uncle
Isaac," Elias said. "I was seeing ghosts, too, everywhere I
turned."

Elias and I often reacted to things in the same way. The lay-
out of the ruins made it possible to roam through every nook
and cranny of the town, and it had been all too easy to imagine
centuries-old phantoms still going about their daily business,
their sandals rustling through the sparse green grass and broken
stones, paying the living no heed.

"Maybe it was an acid flashback from your hippy days," Ty
teased.

"I'm serious," Elias said. "Glanum is cool, but it's also really
creepy."

"Nonsense," Aggie chided. "Shame on you, Elias, for indulg-
ing your uncle in yet another of his morbid occult fantasies."
She turned to me. "Isn't your midlife crisis absurd enough without dressing it up in a Roman toga and making it say '*boo*'?"

She had a point. I'd become obsessed lately, with thoughts about death and the afterlife. I knew, of course, as did everybody at the table, what was behind this fixation: I hated that my body was beginning to slow down, hated that my memory was no longer unimpeachable, hated growing weary so early in the evenings. It didn't help that Bo and Aggie, by contrast, were aging so gracefully. We were all fifty-six, but they looked ten years younger.

"To be fair," Karen said, "Uncle Isaac and Elias aren't the first ones who've ever found things a little out of the ordinary around here. Van Gogh apparently thought so, too."

"Van Gogh was clinically insane," Aggie reminded her.

The hospital where Van Gogh had been institutionalized was very near Glanum, though most of the Roman ruins hadn't yet been unearthed back then. The paintings he'd made of the landscape around the hospital were as haunting in their way as Glanum, full of vibrant life and light, but also with disturbing shadows beneath the trees, and along the walls and fences.

Bo bumped my knee with his own, lightening my mood. "You're brooding, buddy," he said. "What's going on in that grizzled old head of yours?"

I smiled at him. "The usual three-ring circus. Dancing bears and bearded ladies."

The day was hot but not oppressive, with a cooling breeze and a clear blue sky. I was seated at one end of the table, facing Ty at the other end; Bo and Aggie were on my left, across the table from Karen and Elias. All of us were dressed lightly, in short-sleeved shirts and shorts. As always, the beauty of Karen and the two young men moved me, as did their obvious affection for each other. At the moment, Elias was using Ty as an ottoman, his bare right foot resting on Ty's knee, and Karen was absently twirling a strand of Elias's shoulder-length hair in her fingers as she turned to study me.

"Did you break your promise and start writing again last night, Uncle Isaac?"

I blinked stupidly, stalling for time. I had indeed gotten up in the middle of the night to jot down a few thoughts at the small desk in my room, but I had no idea how she knew that. My bedroom was in a cozy nook at the end of an L-shaped hallway on the second floor, well isolated from the rest of the house.

"Of course not," I lied. "Why do you ask?"

"I was spying on you and saw the light under your door."

"You were *spying* on me?"

"Yep," she said cheerfully. "We've been taking turns."

"Isaac Dahl!" Aggie snapped. "You *promised*!"

Up until we came to France, I'd been putting the final frantic touches on an overdue compilation of essays; I'd also been running myself ragged for *The New Yorker*, digging into the Machiavellian mess of Watergate. After a string of sleepless nights, I got dizzy at a restaurant in D.C. and briefly fainted, scaring the hell out of my neurotic, overprotective editor, who then joined forces with my neurotic, overprotective family, making me promise to refrain from writing while on vacation.

"I only wrote for a minute or two," I whined.

"Liar," Agnes said. "An hour or two is far more likely."

I looked away, flushing. "I shouldn't be held to that ridiculous promise."

"You're still not fully recovered, and you know it."

"She's right, Isaac," Bo said. "Please, *please* don't push your luck until we get home and Doc Oliver says you're okay."

I reminded them I'd gone for a three-mile hike with Ty and Elias just that morning and had no problems keeping up. My appetite was almost back to normal, too, and I hadn't had a dizzy spell since arriving at the airport in Paris, three weeks before.

"Yeah, but you know enough to rest when you're hiking," Bo said. "You don't stop writing until you're half-dead."

I opened my mouth and abruptly closed it, and everyone laughed at me.

* * *

All three kids were still unmarried. Each had fallen in love several times, but few of their relationships lasted more than a month or two. Ty had come the closest to marriage, living for a couple of years with another painter in New York, but when she insisted on getting engaged, he broke it off. Karen was relentlessly pursued by would-be suitors, but she seldom dated, happier by far as a single woman. Elias, on the other hand, would've liked nothing better than to find a lifelong partner, but the men he'd thus far been drawn to were, to say the least, unstable—one was schizophrenic, another a chronic liar, and so on. Elias was currently "taking a break" from dating, but if his past history was any indication, he'd be on the prowl again any day now.

I was also single. Since my ill-fated relationship with Paulie twenty-some years before, I'd been alone—save for an occasional dalliance here and there—-and I was highly skeptical that would ever change. Aggie blamed me for being a poor role model for the kids, and I feared there was some truth to that, though until she and Bo had finally figured out how they felt about each other, she had no room to talk.

I was still getting used to their marriage, even after four years. In some ways it made perfect sense: Since Johan's death, Bo was the only man Aggie truly respected—she'd even considered taking his last name as her own, though in the end she didn't, since her readers knew her as Agnes Dahl—and he was also the only person on the planet with the patience to put up with her. They'd always been in love, I think, but because they'd essentially grown up as siblings, they'd never acted on the attraction until one evening when I was out of town, and their mutual desire finally spilled over, or so I was told when I returned. I found them waiting for me at the airport, holding hands and blushing like middle-schoolers. I was shocked at first, but soon realized that nothing had really changed, save that they now shared a bed. I'd offered to move out of our house to give them more privacy, but they'd flat-out refused to consider it.

"Don't be ridiculous," Aggie had said. "This is your home."

"There's no way in hell we're letting you go," Bo said. "We don't see you enough as it is."

Before coming to Provence, we'd stayed a few days in Paris. The others roamed the city, but I stuck to the Latin Quarter, treating myself to baguettes, wine, and frequent naps at our B&B. I'd been to Paris often and dearly loved it, but I didn't have the stamina this time to deal with crowds. I made one exception, however, to spend an hour or so at the Rodin Museum: No matter how exhausted I was, I couldn't bear to miss it. When we first arrived, my family buzzed around me like flies, fretting that I wasn't strong enough for this outing, but I finally managed to shoo them away. They warned me not to tire myself, then wandered off to gawk at everything the museum had to offer.

I was slowly circling *The Age of Bronze* when a slender, elderly gentleman spoke to me in French, much too quickly for me to keep up. I apologized, asking if he spoke English.

"Of course." He had a flawless British accent. "I asked if you were a sculptor."

I shook my head and smiled. "I can barely form a ball with Play-Doh."

"Truly? You surprise me," he said. The blue veins at his temples made me guess him to be at least seventy, though he had a full head of salt-and-pepper hair. He was neatly dressed in a blue scarf, dark pants, a white shirt, and black leather shoes. "In my experience," he continued, "the only people who study a work of art so intently are fellow artists. Everyone else on this godforsaken planet cares about nothing but television and sex."

I laughed and said I didn't think that was true; if it were, we'd be alone here today, instead of surrounded by a sea of humanity.

He eyed the people passing by with open disdain. "These poor souls are only here so they can boast to their friends back home about seeing such and such a famous work of art, in such and such a famous building, in such and such a famous city," he said. "Believe me, they're all wishing they were elsewhere."

His snobbery reminded me of Aggie, but many people walking by us *did* look bored.

"Not you, though," he said. "You've been fixated on this statue for fifteen minutes. What fascinates you so?"

I was unnerved to find he'd been watching me without my noticing, but I shrugged, returning my attention to the Belgian soldier. Every muscle, every tendon, every vein, every toenail was perfectly rendered; the face was every bit as complex and real as a living man's. I was half-convinced if I put my palm on his chest I'd feel a heartbeat.

"He's so real it's frightening," I said. "I keep expecting him to breathe."

He nodded. "I read somewhere that Rodin wished him to be seen as a man slowly awakening from a deep dream. That he's naked doesn't matter to him, because he's still half-asleep and has no more modesty than a cat. That's why he's so compelling to me. He's completely unconscious of his own beauty."

I asked him why he'd been watching me.

He smiled. "I, too, am an admirer of unconscious beauty."

I colored, belatedly catching on. "Uh, thanks," I said. "I'm flattered, but—"

"Not to worry," he said, unembarrassed. "I'm perfectly harmless."

His good-natured aplomb was appealing. We fell to talking and he introduced himself as Michel Guilhaud; he told me he was a retired art teacher from Bordeaux. Elias materialized next to us as we were chatting.

"Dammit, Uncle Isaac," he said. "Have you been standing this whole time without resting? You're pale and sweating again."

"Oh, my goodness," Michel said. "Who is this handsome young man?"

I sighed. "My godson, Elias. He's training to be a wet nurse."

"Very funny," Elias said, unfazed by Michel's flattery. He was used to older men flirting with him. "It'll be even funnier when you pass out on the floor again, like you did in D.C." He took my elbow and propelled me to a bench to sit; I was annoyed to discover my legs were indeed trembling a little.

"I knew it was a dumb idea to let you come here," Elias scolded, putting his hand on my forehead. He turned to Michel. "We all told him to stay at our B&B today and rest, but he was too stubborn to listen."

"We?" Michel asked.

"Our family," I said. "They're all here someplace."

"Indeed?" His eyes twinkled. "And are they all as attractive as you and your godson?"

"Sadly, no," I said, pretending not to notice Aggie approaching at that very moment, holding hands with Bo. "My twin sister, Agnes, for one, is downright hideous. She has a goiter, as well as elephantiasis."

"Don't forget the genital warts," Aggie added, startling Michel. "It's usually the first thing you mention."

"Oh, my," he said, laughing. "Agnes, I presume?" He took her hand and introduced himself. "Isaac should be horsewhipped for defaming you, dear. You're every bit as gorgeous as he is."

"Thank you, I think," Aggie said.

Bo saw I was wearing out and insisted it was time to take me back to our B&B for a nap. We invited Michel to join us for dinner, but he declined, saying he already had plans. As we said goodbye, he took my hand and held it gently in both of his. I told him I'd enjoyed meeting him.

"Likewise, Isaac. Thank you for your kindness to an old man this afternoon," he said. "I'm horribly jealous. You were only mine for a moment, but your family gets to keep you forever. Life is unfair, yes?"

I didn't know what to say to that, but he didn't seem to expect an answer; he squeezed my hand one last time and then left us. Bo stood beside me, and we watched him walk away.

"Interesting friend you made there," Bo said. "What's his story, I wonder?"

I shook my head, feeling oddly bereft. "Guess we'll never know."

Journal entry, Saint-Rémy-de-Provence, France, June 8, 1974.

It's late, but I can't sleep.

When I was dumb enough at today's happy hour to confess I'd resumed writing, everyone at the table—even Bo—chewed me out, worried I was going to make myself sick again. I hung my head and mumbled apologetically, but I'll be damned if they're going to keep me away from my notebook any longer. Until last night I hadn't written anything for weeks, and I was beginning to feel like a dangerously overinflated balloon. When I picked up my pen, the pressure eased immediately, and the more I wrote the better I felt.

Ergo, there's now a rolled-up towel at the base of my door, blocking the light from being seen in the hall.

I'd gladly live like this forever—in this place, with these people, even if they are a gaggle of mother hens. Karen and Ty served a simple, elegant dinner tonight of roasted chicken, red potatoes with garlic, and asparagus, all drizzled with olive oil and balsamic vinegar; we gorged ourselves, watching the sunset as we ate at the table under the grapevines. At full darkness, the air was so still that the flame of the candle Bo lit barely flick-

ered. *The six of us talked until bedtime, rehashing old stories and passing wine around the table, occasionally drinking directly from the bottle, hobo-fashion. It seems like a lifetime since we've all been together, carrying on like juvenile delinquents out past curfew.*

Even Aggie was on her good behavior. She seldom laughs these days, but Ty's impression of a quarrelsome old man he met on the subway in Soho last month had her in stitches, head thrown back and tears streaming down her face. It's impossible not to adore her when she laughs like that. Someone who didn't know her better would never dream that she's typically an inveterate pain in the ass. She was just as disarming later, when her mood turned wistful. She sang a lullaby in Swedish that our mother sometimes sang to us when we were children in Utah. Aggie didn't remember what the words meant, nor did Bo and I—as kids we all knew a little Swedish, but it's only gibberish now. The melody brought tears to my eyes, however. For a moment, I could've sworn I heard Mama's voice, twined around Aggie's as she sang in the candlelight.

Nor was that the only music of the night.

Bo, Aggie, and Karen went to bed at ten (we turn in early here), but I wanted to stretch my legs before sleeping, so Elias and Ty came along to babysit. We ambled down the road to the old mansion/hotel, pausing every few yards to gape at the stars and talk. When our voices fell still, the only sounds were our sandals on the gravel, and a forlorn owl, hooting somewhere in a small grove of pine trees. As we drew near the entrance to the hotel's courtyard, though, the silence was broken by three young men in jeans and T-shirts, smoking under a streetlight and chattering in French. They didn't see us coming. They were a little unsteady on their feet, so I assumed they'd visited the hotel bar; one of them had a cheap travel guitar slung around his neck, and after he lit his cigarette, he strummed a few chords to a tune I couldn't place until he started singing, in English.

"Oh, girl
I'd be in trouble if you left me now
'Cause I don't know where to look for love
I just don't know how."

His friends sang with him; they only knew a quarter of the lyrics but that didn't deter them. When the guitar player, too, forgot the words to the second verse, Elias helped them out, his sweet, clear tenor voice floating out of the darkness. They all spun around in surprise, clapping and cheering as we stepped into their circle of light.

"Oh, girl
How I depend on you
To give me love when I need it
Right on time you would always be."

Elias inherited every ounce of his mother's musical talent. (I hate to give Janet all the credit, but Bo has a three-note range, at best.) The French boys had decent voices, but Elias was in another league entirely, and they were delighted to let him take the lead, humming along and snapping their fingers like backup singers. Ty and I applauded when the song ended, and we all laughed and shook hands. The guitar player told us in French that his name was Charlie, but their taxi arrived before he introduced his friends. Charlie invited us to join them at a nearby house party. His genuine, if woozy, warmth was charming, and if I'd been less tired I might've said yes. I begged off, however, saying I wanted to go to bed. Ty and Elias were clearly itching for a night out, but they were worried about me getting back to the farmhouse on my own.

"Don't be silly," I said, grinning as their faces brightened. "I'll be fine, I promise. Go have fun."

"You sure, Uncle Isaac?" Elias asked.

"Absolutely." I laughed as he and Ty each planted a drunken kiss on my cheek, then watched them wedge themselves into the packed vehicle with the enviable disregard for physical discomfort that only the young and intoxicated are capable of. It

suddenly occurred to me that Ty was thirty-seven and Elias thirty-one, but they seemed barely older than the French boys.

Under the stars, I took my time walking back to our farmhouse, humming the Swedish song Aggie had sung earlier. I remembered a few words, though not their meaning: "Byssan lull, koka kittelen full." The owl in the pine trees hooted again as I passed by, and I hooted the lullaby back at it. When I reached the farmhouse driveway, Nicky the dog and Guillaume the cat came to greet me. Both animals belong to our elderly landlady; she lives in a separate part of the house, but we never hear her through the stone wall separating us. As I leaned over to pet them—Nicky's an Australian shepherd with bad breath and a wet nose; Guillaume is a love-starved, ginger tomcat with matted fur—I could smell the single lemon tree on the property, scenting the night air like a candle.

Anyway, that was all an hour ago, and now I'm back at my desk by the open window of my bedroom. My handwriting is somewhat sloppy from all the wine I had tonight, yet I don't feel overly impaired.

Random meetings with strangers—like the French boys in front of the hotel tonight, and Michel at the museum the other day—often trigger odd emotions in me. It has something to do with the fleeting nature of the connection, and the bittersweet realization that we'll likely never see each other again, but it's more than that, too. I've begun, recently (even while sober), to entertain the notion that people who believe in reincarnation may not be as kooky as I used to think.

I have one of Uncle Johan's old flannel shirts at home in my closet. I wear it often—we were the same size—and every time I pull it on, the love I had for him stirs, reawakens, as if he's still with me, in the fabric on my skin. Similarly, when I met Charlie the guitar player tonight, something about him was as familiar to me as Johan's shirt. He doesn't remind me of anyone in particular, and I know I've never met him before, yet I think he'll haunt my dreams for a long time, wandering around in my psyche like the figments I imagined among the Roman ruins. Part of me recognizes that boy, stranger or not; part of me somehow remembers him, though imperfectly, just as I remember my mother's lullaby.

It's a different sensation from sexual attraction, but the psychic charge is similar. For instance, many years ago, I kissed a stranger in an alley behind a bar in Dallas, and it turned out to be an equally lovely, unsettling experience. To this day, I can still feel his warm hands on my waist, and I can also smell the rum and Coke on his breath. I never learned his name, and all we did was kiss, but my God, I've conjured that make-out session in my mind at least a thousand times in the intervening years. I don't really remember his face, save that he had a ridiculous little mustache and a big nose.

It was reckless, of course, and illegal, and could all too easily have led to arrest, public scandal, and God knows what else, but I was helpless to stop. I can't say how far things might've gone, but we weren't given the chance to find out: The exit door banged open again, startling us apart; we both panicked and took off running, him to the right and me to the left. It was the last time we ever saw each other.

And no kiss has ever disturbed my sleep like that, before or since.

As such things are measured, it was a relatively chaste encounter: There was no time for more. Yet the hungry, sweet, aching pressure of his lips on mine has stayed with me for two decades, along with an odd feeling—based on nothing but intuition and a lingering sadness—that the two of us made a terrible mistake by not running in the same direction.

Lost opportunities are the death of sleep.

To be fair to my younger self, that decades-old alley kiss, like all the other woulda-coulda-shoulda moments in my love life, was created as much by social mores as by my personal cow-

ardice. Since the Stonewall Riots five years ago—which I missed reporting on, sadly, having been elsewhere at the time—things have marginally improved for gays in America, but (A) homosexuality is still illegal, and (B) it can still get me fired, particularly since my job makes me something of a public figure. If I were a braver, more talented writer, like say Vidal or Baldwin, maybe I would've taken greater risks and, as a result, found more peace with myself by now. Then again, we journalists are given far less latitude for sexual "eccentricity" than novelists and poets, and have little choice but to conform if we want to keep working.

Or at least that's what I tell myself when regret gets its teeth in me.

Oh, Christ. Voices in the backyard: Ty and Elias are already back from their party. They'll see the light streaming from my open window and tomorrow they'll tell the whole damn family that I was working in the middle of the night again. I'll have to find someplace to hide my notebook, or Oberführer Aggie will confiscate it.

Well, shit.

DAY EIGHT

October 11, 1982. Aboard the Sea Major, in the Solent.

"God, she looks like a drowned rat," Terry McMillan said, yelling over all the horn blasts and cheering. His wife, Jeanne, stood between us at the stern rail of their sailboat, and their six-year-old son, Philip, was perched on my shoulders, hoping to get a better view of the *Mary Rose* rising from the water, lifted incrementally by a massive floating crane. To protect the fragile hull of the ancient warship—now little more than a pile of saturated wood—she'd been encaged in a metal frame and placed on a cradle, padded with water bags.

"If you'd been underwater for four centuries, you'd look rough, too," I yelled back.

Philip's small hands were resting on mine as I gripped his thighs to keep him from falling. The boy had been glued to me since I came aboard; Terry and Jeanne had told him repeatedly to quit pestering me, but I didn't mind. He was a funny kid, small for his age and smart as hell, already reading books intended for teenagers. He appeared to have adopted me as a surrogate grandfather: When he found out I was sixty-four, he informed me I was the same age as "Grandpa Stan," who had "smoked cigarettes and coughed up blood before he died." It had been a while since I'd spent time with a young child, and it brought back a flood of memories of Ty, Karen, and Elias as kids.

The morning was chilly, damp, and gray, and we were among a chaotic armada of boats, dozens strong and circling the *Mary Rose* as she dangled in her cage. Terry and Jeanne's seventy-five-foot sailing yacht (the *Sea Major*) was one of the most elegant crafts there, with twin engines, twin steering stations, six large sleeping cabins, ingenious interior woodwork, and a luxurious cockpit for entertaining. Terry and Jeanne lived onboard with Philip and two hired crewmen. I'd met Terry in Portsmouth Harbour, and he'd generously offered to host me while I wrote a story about the raising.

Of all the enthralled spectators crammed in the various boats in the Solent for today's resurrection, the most famous was Prince Charles, who'd gone diving earlier that morning to view the underwater proceedings. The spectacle was worthy of a prince: The archaeology team tasked with bringing the Tudor-era ship to the surface had been at it for years, and most of their work had been accomplished in wetsuits, fifty feet beneath the water's surface. Journalists from all over the world were on hand today; the television audience watching was predicted to be as many as sixty million. Though I understood the fascination, I couldn't help feeling sorry for the battered old ship, now on display like a disgraced noblewoman, pilloried in her underthings.

"What is it about a shipwreck that makes us all ghouls?" Jeanne asked, evidently thinking along similar lines. "Hundreds of men drowned in that godforsaken ship, and everyone is carrying on like cheerleaders."

"Don't overthink everything for once, babe," Terry said. "Just enjoy the show."

"How many men drowned, Mom?" Philip said, leaning over

precariously to join the conversation. "I mean *exactly* how many?"

"No one knows for sure, Phil," Jeanne answered, "but yesterday's paper said it was close to five hundred."

"Wow." The boy straightened again, mercifully allowing me to loosen my grip on his legs. "Is it haunted?"

"I doubt it, honey," Jeanne said, smiling at her son's hopeful tone. She'd told me earlier that Philip adored ghost stories. "The remains of her crew have already been removed, so their ghosts don't have any reason to stick around."

"Ghosts aren't real, Phil," Terry said. "But if they were, they'd be bloody great twits to stay on the bottom of the ocean all this time, waiting for somebody to dig up their soggy old bones."

Jeanne sighed. "Terry doesn't believe in anything he can't see, smell, or shovel into his mouth with a fork," she told me wryly, and Terry blew her a kiss.

I glanced at Southsea Castle on the nearby shore, where Henry VIII had watched the sinking of the *Mary Rose* during the battle against the French navy; the stories said he'd heard the screams of the English sailors as their ship went down. I couldn't help thinking how the deaths of the men on the *Houston* had troubled my own sleep for forty years, and I wondered how many sleepless nights the *Mary Rose* had given Henry. Maybe not many, considering that (A) he only lived for a brief time after she sank, and (B) he was a twisted son of a bitch, having famously beheaded two of his own wives. Still, if he possessed a pulse, I'd be surprised if the *Mary Rose* hadn't occasionally sailed through his nightmares.

"Uh-oh," Terry said. "Isaac's frowning again, Jeanne."

"Yes, he is. He does that a great deal, doesn't he?"

Philip leaned his torso over my head as far as he could, peering upside down into my face, his suntanned nose inches from mine. He'd inherited Jeanne's dark brown eyes and Terry's mop of unruly brown hair. "Are you mad at somebody, Isaac?"

"No, I'm not mad, monkey," I said. My shoulders were aching, so I swung him to the deck with a groan. "I just realized that nobody will ever read a word I write about this, since the entire planet is watching it on television."

"Poor guy," Jeanne said, patting my arm. "I suppose you'll just need to find an angle that no one else has thought of."

I made a face. "Is that all?"

"Poor guy," Terry echoed. "How about another drink for courage?"

I still had a pleasant buzz going from the Bloody Mary that had accompanied our breakfast (scrambled eggs, sausage, bacon, and French toast), but I told him I wouldn't say no to another round. Terry turned toward the pilothouse, where Aaron Prall and Mick Donovan—the two young men who crewed the *Sea Major*—were steering us on engine power. Terry called out to Mick and asked him if he'd do the honors of mixing another pitcher.

"Sure thing, Skipper." Mick's homely, friendly face broke into a sly grin as he glanced sideways at Aaron. "How come you don't ask Aaron to make the drinks?"

"Screw you, Mick," Aaron said, scowling, as Mick chortled. "That goddamn story stopped being funny a year ago."

"What story?" I asked.

"The last time Aaron played bartender for us," Terry said, "we all puked our guts up. He claims the tomato juice was bad, but we're pretty sure he just peed in the pitcher."

"You guys are buttholes," Aaron grunted, making Terry laugh, too.

Aaron and Mick were far more than hired help to the McMillans, having sailed with them for two years, ever since the

McMillans had quit their jobs in London, sold their home, and taken to living on the water. Mick was twenty-seven, red-haired and red-bearded, with uneven features, crooked teeth, and acne-scarred skin; Aaron was twenty-four, clean-shaven, blond-haired, and distractingly handsome. The two were inseparable friends, having crewed together on half a dozen similar boats.

"Good for you, Aaron. Don't let Terry and Mick give you a hard time," Jeanne said, smiling sweetly. "Even if it *was* rather childish of you to urinate in our drinks."

Aaron smiled back at her. "You're a butthole, too, Jeanne."

The week before I flew to England, Aggie was at the kitchen table, surrounded by at least a dozen crumpled balls of notebook paper. She was a regular contributor to *The New York Review of Books*, but her writing muse appeared to require, per article, the sacrifice of a full ream of paper. She looked up balefully as I wandered into the kitchen from the living room, where Bo and I were watching a football game on TV.

"Tell me again why you agreed to do a story about the *Mary Rose*," she demanded. I'd accepted the assignment earlier that day, and Aggie had been sulking ever since. "You know absolutely nothing about it."

"Says who?" I took two beers from the refrigerator for Bo and me, then raised my eyebrows at her inquisitively; she nodded and I retrieved another for her. "I know all sorts of things about the *Mary Rose*."

"Indeed? Do tell."

"I believe it sank."

"Very amusing. What else?"

"I'm pretty sure it had sails, and a rudder."

She sighed. "I wish to God you'd stop taking overseas assignments. You're barely ever home, and we miss you terribly when you're gone. Bo mopes around the house like an abandoned puppy."

"*Arf arf,*" Bo barked from the living room. We had the television muted, since sportscaster chatter drove Aggie mad.

"Just give him one of my old slippers to chew on and he'll be fine," I told her. "Besides, I'll only be gone for four or five days this time, tops."

Aggie was still as lovely as ever. The only indications that she was sixty-four were a few wrinkles around her brilliant blue eyes, and a smattering of white in her long blond hair. The wrinkles softened her face somewhat, making her look gentler and wiser, though in truth she hadn't mellowed one iota with the passage of time.

"Four or five days, my foot," she called after me as I made my escape back to the living room. "Since when have you ever finished a story that quickly?"

"There's no choice this time," I called back, handing Bo his beer. "I promised Elias I'd be home before Halloween, to help him plan his anniversary party."

Bo winced involuntarily. None of us cared much for Elias's current lover, Larry, but unlike Aggie and me, Bo tried not to show it. Larry was friendly and clever, but there was something about him none of us trusted, though we couldn't say what exactly. Elias's track record with boyfriends was no doubt largely to blame; it was hard to believe him when he declared he'd finally found someone who wasn't as feckless and unstable as all the rest.

"Bo promised to help with the party, too," Aggie said, appearing in the doorway. "He's as insane as you are."

"Elias will talk you into helping, too, eventually," Bo said, snorting. "When have you ever said no to him?"

"There's a first time for everything." She flopped down between us on the sofa, scowling. "I'd rather have a hysterectomy than go to that party."

"Come on, now," Bo said. "Larry's not so bad."

"Yes, he is," Aggie whined. "He smells like sour cream."

"He does not."

"Yes, he does. Every time I'm around him I want a baked potato."

"You're being ridiculous."

I picked up a deck of cards to play solitaire on the coffee table in front of us. "He smells like baby food to me."

Bo sighed. "Do you two ever listen to yourselves?"

"He's somehow brainwashed Elias," Aggie said. "We should stage an intervention."

"Okay, fine. I don't like him, either," Bo snorted, surrendering. "But I don't know what we can do about it, other than wait for Elias to wake up."

"That's not going to happen anytime soon," I said. "Not unless Larry really screws up. I've never seen Elias this head over heels before."

"Me, either." Bo put his arm around Aggie's shoulders. "Who knows? Maybe we're all wrong about Larry, and he'll start to grow on us."

"Like leprosy," Aggie muttered.

"Or mildew," I added.

The lift crew eventually secured the *Mary Rose* on the barge that would carry her back to Portsmouth Harbour, two miles away, then every boat present escorted the sodden old girl back to shore, following in her wake like devoted ducklings.

"How much longer do we get to keep you, Isaac, now that you've gotten the *Mary Rose* this far?" Jeanne asked, as we neared the dock. Before that morning, I'd been doing the bulk of my research on land, then sleeping on the *Sea Major* at nights, in the harbour.

"I should be able to wrap things up in a day or so," I said. "But I was thinking I should get a hotel room ashore tonight and leave you all in peace. I've abused your hospitality long enough."

"Don't be silly," she said. "Stay as long as you can. We love having you aboard."

"Yeah, Isaac, don't go," Philip pleaded.

"Hear ye, hear ye," Terry said. "The queen of the *Sea Major* has spoken, and the heir to the throne has concurred."

In truth, I was more than happy to stay aboard; I'd become fond of all of them over the past few days, and a lonely hotel room held little appeal. I said I'd be delighted to keep mooching off them, provided I wasn't the only reason they were sticking around. I knew their next destination was Corfu, Greece, and they wanted to leave soon, to escape England before the winter.

"We're not in any rush," Terry said. "We all could use more time in port before we head out again." He leaned close to me so that Philip couldn't hear him. "Especially Aaron. He and his girlfriend have been screwing their brains out."

Aaron apparently had someone on shore he'd been spending time with, when he wasn't needed on the *Sea Major*. He hadn't slept aboard the boat since arriving in Portsmouth, and he'd thus far refused to reveal what he was up to in the evenings.

Jeanne had heard Terry's murmured comment to me, and she leaned in as well. "Why do you think Aaron's making such a big mystery of this girl?" she asked, glancing over at the mystery man himself, who was piloting the *Sea Major* while Mick was in the galley, brewing coffee to sober us up. "It's not as if we disapprove."

"Damn right," Terry said. "I told him this morning that he should bring her aboard for dinner tonight, but he pretended not to hear me."

Whatever Aaron's reasons for secrecy, he was clearly enjoying driving his employers crazy. He looked over his shoulder and caught us all looking at him, and he smiled wickedly before returning to piloting the boat.

"Why doesn't he just *tell* us?" Jeanne complained.

Mick reappeared from belowdecks with six mugs on a tray; he paused to hand one to Aaron. Aaron looked over his shoulder again and said something we couldn't hear, and Mick grinned before walking back to join us.

"What did Aaron just say?" Jeanne demanded.

"He said it's rude to talk about people behind their backs," Mick said.

"He did, did he?" Jeanne pitched her voice to carry. "For your information, wiseass, we're not talking about *you* at all."

Aaron chortled.

"Way to put him in his place, sweetheart," Terry said.

"Shut up," she said, retrieving Philip's hot cocoa from Mick's tray.

Ty and Karen now shared a loft apartment in the Bronx. Karen was teaching German at Hunter College, and Ty's paintings were, at long last, selling enough to earn him a decent living. Even though our whole family was getting together in Iowa at the end of the month for Elias's anniversary party, I'd stopped for an overnight visit at Ty and Karen's loft, on my way to England for the raising of the *Mary Rose*. Ty met me at La-Guardia when I landed; he was dressed in old jeans and a sweatshirt, and he'd grown a scraggly beard since I'd last seen him.

"You look wonderful, Isaac," he said, pulling me into a bear hug at the gate.

"My dissolute lifestyle treats me well." I pushed him back to scrutinize him. His thick hair was now more brown than blond, and I was jolted to see a few strands of white as well. "That beard is grotesque."

He laughed. "Yeah, I know, but I'm keeping it until I see Mom."

Aggie detested facial hair; whenever Bo or I ever dared to let a day pass without shaving, she'd threaten to depilate us herself, as inhumanely as possible.

"Do you have a death wish?" I asked. "She'll have a fit."

"That's the plan," Ty said. "Elias is going to take a picture of her face when I walk in the door."

I laughed. "That kid *definitely* has a death wish."

"Nah. He could set her shoes on fire and she'd still think it was funny."

Though unrelated by blood, Elias was Aggie's favorite family member, by far. She loved us all, of course (possibly even me), but she never held a grudge against Elias the way she did with the rest of us.

We took a taxi to Ty and Karen's one-room loft, and Karen was at the stove when we walked in the door. She squealed in delight—very much like the young girl she'd once been—and ran over to greet me. I held her tightly, then pushed her back to study her, as I'd done earlier with Ty. At forty-five, she'd become a highly respected teacher and linguist.

"Thank God you don't have white hair like your brother," I told her. "The two of you are strictly forbidden to age, but Ty appears to have forgotten that rule."

"I plucked out all the white this morning, just for you," she said. "I tried to get Ty to shave off that stupid beard, too, but he enjoys looking like a disreputable billy goat."

Their rent-controlled loft was enormous by NYC standards, with high ceilings and an entire wall of windows. They'd divided the space evenly, with a common living area in the middle, next to the kitchen and bathroom. Ty's side of the room was a jumble of paintings, easels, books, records, and magazines; Karen's side was almost entirely books and bookcases. To conserve space they each had a Murphy bed. (Privacy wasn't an issue when it was just the two of them, and they had an agreement to sleep elsewhere when either had a date.)

Karen had our meal well in hand—there was an aromatic red sauce bubbling on the stove, with sausage, red and green peppers, mushrooms, garlic, and anchovies. There was nothing left to do at this point but boil the pasta, so after Ty popped the cork on a bottle of wine and poured me a glass, I wandered over to his corner of the loft. A dozen or so of his most recent paintings were leaning against the wall, side by side, and I moved slowly down the line, Ty trailing behind.

Most of his paintings were of New York, but that was only because he happened to live there. If he lived in a remote fishing village, he would've painted that instead. Skyscrapers, roses, streetwalkers, the ocean, pigeons, food, churches, bartenders, parks, clocks, porches, insects—if it caught his eye, he painted it. His style was almost impossible to describe, as he was wary of repeating himself. His use of color, for instance, varied wildly from painting to painting, sometimes reminding me of Andrew Wyeth—washed-out greens, grays, and whites—and other times smacking of Edward Hopper—vivid blues and garish reds.

I paused at a portrait of two children, seen from behind, sitting on the edge of a swimming pool. One was a girl in a bright red swimsuit, the other a boy, and they were skinny and pale, with freckled, sunburnt shoulders. The girl had her feet in the water, but the boy was sitting Indian-style, bony forearms resting on his knees. The skin of his back was so delicate, it was almost translucent, like butter paper, and the girl had a small mole on her elbow, teardrop shaped. The power of the painting was in all the details—a patch of scraped skin on the girl's shoulder, the knobs of the boy's spine, the shadows of both kids on the concrete behind them. It was a perfectly rendered moment of childhood, in all its frailty and beauty.

"I knew you'd like that one," Karen called out. "I told him it's the best he's ever done."

"It's gorgeous," I said.

Ty was standing beside me, now. He was typically hypercritical of his own work, but for once he didn't seem dissatisfied; there was even a trace of pride in his expression. I clinked

my wineglass against his and he thanked me, then told me that
he'd seen the two kids when he was walking by the swimming
pool in late July. He'd snatched a notebook and pencil from
his backpack and began sketching like a madman, losing all
awareness of everything else until the kids broke their pose and
jumped into the water. Ty ran home as fast as he could, tripping
over a curb and skinning both knees, and when he got back to
the loft, he'd tacked the sketch on a wall, set up an easel beside
it, and painted for eleven hours straight.

"It was like I'd just opened my eyes for the first time in my
life," he told me. "I couldn't believe what was coming out of
my brush."

Karen joined us. "It might be healthier for you to take a few
breaks next time that happens," she told her twin, resting her
head on my shoulder. "The last thing we need in this family is
another insomniac overachiever, forgetting to eat and shower."

"Hey, now," I protested. "I never forget to shower."

"No, but Mom does, and you starve yourself to death. I
don't know how Bo puts up with either of you."

Once the *Mary Rose* was safely returned to shore, I spent the
day talking to people who'd taken part in getting her there.
Over the past eleven years, hundreds of workers had been involved in the project, collectively logging thousands of hours
underwater and ashore. Everyone milling around the dripping
hulk of the old ship at the Royal Naval Base was giddy with delight and relief, including Prince Charles, who fielded a few
questions from the press. The specialists now tasked with re-
storing the *Mary Rose* had already begun the next phase of the
project, wrapping her in foam and periodically spraying her
with water to stave off bacteria. This work was the province of
experts, however, so most of the volunteers found themselves
with little to do save celebrate and talk to me.

I wandered back to the harbor late in the afternoon for sup-

per with the McMillans onboard the *Sea Major*. Before I got
there, though, I bumped into Aaron Prall—the good-looking
blond kid who crewed for the McMillans—just as he was coming out of a tiny corner pub, in company with another young
man who apparently needed a little help walking, because
Aaron was more or less holding him up.

"Hey, Isaac!" Aaron greeted me with a surprised smile.
"Fancy meeting you here."

"Holy shit," his buddy said, gaping blearily at me. "It's really you." He glanced at Aaron. "I thought you were just taking the piss, mate, when you said you knew Isaac Dahl."

He was taller and skinnier than Aaron, and had red hair instead of blond, but there was an uncanny resemblance between
the two—the same cheekbones and noses, the same green eyes
and flat chins. Aaron introduced him as Greg, his first cousin.

"Goddamn," Greg said again, shaking my hand. "You're
Isaac *fucking* Dahl!"

"I think he already knows that, boyo," Aaron told him,
winking at me. "Greg just spent the last two hours in Mr. Bush-
mill's fine company, so please excuse his manners."

I told him I was on my way back to the *Sea Major* and he
said they'd tag along. "I'm glad you'll be there tonight," he
continued, falling into step with me. "It'll be a wee bit of fun
when Terry and Jeanne meet my ugly sod of a cousin."

I grinned. "So Greg's the mystery person you've been keeping from them all week?"

"Yep." He grinned back. "I know they think I'm shagging a
pretty lass, but sadly all I've been doing is bunking with Greg
at his flat. I haven't bothered to correct them, though, because
they need to be taught a lesson about nosiness."

Just as we reached the mooring for the *Sea Major*, Mick
Donovan, Aaron's crewmate, popped out of the cockpit to meet
us. He said the harbormaster had just radioed the boat, saying
Aggie was looking for me, and wanted me to phone home right
away.

"Did the harbormaster say why?" I asked, startled. Aggie and Bo had the number for the hotel where I'd planned to stay before I was invited aboard the *Sea Major*, but since I'd neglected to let them know about the change, Aggie must've upended half of Portsmouth to find me. She wouldn't have done that unless something was seriously amiss.

"Sorry," Mick said. "All he told me was that your sister said it was an emergency."

I returned to the *Sea Major* sometime later that evening, not really knowing how I'd gotten there. I was in no shape for company, but being alone with my thoughts was even less appealing, so I'd come back, praying for distraction. It was full dark when I arrived at the dock, but the boat's cockpit was brightly lit, and through an open window I could hear animated voices and laughter. I took a deep breath and straightened my shoulders, then called out for permission to come aboard. There was a chorus of greetings and little Philip burst from the open door of the cockpit as I stepped on deck. He flung his arms around my waist and asked if I was okay.

"I'm fine, buddy." I rested my hand on the boy's head. "What did I miss here?"

"Greg said he pooped his pants in church when he was little, right in front of *everybody*!"

I knew he could see my face in the light from the open door, so I made myself smile. "Wow. That's quite an achievement."

"Yeah. He said his brother told him God hated little kids named Greg, so he got super scared and pooped his pants."

"I don't blame him. God scares the poop out of me, too."

Philip giggled. "You're funny, Isaac."

Empty dishes were still on the table in the cockpit, and the aroma of fried fish and roasted vegetables lingering in the air made my stomach growl, in spite of my precarious emotional state. After everyone welcomed me, they wanted to know about the emergency at home. I was grateful for their concern, but I had no intention of telling them the truth.

"Nothing too awful," I said, hanging my raincoat on a hook by the door. "A water pipe burst in our house and ruined some things, but my sister has it under control. Sorry I'm late for dinner, but we needed to figure out a few things."

Everybody made sympathetic noises, accepting my fabrication at face value. Jeanne said she'd saved me dinner; I told her she was a saint as she went to the galley to warm a plate. Terry poured me a double shot of whiskey and I sat by Philip at the table, deflecting the conversation from my phone call home by asking what they'd been talking about before I interrupted. They said they'd been gossiping about Prince Charles and his interest in the *Mary Rose;* they were curious about the people I'd interviewed at the naval base, and I answered their questions as well as I could.

I had no idea how I was going to get through the next few hours.

Aggie and Bo had spent the better part of two days trying to find me. They'd finally stumbled across a journalist friend of mine also on assignment in Portsmouth who happened to know I was aboard the *Sea Major.* By the time I called home, Aggie was beside herself; she broke down when she heard my voice, and passed the phone to Bo. Bo was a mess, too, but at least he was able to talk. He said a few days ago Elias had discovered a purple lesion on his ankle, and blood tests had soon confirmed the worst.

He had AIDS.

The silence on the phone after Bo finished telling me lasted an eternity; I'd stared through the dirty window of the phone booth, seeing nothing. Though we were four thousand miles apart, I could picture Bo and Aggie sitting at our kitchen table in Iowa, staring at the exact same nothing.

Elias would almost certainly be dead in a year, and I wasn't sure I could bear it.

I'd somehow managed to convince myself that the monstrous virus now rampaging through the gay community like a modern-day Black Death wasn't going to get him. (I wasn't worried for myself; I was sixty-four, single, and not at all promiscuous, so my risk of infection was nonexistent.) I knew how deadly HIV was, of course, and I also knew how quickly it was spreading: The first cases had just cropped up in Los Angeles the year before but now over a hundred thousand people in the U.S. alone had contracted it, and that number was growing exponentially by the day. But Elias had been in a monogamous relationship for some time so I'd told myself he'd be safe. I'd still worried about him, naturally, because we each had friends and acquaintances who were sick and getting sicker, and it was a terrifying way to die. But I'd believed he was out of harm's way, and being careful, and would surely outlive me by decades.

Surely.

I wanted to scream in pain and rage, but I was afraid if I started screaming I wouldn't be able to stop.

Philip tugged at my sleeve and I leaned down so he could whisper in my ear, as the others were talking. "Are you sad about your house getting wet, Isaac?" he asked.

"Yes, buddy," I whispered back. He slipped his small fingers into my hand, and my eyes stung. "I'm pretty sad."

"Sorry there's no roasted garlic left," Jeanne said, reappearing before her son's sweetness could undo me. She gave me a plate of leftover fried shrimp and potatoes that she'd kept warm on the stove. "These savages didn't save you any."

I cleared my throat to thank her. "No worries. This looks terrific."

"Aaron ate the lion's share of the garlic," Terry said. "Thank God he's bunking at Greg's place."

"Nope," Aaron said. "I'm back aboard tonight, skipper. Greg's bloody couch is a nightmare, and now that you and Jeanne have seen what snooping gets you, I see no reason to keep torturing myself."

"Ingrate," Greg grumbled.

"We weren't *snooping*, Aaron," Jeanne protested. "We were just, uh—"

"—just sticking our big fat noses into your personal life," Terry finished, grinning.

"I see," Aaron snorted. "My mistake."

I listened to the banter between the McMillans and the three young men as I ate, and I did my damnedest to join in. It was a damp, cold night, but the cockpit—warmed by the galley stove and the body heat of seven people—was perfectly cozy, even with a couple of windows cracked for air. I was still glad for my sweater, though, and the burn of the whiskey in my throat, and the hot food. I told myself there would be ample time to grieve for Elias; I reminded myself he was still alive, and as long as that was true, there was hope. I also reminded myself that an evening with good company in a safe harbor is a precious thing and should never be taken for granted. Elias himself would tell me not to give him a second thought; he'd call me a fool for wasting a chance to share a few drinks and laughter with these kind and generous people.

So I tried.

I joked with Mick and Aaron about things I have no recollection of, and I talked to Jeanne about British politics. I played a few hands of gin rummy with Philip and Greg before Philip's bedtime, and then played chess with Terry afterward. Aaron and Greg helped Jeanne clean the galley, and Mick messed around on a beat-up guitar, mangling Jim Croce's "Operator." Greg eventually became too tipsy to make it home safely, so after a final round of drinks, Aaron and Mick called it a night, carting him off to the crew cabin. Terry, Jeanne, and I sat up for a while longer, chatting softly about this and that, with the boat gently rocking beneath us.

And then it was time to say good night. I went to my cabin, closed the door, undressed, got in bed, and turned off the light on the headboard. I stared for a while at a shadow on the wall—there was a little illumination coming from the cabin porthole, even though the night sky was overcast, hiding the moon—and I listened to the hypnotic, monotonous slap of the ocean against the hull, steady as a clock.

Nothing on a boat is private, so I heard when Terry and Jeanne began making love in their cabin, though they were quiet. About the same time, someone in the crew cabin commenced snoring—Greg, most likely—and a while later the door across from mine opened. Philip's small, bare feet padded lightly past my door, on his way to the toilet; he left the bathroom door open, and I could hear him humming to himself as he urinated.

I remembered when Elias was Philip's age. I thought of the formal way he used to greet Aggie and me, shaking our hands every time we saw him, and how his mother always made him wear bowties, and kept his hair neatly combed. I thought of how during his senior year in high school he'd gotten into his first serious relationship with a boy in his class, and how he'd come to talk to me about it. I thought of how he'd always loved to sing, even in his sleep. I thought of him in Mississippi, and how brave he'd been when the Klan beat him to a pulp; I thought of him in Provence on our family vacation eight years before, hovering over me to make sure I didn't make myself sick with work.

There was a soft knock on my cabin door before it opened. "Isaac?" Philip whispered. I could make out his sturdy little silhouette. "What's wrong?"

I couldn't answer, and a few seconds later he climbed on the bed and sat with me as I fought to regain control of myself. He was wearing flannel pajamas and radiated warmth like a hot water bottle; he patted my shoulder and murmured comfort, as if he were the old man and I the little boy. I had no idea how he'd heard me crying—I didn't think I'd made any noise—and I prayed he was the only one who had.

"I'm okay, buddy," I finally managed to say. I wiped the tears from my face and pulled him into a hug. "Thanks for checking on me, but you'd better get back to bed, don't you think?"

I expected him to argue, but he didn't. He gave me a final pat on the shoulder, said good night, and slid off the bed. A second later the door closed behind him. I drifted off to sleep an hour or so later, surrendering to the endless tide.

DAY NINE

June 25, 1990. Romola, Italy.

On land, Danny seemed a bit ungainly, his arms and legs too long for his body. When he swam, though, he was graceful and sleek, like some exotic sea mammal. I sat at the edge of the pool behind his villa, paddling my feet in the water and letting the late-afternoon sun bake my skin as I watched him do laps. I had no idea how many he'd completed, but he'd been at it for the better part of an hour. He was finally tiring—he'd slowed down in the past few minutes—yet I knew he wouldn't stop until he grew bored or wore himself out. He was that way about everything: running, dancing, writing, piano, sex.

The Rossetti family had owned this villa for generations, and Danny was the last surviving Rossetti. The centuries-old house had a red-tiled roof and white stucco walls, and was surrounded by seven acres of olive and lemon trees, all tucked away behind a high, gated wall in the sleepy village of Romola, just outside Florence. Danny and I lived there by ourselves, but Aggie and Bo were on their way to join us for a month, theoretically arriving any moment. They'd flown into Rome and were coming to us via rental car, but Aggie would dawdle every inch of the way, so I didn't really expect them to show up for quite a while.

Danny did a last lap, then planted his feet on the bottom of the pool and stood up, shedding water. His mother had been Chinese and his father Italian, and I was profoundly grateful he took after his mother when it came to body hair. (According to Danny, his father had resembled a black bear, but Danny was smooth all over, save for armpits and groin.) From the pictures I'd seen, he inherited the best of both parents: his father's olive-colored skin and Roman cheekbones, his mother's lustrous black hair and long-boned hands. He joked that he was the human equivalent of pasta, "conceived in China, perfected in Italy."

"Go for a swim, old man," he said. He'd just turned forty-seven and was strikingly beautiful, whereas I was seventy-two and resembled a snapping turtle. "You'll get fat if you're not careful."

Save for a slight accent, his English was excellent—he'd lived in Boston in his twenties, while earning a PhD in theology.

"I'm saving my strength," I said. "Aggie will be spoiling for a fight when she gets here."

"No, she won't. When I talked to her on the phone last week she promised to behave."

I laughed. "And you believed her?"

Danny and I had flown back to Iowa for Christmas with Bo, Aggie, Karen, Ty, and Jamie (Karen's young adopted son). Aggie had been in a wretched temper, barking at everybody in the house, but she'd saved her worst tantrums for me. She was still furious I'd moved to Italy the previous spring with Danny, accusing me of "breaking up the family." Ty and Karen only came home themselves once or twice a year, but that didn't annoy her nearly as much; she'd resigned herself decades ago to their absence, but my decision to relocate half a world away had hurt her deeply.

"She may manage to be civilized for a day or two," I said, "but I guarantee she's not done yelling."

Danny and I had met in Florence four years before, when I was researching an article about the San Marco Museum. I'd been sitting alone in a small restaurant, drinking chianti and stuffing myself with prosciutto, olives, and thin slices of Parmesan cheese, as I read over some notes. I looked up, startled, when a man spoke to me in Italian, asking to share my table. The restaurant could only seat a dozen people, and the single empty chair left in the place was across from me. He made no attempt to converse, however; he just sat down, ordered a half carafe of wine from the waitress, and pulled a book from his backpack. It was an Italo Calvino novel, and I grimaced before I could help myself.

"Something wrong?" he asked in English, clearly pegging me as an American.

I shook my head. "Sorry. My sister and I had an argument about Calvino a couple of years ago, and I still haven't gotten all the salt out of my hair."

He smiled. "I beg your pardon?"

I hesitated, aware of how ridiculous the story would sound. "Aggie—my sister—thinks Calvino's a genius, but I think he's pretentious. We fought about it and she poured a jar of salt over my head."

His smile broadened. "Do your literary discussions always involve table condiments?"

I laughed, and we introduced ourselves. I asked if he lived in Florence, and he said he did—he taught religion at the University of Florence—but he was soon moving back to the village where he'd grown up. His mother had died that year, and his father was ill and couldn't live alone. I asked if he'd continue teaching at the university after he moved.

"Oh, yes," he said. "Romola isn't far, and there's an old woman who cooks for my father, while her nephew tends our olive grove. I'm not really needed until they've gone home at night. Dad gets lonely with no one to pester."

Over three bottles of wine—and enough cured meat to choke a St. Bernard—he told me how his father, an Italian soldier, had met his mother during World War II, when Italy controlled a small territory in China. She got pregnant three months later, so after Italy surrendered to the Allies, the hastily married couple returned to Danny's father's home in Romola, just in time for Danny's birth. He said growing up biracial in Romola had taught him valuable life lessons, such as how to run very fast. He was a gifted storyteller, and I would've been content to just sit and listen, but he prodded me for stories of my own. I found myself telling him all about Aggie and Bo, and he was surprised to hear that the three of us still lived together in Iowa.

"You must get along very well, to have stayed together so long," he said.

I made a wry face. "Bo's an excellent referee, otherwise Aggie and I would've killed each other fifty years ago."

"Really?"

"No, I'm exaggerating. We only would've maimed each other." I sipped my wine. "My sister's brilliant—honest to God, she knows *everything*. And now and then she even manages to be kind, too." I grinned. "But when she's angry, she's terrifying. Picture Medusa, with more snakes."

Danny grinned back at me. "And what does she say about you?"

"Sadly, it's not as flattering as you might think."

At first, I didn't have any idea Danny was gay, nor did I dream he might find me attractive—the difference in our ages made that unlikely—so I simply enjoyed his company, free of the awkwardness I usually felt when talking to potential lovers. When we finally finished our meal, we wandered out into the cobbled street and said good night. I held out my hand and he took it, then leaned forward to kiss me on both cheeks, Italian-style.

"Do you have plans for tomorrow evening?" he asked, still gripping my hand. "I've moved the bulk of my furniture back to Romola, but I still have an apartment here in town, with all my kitchen things. I'd like to cook for you." He met my eyes, and I was astonished to see him blush. "I'd really like to get to know you better."

My heart began beating in a way I thought it had long since forgotten how to do.

"I'd like that," I said, as casually as I could. "What can I bring?"

Aggie and Bo arrived in Romola right before sunset. Danny and I were in the middle of cooking dinner, having given up on them getting there in time to join us. I looked out the screen door of our villa and saw their rental car wending through the olive trees, negotiating the potholes in the narrow dirt path that was our driveway. I knew at once Bo was driving; Aggie would've barreled straight ahead, not giving a damn about the car's suspension. I ran to meet them as they parked. Bo was the first out of the car—he was still enviably spry for an old man—but Aggie wasn't far behind, and within seconds the three of us were locked in an embrace, rocking back and forth on the lawn.

"I guess what they say about the Tuscan sun is true," Bo said. "You're brown as a walnut."

"Too brown," Aggie said. "Your skin must feel like cowhide."

I couldn't talk. My throat had closed and I was crying. We'd just been apart for six months, but the only time in our lives we'd been separated so long was during World War II. Bo's once quasi-orange hair was now solid white, but—judging from his grip around my rib cage—he was still freakishly strong, and his smile was as sweet as ever. Aggie's hair, too, was white, but it was still long and luxurious, reaching halfway down her back. In the last couple of years she'd begun to age, finally, but the crow's feet at the corners of her eyes did nothing to diminish their fierce intelligence, nor the beauty of her face.

"You old softie," she said, kissing my cheek. "Stop crying this instant. Your lower lip is curling in a very unappealing way."

"It's your fault for being late," I blubbered. "I'm emotionally fragile when I'm starving."

Bo laughed. "Your sister wanted to stop at every vineyard in Italy."

"We only stopped once, and it was Bo's idea," Aggie said. "Where's Daniel?" She adored Danny, and held him blameless for my move to Italy, as if I'd forced him at gunpoint to invite me into his home and bed.

"I'm here," said Danny, hurrying out the front door. "My gorgonzola sauce was in critical condition." He joined our hug, laughing at me. "Isaac, you are *such* a baby."

The sun was a dazzling orange and red disk on the horizon. Dark green cypress and pale green olive trees lined the gravel roads; mottled gray and brown stone fences separated fields of beans, asparagus, strawberries, and artichokes; lemon trees riddled with vivid yellow huddled together like timid girls at a party; white and tan stucco houses dotted the hillsides; white daisies and red poppies aimed their pistils lazily at the faded evening blue of the sky. Aggie broke away to take it all in, turning in a slow circle. She'd been to Italy before, as had Bo, but neither of them had ever been to Tuscany.

"Oh, my," she murmured. "It's so lovely." She glanced over her shoulder at me and smiled ruefully. "I hope you know how much it kills me to admit that."

I smiled back at her. "You're enduring your death pangs quite well."

"The wine we had at the vineyard fortified me." She stepped back into my arms and rested her head on my chest. "You're an ass, Isaac Dahl, but dear God, how I've missed you."

My relationship with Danny surprised everybody, but especially me. Following our first encounter, I ended up staying that night at his apartment—and every night afterward, for the remainder of my trip to Italy. He wrote soon after I'd returned to the States, telling me his father had died, and asking if I could come back. I flew to Florence and spent several weeks at his villa in Romola. He was distraught and depressed, and I did what I could to help—which wasn't much, save to hold him as he grieved, and watch him sort listlessly through his father's things. He extended his leave of absence from teaching to come with me to Iowa, wanting to meet my family. Karen, Ty, and Jamie joined us there, flying in from New York.

I was grateful no one cared about the disparity in our ages. Danny was, after all, six years younger than Ty and Karen—and the same age Elias would've been, had he lived—and I sometimes felt like a scandalous old pervert, preying on the young. Danny just laughed when I told him this; he reminded me that he'd seduced me, not the other way around. Aggie also found it ridiculous that I could ever imagine myself as a predator.

"You're not a lion, Isaac," she said. "You're a gazelle."

Aggie and Danny hit it off at once. Not only were they both obsessively passionate about literature, philosophy, and history, they were also absurdly well-read. On our first evening there, I woke in the dead of night and, finding Danny missing from our bed, went hunting for him. He and Aggie were in the kitchen, chatting at the table. I asked what they were talking about.

"Charlemagne's children," Aggie said. "Specifically, Pepin the Hunchback."

"No one really knows if Pepin was legitimate," Danny explained. "The jury is still out about the legality of his parents' marriage."

"Oh," I said, yawning. "And is there a reason you're talking about this at two in the morning?"

Aggie rubbed her temples. "Neither of us can sleep, so we decided that listing Charlemagne's kids might be more of a soporific than drinking warm milk."

"Poor Pepin," Danny said, still adrift in the Middle Ages. "As if it weren't bad enough to be a hunchback, his dear old dad shaved his head, too, and made him become a monk."

"He was lucky to have a head to shave," Aggie said. "Didn't he lead a revolt against Charlemagne, prior to being tonsured?"

I yawned again, giving up. "I'm going back to bed. You kids have fun."

"It may be a while before I join you," Danny said, squeezing my hand. "Charlemagne had eighteen children."

Back in Romola.

Bo and Aggie wanted to shower prior to dinner, so I showed them their upstairs room in the villa before helping Danny finish preparing our meal. I decanted some wine and set the table, humming to myself as I rummaged for candles in the pantry.

"I haven't seen you this happy in a long time," Danny said.

There was no reproach in his voice, but I still felt guilty, recognizing the truth of what he'd just said. I know he worried about having asked me to uproot my life to live with him.

"It's just nice to have Aggie and Bo here," I said, joining him at the stove.

"I keep telling you to go home more often." Danny's teaching didn't allow him to travel as much as I could. "It's not like you don't have the time, or the money."

"My home is here," I said.

He took my hand and squeezed it gently. "The three of you have loved each other for seventy-two years. I can't compete with that."

"It's not a competition." I grinned. "Besides, you live in Eden, and they live in Iowa. There's really no contest."

He waved me off with a spoon. "You only love me for my villa. Go tell Aggie and Bo to hurry up, will you? Dinner's almost done."

I poured myself a glass of wine and went upstairs, enjoying the cool stone steps under my bare feet. Bo and Aggie were showering together, and they'd left the door to the bathroom ajar, just as they always did at home. The shower curtain, draped around an old clawfoot tub, kept them from seeing me, so I leaned quietly against the doorframe and eavesdropped, shamelessly, on their conversation. They'd been listening to my private conversations for years, so it seemed only fair.

"Stop hogging the water," Aggie was saying. "I need to rinse off."

"What's your hurry?" Bo asked. "You look super sexy when you're covered in soap suds. You could be a *Playboy* bunny."

Aggie snorted. "I'm a senior citizen, Bo, and you're half-blind without your glasses. I'm as sexy as Henry Kissinger."

"I see just fine, Henry. Change places with me." They shuffled around behind the curtain. "What's Danny cooking, I wonder? It smelled great when we walked into the house."

"Yes, it did," Aggie agreed. "I'm jealous of Isaac. Why can't you cook like Danny?"

"No one ever lets me near the kitchen. Johan did all the cooking when we were kids, and Janet did the honors when we were married. You and Isaac never let me cook, either."

"That's because you can't even make oatmeal without it tasting like glue."

I laughed, and the curtain parted; they weren't in the least surprised to see me.

"She's right," I told Bo. "You're a godawful cook."

"Y'all are just plain mean," Bo said.

"I should think you'd be used to that." Aggie disappeared from view again as Bo stepped from the tub, reaching for a towel. The three of us had long since discarded modesty, having shared a bathroom forever. Bo might have lost a little muscle tone since I'd last seen him without clothes, but he still looked lean and fit.

"Time doesn't pass for you the way it does for the rest of humanity," I told him as he dried off. "You make me feel like a fossil."

Aggie snorted behind the curtain. "It's a wonder you don't crumble into dust."

"Give it time," I told her. "I've started falling asleep during sex, so dust is the next step."

Bo moved to the sink, wiping steam from the mirror with his towel. The scars on his lower back and hip, though somewhat faded since he got them, reminded me forcefully of the last time he'd been to Italy.

"How does it feel to be back in this neck of the woods?" I asked. "I mean, no one's shooting at you this time around. Aren't you bored?"

He grinned over his shoulder. "To tell the truth, it's a little weird, but I'm okay. My unit never fought hereabouts." The window next to him was wide open; he peered out at the full moon lighting Danny's olive grove with astonishing clarity. "It's a damn good thing you don't live in Bologna, though. I still have nightmares about that goddamn place."

Aggie turned off the shower and pushed aside the curtain, reaching for a towel. My twin's body, unsurprisingly, was also aging better than mine.

"Do you guys always talk about Henry Kissinger when you shower?" I asked.

"Not always," she said. "Yesterday we argued about Margaret Thatcher."

"That's very disturbing."

"You have no idea." She glanced at my wineglass. "Where's mine?"

Shortly after Elias was diagnosed with HIV, he learned that his boyfriend, Larry, had been sleeping with strangers for much of the time they'd been together. Elias moved back in with Aggie, Bo, and me; he died thirteen months later. Near the end, we were caring for him in shifts to keep from exhausting ourselves. Bo and I often had to drag Aggie from the room when her shift ended, to make sure she slept. Ty and Karen came home, separately and together, to help when they could, and they were with us when Elias passed. Elias's mother, Janet, was there, too, having flown in from Ireland. Miraculously, she and Aggie managed a temporary truce; they were both too heartbroken to indulge in their habitual animosity.

There was no dignity in Elias's death. There was just shit, piss, vomit, and a lot of feverish mumbling, and there was next to nothing that any of us—including the full-time nurse we'd hired—could do to ease his suffering, though God knows we tried. In a bedroom full of flowers, cards, IVs, syringes, bedpans, plastic sheets, washcloths, pain pills, and diapers, we read aloud to him when he was lucid; we sang his favorite songs; we cried with him; we held him in our arms; we told him how much we loved him.

And then we said goodbye.

The scarred, sturdy oak table in Danny's kitchen could easily seat ten people, and generations of Rossetti buttocks had worn faint grooves in the two long, equally solid benches that went with it. The kitchen ceiling was crossed by wooden beams, the floor was stone-tiled, and there was a large double window over the sink, looking out on our valley. The evening Bo and Aggie arrived in Romola, the four of us lingered at the table after dinner, drinking prosecco. The night was hot and sticky, but we were all barefoot and dressed in shorts and short-sleeved shirts, and there was a light breeze blowing through the open doors and windows of the house, helped along by the kitchen ceiling fan.

"That was an amazing meal, Danny," Aggie said, topping off her prosecco. The recipe that Danny had prepared for us that evening—gnocchi in a gorgonzola sauce—was one his grandmother had made for him countless times when he was a child. Aggie told him it was grossly unfair that he'd grown up eating food like that on a regular basis.

"It sure is," I agreed. "Every time I tell him about our diet during the Depression, he starts to gag."

"You all might've missed out on good food when you were kids," Danny said, "but I think it's fair to say that you never lacked for good company."

I exchanged a look with Bo and Aggie that carried all the convoluted memories of our childhood. We smiled at each other.

"The company was okay, I guess," I said. "Except when Aggie was possessed by Satan."

"Damn straight." Bo laughed, clinking his glass against mine. Aggie sniffed primly, and I snorted into my wine.

An urgent rapping at the front screen door made us all jump. Danny and I looked at each other, puzzled. He knew everyone in Romola, but many of our fellow citizens disapproved of our relationship and went out of their way to avoid us—which wasn't particularly difficult, as our nearest neighbors were half a kilometer away, on the far side of Danny's olive grove.

"*Chi è?*" Danny called out.

No answer, save for another burst of rapping. Danny frowned, swinging his legs around the end of the bench and rising to his feet. He called out again as he disappeared down the hallway.

"Please don't let it be that Jehovah's Witness couple who've been stalking me all year," Aggie joked. "They're very persistent."

We could hear Danny speaking to someone, but not what they were saying. He popped back into the room a moment later. "It's Alessio Greco," he said, grabbing a flashlight from the top of the fridge. "He says his brother, Claudio, was climbing one of our trees and fell, and now he's not moving at all."

I knew both boys; they and their parents were somewhat more sociable than their fellow townsmen. The elder Grecos owned a small vineyard, abutting our olive grove. Alessio was about six; his older brother, Claudio, was nine or ten.

I hurried down the hall after Danny, with Bo and Aggie at my heels. We ran out of the house barefoot, nearly trampling Alessio at the base of the steps before the beam from Danny's flashlight found him. He was a stocky little boy, dressed in light blue shorts and a pair of white sneakers. Danny asked him to take us to Claudio and he sprinted down the driveway, into the trees. He was amazingly fast for having such short legs, but Danny managed to stay close enough to keep the light on his naked back. The boy led us about a hundred yards farther into the grove before veering off the driveway to the right. Danny called him back, afraid of losing him, and he reappeared, hopping with impatience. Bo, Aggie, and I were all breathing hard; the moon and stars were bright enough that I could see their faces, and they both looked oddly exhilarated. I felt the same, even though I was worried about the injured boy. I couldn't remember the last time I'd been outside running on a summer night.

"Thank God there's no gravel on your driveway," Aggie panted as we caught up to Alessio. "My feet would be hamburger."

The kid took off again, darting down a row of olive trees. A little way in, he abruptly dropped to his knees, and Danny's flashlight picked out Claudio's body next to him. When we reached them a few moments later we all squatted beside the prone boy. He was on his stomach, face in the grass, with one arm twisted awkwardly beneath him. He was wearing a white tank top, black soccer shorts, and no shoes; he was almost a foot taller than his brother, and just as stocky. I felt a surge of relief when I saw that he was breathing, though he appeared to be unconscious.

Bo calmly checked the boy's pulse, his fingers sure and gentle. I shouldn't have been surprised that he looked like he knew exactly what he was doing; God only knew how many wounded young men he'd knelt beside during the war. "Danny, can you ask the little guy—what's his name, Alessio?—if his brother moved after he fell, or did he land just like this?"

Alessio told us that Claudio had first fallen on his back, so he'd rolled him on his stomach, thinking the older boy was playing a prank. Danny translated as Alessio began to cry, and Bo took the flashlight from Danny, gingerly exploring Claudio's skull through the boy's black hair.

"Danny, you better go call an ambulance," he said. "Tell them his pulse is okay, and he's not bleeding much, but there's some swelling on the left side of his head, and he's out cold. I think he may have a skull fracture."

Danny ran off at once, yelling back over his shoulder that he'd call Claudio's parents, too.

"I hate like hell to move him more than he's already been moved," Bo said. "But maybe we should try to make him more comfortable?" He gave the flashlight to Alessio and asked me to tell him to shine it on his brother. Bo lifted Claudio's head gently, then had me turn the boy on his right side, maneuvering Claudio's arm out from under his stomach and keeping his back as straight as possible, protecting the spine.

"So far, so good," Bo said. He removed his own shirt, rolled it into a ball, and slid it under the boy's head for a pillow, then reclaimed the flashlight and lifted Claudio's eyelids, shining the light in his pupils. I started to stand but he stopped me.

"Stick close, buddy," he said. "If he wakes up, I'll need help holding him still. Can you ask Alessio if his folks are home, for when Danny calls them?"

The flashlight in Bo's hands cast a small dome of light around us, like a campfire, as I spoke to the boy. He told me his parents were watching TV; Claudio and he were supposed to be in bed but had snuck out of the house to play. He asked Bo if Claudio was going to die, and I translated.

"Your brother's going to be just fine, son," Bo said, with a reassuring smile that would've convinced anyone besides Aggie and me. "Aggie, can you and Alessio go back to the driveway and keep an eye out for his parents, and the ambulance?"

"Of course," Aggie murmured, putting an arm around Alessio's bare shoulders and gently leading him away. Bo watched them until we lost sight of their backs in the trees and the darkness.

"I sure hope I didn't just lie to that little kid," Bo said quietly. I asked how bad it was, and he checked Claudio's pulse again before answering. "His left pupil's blown, and that big damn bump on his head scares me."

The cicadas were in full voice in the olive trees around us. Bo rechecked the swelling on the boy's head as I looked on. Something about Bo's expression reminded me of the boy he'd once been, when we were Claudio's age. It didn't seem so long ago, yet somehow more than six decades had gone by, and we'd become old men. I thought of his face when Elias was dying in his arms, and I couldn't bear the thought of him witnessing another child's death.

"He'll be okay," I said, knowing how inane I sounded. "Italian kids have hard heads."

He managed a shadowy grin but stayed silent. I swatted a mosquito on my neck that turned out to be an advance scout;

within seconds a legion of them attacked. It was worse for Bo with no shirt, but I took the assault less stoically. Claudio must've been wearing insect repellent, thankfully, because the swarm was avoiding him.

A quickly approaching flashlight between the trees was a welcome distraction. It was Danny, followed by Claudio's parents. Emilio was a hefty, balding man in his thirties, Sofia a thin, nervous woman who always reminded me of a hummingbird. Emilio was towing little Alessio by the hand, and the boy looked miserable. Aggie must've volunteered to wait for the ambulance in the driveway.

"*Dio mio*!" cried Sofia, falling to her knees on Claudio's other side. "Claudio!"

Bo put a restraining hand on her wrist, preventing her from throwing her arms around the boy. "Warn her to be careful, Danny," he said. "We can't risk moving him anymore."

Sofia looked with anguish at Bo as Danny translated, but she nodded, gripping Claudio's fingers and bending down to kiss his cheek. Emilio released Alessio's hand and sank to his knees beside his wife as Danny relayed what Bo was able to tell them. Emilio listened until Bo finished, then turned to Alessio, demanding to know why the boys had snuck out of their bedroom to climb trees; he also asked why Alessio had come to Danny's villa for help instead of returning home. Alessio's blubbered answer was largely incomprehensible, but the gist was that he'd been afraid of getting in trouble, so he'd come to get Danny and me, hoping we'd be able to "fix" Claudio. Emilio scowled and began chiding the boy, but Sofia shushed him, saying something I couldn't catch.

"Boys sneak out at night to do dumb things," Danny translated.

"Yep," Bo agreed. "That's a fact, and then some."

His steady, watchful presence seemed to calm Emilio, and I marveled, as always, at how readily people trusted him. Aggie and I had often joked that Bo would've made a great Jesus if the role hadn't already been taken by that flashy Mediterranean usurper.

A siren finally began to wail in the distance. Romola's volunteer emergency service was seldom required and must've needed a few minutes to pull itself together. Emilio's eyes met Bo's, and then mine, over the unconscious body of his son, and in spite of his obvious anxiety, he nodded and gruffly thanked us in broken English, for helping. Bo said that we hadn't been able to do much at all, but Emilio waved his words away.

"You here, you help," he said. "Thank you."

Claudio's legs spasmed, and he cried out. Bo clamped down on his shoulder and waist and told me to grab his legs, and Sofia spoke to him, telling him she was there, and not to move. He didn't answer, but his legs spasmed again, and went rigid. I couldn't get a good grip on him, even after Emilio seized his ankles, because the boy's skin was sweaty and so were my hands. The siren grew louder, and then we could see headlights through the trees. Car doors opened and slammed shut; Aggie's voice carried in the night air, as well as the voices of two men, although I couldn't hear what was being said. Claudio kicked again and moaned, but he didn't answer Sofia, and his eyes remained shut.

"I think he knows we're here," Bo said. He leaned close to the boy's ear and spoke softly to him. Claudio quieted almost at once, though Bo was speaking English and the words could only have been gibberish to him, conscious or not.

Late that night, Aggie was sitting by the swimming pool, smoking a cigarette, when I joined her. "I thought you'd given up those damn things for good," I said, sitting beside her and slipping my bruised feet in the water.

"I did," she said. "But I still keep a pack in my purse for emergencies."

I glanced at her. "And how many emergencies have you had since you quit?"

She snorted, expelling a cloud of smoke. "Three or four a week. Sometimes more."

Behind us in the villa, Bo and Danny were at the kitchen table, drinking wine and hoping for a call from Emilio at the hospital. Danny had phoned the emergency room in Florence three hours before, but all he'd been told was that Claudio was in surgery, and the operation was expected to take half the night.

"I'm really sorry," I told Aggie. "This isn't exactly what we'd planned for the first evening of your visit."

"I'm relieved to hear it," she said, tilting her head back to look at the stars. "I was afraid you might have orchestrated the whole thing just to give me a stroke."

I smiled. "It's your own fault. This was a quiet little town until you and Bo showed up." I scratched at one of the myriad mosquito bites on my neck. "Seriously, thank God you're here. Danny and I would've been useless by ourselves."

"Me, too," she said. "Bo's the only one who knew what to do."

The cicada chorus was still at fortissimo in the grove, but here behind the house their song was less intrusive, enough so that we could hear crickets, and a couple of wolves barking in the distance. We sat without talking, lazily kicking our feet in the water, until she grew restless and lit another cigarette. "Have you heard from Ty or Karen recently?"

"They sent a letter last week. Jamie added a couple of illustrations."

Karen's adopted son, Jamie, was benefiting from living with his artist uncle, Ty. His drawings were quite accomplished for a five-year-old.

"You're lucky," Aggie said. "I don't get letters. We speak on the phone, of course, but I wish they'd write. We can never get through a phone call without fighting."

I snorted expressively—Aggie fought with everyone on the phone—but all she did by way of punishment was to tweak my earlobe. I raised my eyebrows at her mildness. "You're in a forgiving mood. What's gotten into you?"

She shrugged. "To be honest, I'm not sure. I can't seem to get angry at you, even though I want to."

"My God," I marveled. "Did you have a lobotomy?"

"No one's more shocked than I, believe me." She blew a plume of smoke over the water. "But being angry with you is a luxury I can no longer afford. We live so far apart now, and I find myself wishing we hadn't spent so much of our lives bickering." She met my eyes. "It seems a waste of a perfectly decent brother."

We'd never been particularly affectionate with each other, but the sadness in her voice made it easy to put my arm around her shoulders.

"Will you look at us?" I murmured as she settled against me. "Two old porcupines from the same litter, finally figuring out how to touch without killing each other."

I heard her swallow, fighting tears. "Porcupines don't have litters," she said gruffly.

I rested my chin on her head. "How about twins? Do they have those?"

"Almost never."

"Lucky bastards."

She laughed in spite of herself, then caught me by surprise with a shove, unbalancing me. I grabbed her wrist as I tumbled into the water, dragging her in after me, cigarette and all. When we both resurfaced, spluttering, Bo and Danny were standing by the pool, looking down at us, but I couldn't see them well: My glasses had miraculously stayed on my face but were of little use at the moment.

"Is this one of those cultural differences we've talked about?" Danny asked. "We Italians don't usually swim in our clothes."

"You don't know what you're missing," I said, holding up my hand. "Help me out?"

He took a nimble step backward. "So you can pull me in, too? No, thank you."

"Bo will help me, though, won't you, Bo?" Aggie asked sweetly, extending her hand.

"No way in hell, my dearest love," he said, also scuttling out of reach. "You're even less trustworthy than Isaac."

"What an appalling thing to say." She put her hands on the pool edge and began to lift herself out, but I seized her around the waist and dragged her underwater again. We both came up winded and coughing.

"We may be getting a little old for this," I gasped.

"Speak for yourself, Grandpa," she said, attempting to dunk me.

The phone rang in the house, ending our horseplay. Danny hurried inside to answer it as Aggie and I clambered out of the pool and stood dripping on the patio, waiting with Bo for Danny.

"It's too soon for the surgery to be over," Bo said. "Any chance it's someone else?"

I shook my head. "Doubt it. It's nearly midnight."

None of us made a move to go inside. I took off my glasses, forgetting I didn't have anything to dry them on, and Bo plucked them from my hand and wiped them on his shirt before returning them to me.

"Maybe the operation didn't take as long as they thought it would," Aggie said.

Danny stepped back outside. He didn't say anything; he just shook his head and rejoined us. There were tears in his eyes, and I put my arms around him. He buried his face in my neck and I looked over his shoulder at our dark, quiet valley.

Aggie took Bo's hand. "Don't you dare beat yourself up for this Bo Larsson," she begged. "You did everything you possibly could."

He didn't respond. Aggie was right, of course, but it wouldn't make a difference; Bo would second-guess himself forever. I knew his heart was hurting for Claudio's family, as was mine. Only a few hours before, I'd held the boy's legs to keep him from injuring himself, and the memory of his warm skin was still imprinted on my hands. All I could think about was how that warmth was now gone from the world. His family was no doubt huddled around his remains at that very moment, feeling his limbs grow cold to the touch, and I couldn't fathom how they would survive the awfulness of that transition.

Hell isn't fire. Hell is ice.

"I don't know about anyone else," Danny said dully, "but I need a drink."

I told him to lead the way. He took one of my hands and Aggie claimed the other as we went by; she was still holding Bo's hand, too, so the four of us ended up in a single line as we returned to the house, linked together like children.

DAY TEN

December 13, 1998. Westport, Massachusetts.

I left Boston just before sunrise, heading south to join Karen and Jamie in Westport. It was Sunday so the traffic was light, and I was grateful for the lack of congestion. I'd only been in Boston for a few days, researching a piece for Harper's, but I was already tired of the noise and the crowds. I'd grown addicted to peace and quiet in Tuscany, and even though I now only lived with Danny about half the year, I couldn't seem to shake the addiction. Cities made me claustrophobic; I missed breathing fresh air, and seeing the stars at night, and stepping out the front door without tripping over my neighbors. Aggie accused me of becoming crabby and provincial, and she was probably right.

Danny and I were still together, more or less, but we'd discovered we did better if we didn't always inhabit the same continent. This being the case, whenever we began getting on each other's nerves, I flew back to the States to live with Aggie and Bo; whenever Aggie and I started quarreling, I returned to

Italy. If Italy and Iowa both happened to be ill-advised destinations, I went elsewhere. This last week, I'd fled to Boston, until Karen asked me to meet her and Jamie at a small rental cottage in Westport Harbor. They'd vacationed there before, with Ty, but this time they drove up from New York by themselves, since Ty and Jamie were currently at loggerheads.

Ty and Karen had just turned sixty-one, Danny was fifty-five, and Bo, Aggie, and I were all eighty. Jamie was thirteen. His newly acquired adolescent hormones were playing holy hell with his personality, and having no one in the family remotely close to his age wasn't helping. Until recently, he'd been a funny, well-adjusted kid with a sunny smile and a sweet disposition, but in the past few months he'd become sullen and contrary, prone to lashing out at anyone resembling an authority figure. Ty, especially, was having problems adapting to the pubescent demon who'd taken possession of the gentle nephew he'd helped raise. Karen was slightly more patient with the boy's orneriness, but their once-happy home (they'd given up their loft apartment and bought a duplex in Brooklyn) had become unstable, with furious arguments and brooding silences.

Though Jamie vented his spleen mostly at Karen and Ty, the rest of us were by no means safe. Even Aggie—who wouldn't think twice about poking a rabid badger with a stick—treaded lightly around the kid. Why adolescence was hitting him so hard was a mystery. Karen and Ty weren't perfect, of course, but they openly adored him and were far better role models than Aggie and I had been for them. His physical transformation into adulthood was treating him more kindly than most: His complexion remained clear, and his wiry little body was maturing gracefully, without the comical growth spurts that can make junior high such a torment. He was blessed with clever hands, too; he played the violin beautifully, and was nearly as gifted a painter as Ty had been at that age. In short, if he had a reason to hate the world, I couldn't see it.

I had mixed feelings about spending time with him until he became civilized again, but Karen had sounded desperate on the phone when she asked me to join them, so I couldn't say no—especially when she sweetened the deal by mentioning that the cottage where we were staying was three minutes from the beach. I figured if Jamie became unpleasant, I could make a cowardly escape to the ocean, leaving Karen to fend for herself. The beach would be cold and deserted this time of year, but I had a warm coat, insulated boots, and a large flask of Bushmills, and I loved nothing more than walking a lonely shoreline in the winter.

I knew nothing about Westport, Massachusetts, save that Karen had said it was a small, precolonial town, not far from Fall River. (Passing by Fall River that morning, I thought of Paulie, my former lover, a Fall River native. The two of us hadn't spoken for years, and the realization that he would now be quite old—or dead—hit me hard.) Karen's directions took me down a deserted highway and eventually onto a gravel road, recently cleared of snow. The cottage was hidden behind a large sand dune, and when I first saw it I smiled. It was a charming Cape Cod house, with weathered wooden shingles, a white picket fence, and a brick front walk. It sat on a hill at a bend in the Westport River, and its closest neighbor was an empty boat dock. There was woodsmoke rising from a black chimney pipe on the roof, but the window curtains were still drawn. I glanced at my watch and saw it wasn't even nine yet; it was a good bet that Karen and Jamie, both late sleepers, were still in bed.

I got out of the car and stretched in the cold. A lone seagull hovered over the partly frozen river, hunting for breakfast where the current still flowed, midway between the banks. The wind rustled through the brown reeds at the river's edge, and I breathed deeply, taking in the peaceful morning. To the west, in the distant harbor, a few scattered fishing boats were headed out to open water, where the mouth of the river met the ocean. I wondered idly where they were going, and what kind of fish were crazy enough to make their home in the icy northern Atlantic. The fishermen seeking them had my sympathy: Outside the harbor the wind would be brutal.

I knocked on the cottage door and no one responded, so I tried again. I hadn't told Karen what time to expect me, but she'd promised coffee and pancakes when I arrived. I waited a bit, then knocked more persistently, finally summoning Jamie to the door. He was dressed in black sweatpants and a rumpled, Pink Floyd T-shirt; his thick black hair (his birthmother was Filipina) was several inches longer than the last time I'd seen him, and he was sporting three distinct cowlicks on the crown of his head. His feet were bare.

"Good morning, sir," I said, as he blinked up at me owlishly, rubbing his eyes. "I'm afraid I'm lost. Is this San Antonio?"

"Hi, Isaac," he said, with no trace of a smile. "You woke me up." I apologized, telling him I'd thought the drive would take longer, and he shrugged, stepping aside. "I told Mom to leave the door unlocked in case you got here early, but she locked it anyway. She's still in bed."

Affection between us had been an early casualty of his puberty, so I didn't risk a hug. He led me down a short, dark hallway and into the kitchen, where a cast-iron stove was churning out welcome heat.

"I got up a while ago to stoke the fire," he said. "If I don't do it every couple hours, we freeze our butts off. There's a furnace in the cellar but it sucks."

He was used to me making myself at home whenever I visited them in Brooklyn, so I assumed he wouldn't mind if I did it here, too. The coffeepot—a blue electric percolator, at least forty years old—was by the sink, and I started poking through the cabinets for coffee as he rechecked the fire. "You want breakfast?" I asked. "I'll cook."

He shrugged again. "There's eggs, and pancake mix, but no bacon. We ran out."

"I'm devastated." I interrupted my cabinet search to assess the contents of the refrigerator. "Hallelujah. You've got butter." I asked if he knew where the coffee was hiding, and he pointed to a cabinet I'd overlooked.

"Why were you in Boston?" he asked, sitting at the table and yawning. I told him I was doing a follow-up to a story I'd first written in 1990, about the infamous art heist at the Gardner Museum. He rolled his eyes.

"Oh, yeah, I forgot. Blah, blah, blah, Vermeer, Rembrandt, Degas, two-hundred-million dollars, blah, blah, blah, a great loss to the art world. It's all you and Ty have talked about for the last eight years."

I grinned in spite of his offhand dismissal of the most notorious (and still unsolved) art theft in history. That he'd clearly already known what I was doing in Boston—and had pretended otherwise, setting me up for ridicule—struck me as funny.

"I guess Ty and I *have* been a teensy bit obsessive," I conceded, plugging in the percolator. "I won't say another word about it while I'm here."

He wasn't mollified. "I mean, I know it's a big deal, but why do you guys always have to go on and on about it? It gets really old."

"Hence my solemn promise not to bring it up again." We were fast approaching the danger zone, though his tone was still mild. Most of his outbursts started with a tiny wave of pique just like this one, then burgeoned into a tsunami of hostility. "How do you want your eggs?" I asked.

He blinked, sidetracked. "It doesn't matter. Scrambled, I guess. We've got cheese, too."

We both fell silent as I began whipping the eggs. I knew the smell of coffee would wake his mother, and sure enough, she appeared in the doorway two minutes after the pot started percolating. She was bleary-eyed, and dressed in a ratty pink bathrobe, but she was as lovely and willowy as ever. Her once-blond hair was now brown and streaked with white, but she still wore it long; she had it tied back in a ponytail at the moment, making her look half her age.

"Good morning, Professor Slacker," I said. "It's about time you got up."

"Ha," she said. "My diabolical plan to make you cook breakfast worked." She gave me a hug. "Jamie hates the way I cook his eggs, but he loves yours."

"No, I don't," Jamie said. "I just *like* them."

Karen sighed. "Thanks for the clarification. Did you ask Uncle Isaac if he wanted help?"

He became absorbed in tying a cloth napkin in a knot, but his eyes briefly met mine. "Do you need help, Uncle Isaac?"

"I've got it under control, thanks," I said, grinning as Karen planted herself in front of the still-percolating coffeepot and waited impatiently for it to finish. "Rough night?" I asked.

"Very," she said. "The wind blew like crazy. I kept thinking we'd end up in Oz."

"Why do you have to exaggerate all the time?" Jamie muttered.

Karen ignored him, turning to watch me mix the pancake batter. "How was Boston?"

"Loud. From here on I'm only writing articles about nice, quiet places like Romola."

She laughed. "Nothing's happened in Romola since the Gallic Wars." Jamie opened his mouth, and she held up a hand to forestall him. "Yes, Jamie, I'm aware I'm exaggerating again."

"I mean it," I said. "I'm done with cities. Hell, I may be done with traveling altogether. I just wish I could talk the rest of you into moving in with Danny and me in Romola, so we can all live happily ever after."

She snorted. "Fat chance. Mom would drive us all stark raving mad in two weeks flat."

"Good point. Aggie is hereby disinvited from our happily-ever-after party."

"Don't invite Uncle Ty, either," Jamie blurted. "He hates my guts."

This was a preposterous statement; there was no one on the planet Ty loved more than Jamie. I expected Karen to say something, but she didn't. She no doubt had to field similar remarks from him a dozen times a day. The percolator finished burbling with an operatic flourish, and she poured a mug for herself and me, and half a mug for Jamie.

"Since when do you like coffee?" I asked him.

"Since always, but Mom didn't let me start drinking it till my birthday this year."

"You're still too young," Karen said, "but I figure half a cup a day won't kill you." She smiled. "We may have to peel you off the ceiling this morning, though. Isaac's coffee could make a penguin fly."

And just like that, she'd crossed an invisible line. Jamie flushed bright red and pushed back from the table. "Fine, I don't want any *fucking* coffee!" he raged, stalking from the room.

I raised my eyebrows, but Karen only sighed again. "Care for a shot of vodka in your orange juice?"

In spite of my desire to avoid my surly great-nephew at all costs, Karen's need for a little alone time was painfully obvious, so after breakfast—which Jamie skipped, as Karen had given him a choice of either apologizing for his outburst or not eating—I made myself ask if he'd like to go to the beach with me, for a walk.

I'd hoped he wouldn't accept, but he did.

Karen's gratitude was palpable as she waved goodbye at the

cottage door. Jamie and I drove in silence over the long bridge separating Westport Point from the Horseneck Beach State Reservation. He was still sulking about his lost breakfast, and I was in no hurry to start a conversation either, so when we arrived at the beach parking lot, we remained mute as we got out of my rental car. The empty lot was sheltered on all sides by high sand dunes, but even so the wind was vicious.

At eighty, I knew I was getting more feeble by the second, but I still occasionally forgot how untrustworthy my body had become. I was fine on the boardwalk leading to the beach, but when Jamie and I emerged from the protection of the dunes and came face-to-face with the Atlantic in all its wintry, frothing glory, the full force of the wind hit me just as I stepped in loose sand. My knees buckled and I lurched into Jamie, who mercifully caught me before I fell.

The strength of his thin arms around my waist was comforting, if also humbling. The top of his head only came up to my shoulders, and he barely weighed a hundred and twenty pounds, yet he was now more solid than me, and the wind didn't appear to faze him. I suddenly remembered teaching him how to swim when he came to visit Danny and me in Romola, only a few years before. He'd clung to me like a koala bear, and even after I'd taught him to stay afloat on his own, he didn't let me out of arm's reach. He wasn't that same little boy anymore, of course, but I was still shocked to find myself in his hands, now, instead of the other way around.

"Thanks," I said. "If I'd hit the ground, my new nickname would be Humpty Dumpty."

"You and Mom should have an exaggeration contest," he said, releasing me. If my fragility unsettled him, too, he gave no sign of it. "You okay?"

"I'm fine, just old." I sighed, wishing we were already on the smooth sand by the water. "I'll do my best not to fall on you again, but no promises."

We were both swathed in multiple layers of warm, hideously colorful clothes. Karen had taken one look at my hat, scarf, and gloves—all of which matched my winter coat—and deemed them inadequate for the cold beach. She'd rooted through what looked to be a lost-and-found box in the cottage's hall closet, and the result of her search was that I now had a canary-yellow hat, a purple scarf, and orange mittens, all fit for a circus clown. Jamie had fared no better: He had a green wool stocking cap pulled down over his eyebrows and ears, and a long pink scarf, embroidered with apricot-colored rabbits. The scarf was wound around his mouth, nose, and neck, leaving only his eyes visible. I'd accused Karen of making us look like color-blind mummies, but I shut up when she pursed her lips and raised an Aggie-like eyebrow in warning.

"Is this the first time you've been to the beach since you got here?" I asked Jamie when we reached the tideline.

"On this trip, yeah. We came every day when Ty was with us before, but Mom hates the cold." By unspoken consensus, we turned right and began meandering down the shore. "She won't let me come here by myself, either, so I'm stuck at the cottage all day. It's boring as hell."

This complaint aside, he seemed less prickly in the open air. A trio of plovers was on the sand in front of us, hunting food and playing tag with the tide as it repeatedly chased them inland and withdrew, and Jamie chuckled as they scuttled back and forth on their thin, tiny legs. Two of the birds got into a squabble over a mollusk shell, but the ocean abruptly confiscated their prize. Jamie and I both laughed at the bereft look on their faces, and I relaxed a little, thinking maybe this outing might not go as badly as I'd feared.

The beach was clean and well-maintained, even in the dead of winter. The pale blue sky was cloudless, the sand was nearly as white as the sprinkling of snow on top of it, and the ocean was blue-green and agitated, with row after row of icy whitecaps charging the shore. There was a potent smell of seaweed and fish, but no hint of the decay that usually accompanies those odors in the summer. Aside from the greedy plovers and a few gulls, we had the place to ourselves, and I raised my hands over my head and reveled in the open space.

An old memory surfaced of another deserted beach, with another boy about Jamie's age: forty years before, in the Marshall Islands on Wotho Atoll. Ty and Karen had been there, too, but what I most remembered was walking with the boy, late at night, beneath a glittering array of stars. He'd been Marshallese, of course, but now, four decades later, I couldn't recall his name. I remembered him running barefoot on the shore and giving me a snail shell; I also remembered us staring up at the stars together, and listening to the ocean roll in, time and time again. The shell he'd given me was on my desk in Iowa, and it bothered me that I could no longer think of his name. His memory was dear to me, though I'd barely known him.

"Isaac?"

Jamie's voice interrupted my reverie. He was several yards ahead, waiting for me.

"Sorry," I said, rejoining him. "I was woolgathering."

Jobel. The boy from Wotho was Jobel. If he were still alive, I realized, he'd be nearly the same age as Danny. And Elias, too, of course, had he lived.

I blinked, glad that the wind provided an alibi for wet eyes. My tear ducts had become as untrustworthy as my legs. The past was loose sand, threatening my balance every time I let my guard down. I briefly considered telling Jamie about that long-ago night on Wotho, but was afraid he wouldn't care. It was, after all, a story with no point—the kind of story Uncle Johan used to tell as he got older—and stories with no point are deathly boring to the young. Thinking of Johan intensified my heartache, because I missed him, too, as I missed Elias.

"If we walk all the way to the end of the beach," Jamie said, "we'll get to the Westport River." He pointed ahead of us and I followed his finger. "See that big rock on the other side of the river mouth, and that mansion just a little farther up the hill? The rock is called the Knubble. We tried to find out who owns the mansion, but no one could tell us. I love that weird little tower next to it, but I don't know what it's for."

He sounded for a moment like the boy he'd been before this past year: chatty, cheerful, eager to please. Even at this distance—at least a mile, maybe more—the mansion looked imposing, like something Gatsby would've purchased. "Let's go see it up close," I said. "I'm game if you are."

"It's really far." He eyed me skeptically. "Are you sure you can make it all the way?"

I hesitated. A mile forward meant a mile back, and I'd wear out quickly on sand. "How about we keep going for a bit and see what happens?" I suggested. "I'll let you know if I'm getting to the point where you might have to carry me back on your shoulders."

"Okay." He still sounded dubious. "I can't carry you very far. You're too big."

His seriousness tickled me. "If I collapse, just roll me back to the car like a beach ball."

"Why does everybody in this stupid family have to make jokes about *everything*?" he demanded, rounding on me with sudden ferocity. "It gets so *fucking* old!"

The change in his mood was startling, the more so because I could only see his eyes. I knew unprovoked outbursts were a specialty of his these days, but his volatility was alarming. Was it just hormones, or something more serious? I toyed with the idea that he might actually have some kind of psychosis, but it seemed unlikely, considering that Karen and Ty swore he didn't erupt like this around his friends. Drugs, maybe? I was no expert, but aside from emotional instability, there were no telltale symptoms of abuse. I wondered if he was actually waiting for an answer to his question, given that he was still staring at me.

"Why are you so upset, Jamie?" I asked quietly. "Do you even know?" Something in his posture reminded me of Aggie's obstinance, and I found myself getting irritated. "Is it because you're wearing a pink scarf with bunnies on it?"

"Goddammit!" he cried. "What does this stupid fucking *scarf* have to do with anything?"

"Nothing, I guess," I said, sighing. I should've known better than to goad him. "It was a dumb joke, kid. You used to laugh at dumb jokes."

"I wish I hadn't come here with you. I thought you were different." He spun around and sprinted away before I could respond.

I sighed again, watching him go. A solitary plover darted in front of me and stuck its bill in the sand within inches of my left boot. "I suppose you think I should've kept my mouth shut," I told it. "Don't be so judgmental. You saw how he was behaving." It tilted its head and looked at me, then went back to rooting for food.

The beach ran from east to west. Jamie was still headed west, to the Knubble, but chasing after him held no appeal. I needed to get moving again, however, or I'd freeze solid, so I turned around and went east instead. His fury would burn itself out eventually, I assumed, and if he wanted a ride back to the cottage, he could either catch up with me or wait by the car.

We hadn't come far, so I soon passed the boardwalk where we'd entered. The stretch of beach nearby appeared to be the main swimming area during the warmer months, with several wooden lifeguard towers in the sand and a concrete cantina/restroom set farther back from the shore, now boarded up for the winter. I didn't let myself look back to see if Jamie knew I was no longer following him; I thought it might do him some good to turn around and find himself alone after having thrown one of his tantrums.

Karen had mentioned earlier that I might enjoy visiting an abandoned World War II submarine watchtower on Gooseberry Island, visible from the east end of the beach. It was too far off to see clearly, but there was definitely a tall, isolated structure of some sort at the tip of a gray spit of land a couple of miles away. It looked like an accusing finger pointing up at the sky. I wondered if the men who'd once stood guard in that tower during the war had ever spotted an enemy sub. I'd never heard of a German naval presence by New England in those days, but I supposed it was possible.

Inevitably, thinking of naval warfare in WWII reminded me of Paulie for the second time that morning. I told myself I should find out if he were still alive, and reach out to him, if so. Surely enough time had passed since his legal troubles back in the fifties, and he would no longer mind hearing from me. Then again, he'd severed all ties to his life—even going so far as to change his name—and exiled himself to some Podunk town in Oregon, so maybe it would be too painful for him to reconnect.

A harsh gust of wind made me stagger, and I wondered again if Jamie had discovered my change of course. The farther apart we drew before he noticed would add to his feeling of isolation, and I started to feel badly for leaving him to his own devices. I did love the little shit, after all, even though he wasn't particularly lovable at this stage of his life.

"He's *thirteen*, for Christ's sake," I scolded myself. "What did you expect?" I glanced over my shoulder as surreptitiously as I could, hoping to find him trailing after me with his tail between his legs.

He was nowhere in sight.

After searching for Jamie in the sand dunes for nearly an hour, I decided I needed help, and went to fetch Karen at the cottage. We returned to the beach, split up, and began a systematic hunt, but two long hours later he was still missing. We met at the car to warm up—trading sips from my flask of Bushmills—

then resumed the search, our voices mingling with the cries of seagulls as we circled one dune after another, calling Jamie's name. By then it was midafternoon, and we were both worried, worn out, and chilled to the bone. We were exasperated, too, because we knew he was likely playing hide-and-seek with us the entire time, nursing his grudges like a hen brood's eggs. But Horseneck was a long beach, with countless dunes to conceal a teenage boy, and we couldn't keep going forever without a little food and rest. We didn't want to call the police, but nightfall was coming, and we were running out of options. At 3:30, we met again—this time on the lee side of the boarded-up cantina—to figure out what to do.

"I'm sorry, Karen," I said. "This is my fault. I shouldn't have let him out of my sight."

She took my arm as we leaned against the wall. "Don't be silly," she said. "My ridiculous son had a meltdown, and all you did was go for a walk to let him cool off. I would've done the same thing."

"I knew he was mad, but I didn't think he'd just disappear like this."

"It's not the first time. He ran out of the house last month when he and Ty argued at breakfast, and he didn't come back until midnight." She shaded her eyes with a mittened hand to scan the crest of a nearby dune. "In retrospect, maybe I should've adopted a guinea pig."

"Think it's too late to make an exchange?" I asked, earning a tired smile.

When she was younger, she'd always said she didn't want children, so Aggie, Bo, Ty, and I were all shocked when she changed her mind, at age fifty, and decided to adopt a little boy. She told us it was turning fifty that had actually triggered the decision; she said she'd suddenly realized her life was more than half over, and she'd likely outlive us all—even Ty, since women typically last longer than men—and the idea of watching the rest of us grow old and die one after another terrified her. She said she wanted someone to love who would outlast her as well, so she wouldn't be left alone in an empty house, with just her memories for company. Aggie had tried to talk her out of it at first, telling her that raising a child on her own at fifty would be exhausting, but Karen reminded her that she wouldn't be on her own: Like it or not, Ty and the rest of us would be just as much a part of the boy's world as she was.

"*I was an absent, mediocre mother at best,*" Aggie had protested. "*What makes you think I'll be any better as a grand-mother?*"

I found myself grinning, and Karen raised an eyebrow curiously. I shook my head. "I was just remembering how fast your mom changed her tune about adopting Jamie, once she actually held him for the first time," I said.

Karen snorted, then sighed. "She'd change it back again pretty damn fast if she were here right now."

Thus far, we'd focused most of our efforts on the west end of the beach, where Jamie had disappeared, but our latest foray had been to the east. Karen had taken the service road that ran parallel to the shore on the far side of the dunes, while I patrolled the ocean side. Between the service road and the water, there was a small desert of sand—replete with imposing hills and ankle-twisting dales—and the simple truth was that I was too damn old to be of much use. After four hours of walking, I was hobbling like an invalid.

"He's got to be starving," I said. My own stomach was none too happy about skipping lunch. "You'd think he'd give up, just to get some food in his belly."

"He's impressively pigheaded. He'd rather eat seaweed for a week than admit he was wrong."

Seaweed was starting to sound pretty tasty to me, too, so I suggested one of us take the car to town to get coffee and sandwiches while the other kept searching.

Karen nodded. "Good idea." She glanced at her watch. "Mind if I go? I think I should stop by the police station. I doubt there's much they can do, but I want to talk to somebody who knows the area better than we do."

I gave her the keys to the car and she squeezed my hand, then hurried down the service road to the parking lot. I stamped my feet to restore circulation, then stepped away from the cantina, wincing as the wind found me again. A few hardy souls had joined us on the beach in the past hour: A young lesbian couple holding hands, and a heavyset gentleman with an elderly, half-lame Irish setter. The dog, who had more white in his fur than red, occasionally attempted to frolic but could only manage a jump or two before flopping on its belly to recover. Karen had spoken to the man when they crossed paths a while back, asking him to keep an eye out for Jamie, but neither of us had passed the young couple, who were now at the far west end of the beach, by the Knubble.

"Okay, Jamie," I muttered. "Where are you, you little prick?"

It was possible that he wasn't in the dunes at all. He could've made his way out to the highway while Karen and I were elsewhere, and if so, he could be just about anywhere by this point—especially if he'd been brash enough to hitchhike. He also might've followed the Westport River back to the harbor, though I seriously hoped not. The riverbank was probably icy and treacherous, and he surely wasn't foolish enough to risk it. He was dressed as warmly as I was, so assuming he kept himself dry, he wasn't going to freeze to death anytime soon, yet the idea of him having somehow injured himself and lying on the cold ground for hours, waiting for help to arrive, was appalling.

I turned in a circle, having no idea which way to go. For lack of a better plan, I limped back to the shoreline and stood still, facing the ocean, only giving ground when the water crept close to my feet. We'd tried everything else, so maybe it was time to do nothing. Perhaps he'd found a way to spy on us all that afternoon—maybe he was stretched out on top of a dune at that very moment, watching me through tall grass—and if so, I wanted to make sure I stayed fully visible. If he saw me alone, and no longer actively looking for him, maybe he'd decide enough was enough, and finally show himself. I watched the waves roll in, and I didn't look left or right, even as the cold settled into my bones. I had to hug myself to keep from trembling, but I refused to budge an inch until Jamie put in an appearance, or Karen came back.

No teenager on earth can rival a cranky octogenarian for pigheadedness.

I found myself wishing, not for the first time, that I'd spent less of my life in landlocked terrain. True enough, the ocean had always frightened me, but only when I was in it, or on it. From the safety of the land, I was free to love its power and its mystery, without having to worry about all the hungry, unblinking creatures hidden beneath its surface, wanting nothing more than to sink their teeth in my flesh.

"It's beautiful, isn't it?"

Jamie's voice startled me, but I didn't let it show as I glanced over at him. "Yes, it certainly is."

I was glad to see that he looked as cold and miserable as I felt. He'd pulled the pink scarf down so it was no longer covering his mouth, and his lips were tinged blue. "Can we go?" he asked. "I'm kind of hungry."

I nodded, feeling a little lightheaded from hunger myself. "As soon as your mom comes back with the car. She went to get some coffee and sandwiches. We can eat at the cottage."

He kicked at the sand. "She's really pissed, isn't she?"

"Yep." I turned back to the ocean. "She's not the only one, by the way."

Another kick. "I know."

I suppressed an urge to wring his neck, though once we were

safely off the beach, I would be more than willing to play a leading role in whatever punishment Karen wanted to subject him to. In my current mood, I was rather hoping it would involve thumbscrews.

"I'm sorry, Isaac," he said, wiping his nose on his sleeve. "I know I've been a dick."

His apology surprised me, and my vexation cooled. "Thank you for saying that, Jamie. I'm sorry, too, for giving you a hard time when you were upset." I hesitated. "I just wish I understood why you've been so mad at everything, lately. You used to be such a happy kid."

"You sound like Ty," he said, scowling. "So does Mom, and Grandma, and even Grandpa. You all say the same stuff to me, over and over."

I sighed. "Would it make any difference if we said something new?"

He blinked. "What's that supposed to mean?"

I was finding it hard to focus for some reason; my lightheadedness was getting worse by the second. "It means that I'm not sure it really matters what we say these days. You'd be mad at us, regardless."

"That's not fair."

"Isn't it? Be honest." The beach began to spin. I heard Jamie say my name, but his voice sounded odd, as if my ears were stuffed with cotton. "Uh-oh," I gasped, and the world went black.

When I came to, I was flat on my back on the sand, staring at the sky, and an ancient Irish setter with incredibly foul breath was licking my face.

"Quit it, Tonto." The large man who was Tonto's owner tried to pull him away, but the dog had other ideas.

"Don't move, Uncle Isaac." Jamie was at my other side. "The ladies are getting help."

"What ladies?" I grunted, fending off Tonto as he slobbered on my chin. "Can you please get this damn dog off me?"

"Sorry, Mr. Dahl. He really likes you," said the man, wrapping his arms around Tonto's neck and tugging ineffectively. "Are you okay? Jeez, I can't believe it's really you."

I blinked at him and tried to sit up, but I was too weak. "What happened?"

Jamie put a hand on my shoulder to keep me still. "You fainted. The ladies are calling an ambulance."

"What ladies?" I demanded again.

"The ones who were walking on the beach. One of them has a mobile phone but couldn't get any reception. They went to try to find a place where it would work."

"My wife and I are both huge fans of yours," the dog-man told me. "She'll hate herself for not being here with Tonto and me today to meet you."

That I'd fainted really shouldn't have surprised me. Between the ice-cold wind, hunger, exhaustion, and standing without moving for at least half an hour, it was a wonder it hadn't happened sooner.

"I don't need an ambulance," I said. "I just need food, and someplace warm."

Tonto's owner finally succeeded in dragging him away, allowing me to breathe. I had no idea how long I'd been unconscious, but the sun was close to the horizon. I sat up, ignoring Jamie's protests, and after my head stopped spinning, I rose slowly to my feet, using him as a crutch. Tonto lunged at me enthusiastically and almost knocked me down again before the man regained control.

"How do you feel?" Jamie asked.

"A bit dizzy, but okay." Truth be told, I felt frail and old, with ice in my veins, but I certainly didn't need an ambulance. "How about we head to the parking lot? We should be there when your mom gets back with the car."

"Are you sure you can walk? You don't look so good."

"You should listen to the kid, Mr. Dahl," said Tonto's owner. "You're really pale."

I grimaced. "I just spent the last five minutes with Tonto's tongue down my throat. Of course I'm pale." I draped an arm over Jamie's shoulders and tugged him toward the parking lot.

He sighed, surrendering, and put his arms around my waist. "You're not just pale," he said. "You look like an albino."

"Get me out of this wind, and I'll be fine." I shivered violently. "With any luck your mom is already on her way."

He didn't answer and I glanced down at him as we lumbered through the sand. His face was stony but his eyes were brimming with tears.

"Hey, now," I said, surprised. "Don't cry, kid. I'm fine, I promise."

"I'm not crying. I'm just cold."

I gave his shoulders a squeeze. "Are you sure that's all that's bothering you?"

He was silent for another few steps, then his face contorted. "Are you going to die, Uncle Isaac?"

The fear in his voice moved me. "I just fainted, son, that's all. I am absolutely *not* going to die." *At least not right this second,* I thought.

"It's all my fault," he blurted. "I didn't mean to make you sick!"

"I know you didn't," I said quietly, "and I'm not sick. I'm just tired."

"Everything is going to be even worse now than it already was," he sobbed.

"Whoa, now," I said, stopping in my tracks. We'd just about reached the boardwalk that led to the parking lot, but I temporarily forgot my haste to get off the beach. "What will be worse?"

"I'm so sick of being the family loser!"

I pulled him around so that we were face-to-face. "Look, Jamie. Nobody thinks of you that way, and I mean *nobody*. We all love you very much."

"Yeah, but you all think I'm stupid." Tears were pouring down his face. "It's not just you guys, either. Every time I meet someone new, they start telling me what a genius Mom is, or how talented Ty is, or how much they love your writing, or how much they admire Grandma. Then they look at me like I'm pathetic, because they know I'm never going to be like the rest of you." He wiped his nose on a mitten. "Jesus, you should've seen that guy with the dog back there when he figured out it was you. His eyes about bugged out of his head."

"That's only because I'm dressed like Ronald McDonald." I shook his shoulders gently. "You're multitalented, and you're super smart, and trust me, you're going to end up doing amazing things." I shivered again. "It will just take time, that's all. The rest of us have had a whole lifetime to get good at what we do."

"Yeah, but by the time Grandma and you were my age, she'd taught herself to read in four languages, and you knew more about world history than most college professors."

I snorted. "When I was your age, I thought Caesar invented salad." We resumed walking toward the parking lot. "And as far as your grandmother goes—well, she makes us all feel stupid. Who was telling you stories about when we were kids?"

"Grandpa. He called on my birthday last month and started talking about lots of stuff. It was kind of weird."

"How do you mean?"

He shrugged his shoulders beneath my arm. "I don't know. It was pretty random. One second he was all excited about looking at the stars with that telescope you gave him, but then he started talking about when you guys were growing up. It didn't have anything to do with anything."

I bit my lip. Aggie and I had both been a little worried lately about Bo. His mind tended to wander far afield sometimes, though in most ways he was still as sharp as ever.

"People our age are allowed to be random when we talk," I told Jamie. "Our brains are like old houses, with roomfuls of junk that we don't know what to do with anymore."

He was quiet for a minute. "Yeah, well, Grandpa should maybe think about downsizing," he said, and I laughed, pleased to see that his sense of humor wasn't completely dead after all.

We reached the end of the boardwalk and emerged from the dunes into the parking lot, but Karen wasn't back yet with the rental car. Disappointed, I suggested we retreat into the dunes to get out of the wind, but as we turned around my head began to spin, yet again.

"Oh, hell," I gasped, and the world tipped over.

DAY ELEVEN

April 13, 2006. Iowa City, Iowa.

"When you're a kid it's an adventure if the power goes off," I said, groping my way back into our pitch-black living room. "It's somewhat less stimulating when you're eighty-eight, and on the toilet with your pants around your ankles."

Aggie, Bo, and I had been playing gin rummy until I took a break; I assumed they were still seated at the table on the far side of the room, where I'd left them.

"For God's sake, Isaac, can't you hear the tornado siren?" Aggie said, her voice an inch from my ear.

I jumped in the dark, squealing. "Dammit, Aggie! Don't sneak up on me like that!"

"I was just coming to check on you," she said. "You took so long, I was afraid you'd passed out again."

I hadn't fainted in months, but my sporadic bouts of vertigo—caused by an inner ear malfunction that was the bane of my existence—were never far from her mind; she fussed and fretted every time I left the room. "Blame my gastrointestinal tract," I said. "The word *hurry* is no longer part of its vocabulary."

"The matches are here somewhere," Bo said. From the sound of it, he was apparently rummaging through the drawers of the credenza by the kitchen doorway. "Ah, let there be light." He struck a match and appeared in its glow—white-haired and a bit stoop-shouldered, but handsome as ever—then lit a candle on the top shelf of a bookcase.

"My hero," Aggie said. Amusement crept into her voice. "Where's our flashlight, by the way?"

"Good question," he said, grinning. "Maybe you should ask Isaac."

I sighed in exasperation. "It's beyond sad that the two of you think you're funny."

Two weeks before, Aggie and I had been outside looking for her cat, Wotan. The psychotic creature—named after the Scandinavian god of war and death, and just as cuddly—popped up from under the front porch and darted between my legs, tripping me. I'd dropped my flashlight on Aggie's bare foot, hard enough to bruise a bone, and her big toe swelled grotesquely; the flashlight didn't survive the encounter.

"I count myself lucky that I can still walk, by the way," she said.

At the time, she'd barely even flinched; her tolerance for pain had always far exceeded mine. Since that night, however, she'd milked her injury for all it was worth, dragging her foot behind her like the Elephant Man whenever she caught me watching her.

"I wish I'd dropped the damn thing on your head," I said.

"You may need to carry me to the basement," she said, ignoring me. "I doubt I can manage the stairs in my weakened condition."

"How about I just give you a little push?"

Bo laughed. "I hate to interrupt y'all when you're having so much fun," he said, lifting the lit candle above his head, "but we should probably shake a leg. I peeked out the front door while you were on the john, Isaac, and things are getting dicey out there."

I didn't like our basement. Even though we had lawn chairs to sit on, it was dirty and damp, as well as being home to countless spiders and Wotan's litter box. When we reached the bottom of the stairs, we set our chairs in a triangle and put the candle on the floor between us.

"We left our drinks up on the table," Bo said. "Oh, the humanity."

"I hope Wotan's okay," Aggie said. "He didn't come when I called."

"Maybe his name embarrasses him," I muttered, earning a kick in the shin.

An ominous rumbling noise in the distance—competing with the wail of the tornado siren—made me cringe, and we all fell silent, listening.

"Is it just me," I said, "or should we be worried?"

"We'll be fine," Bo said. The rumble grew louder, and he cocked his head. "Huh, kind of reminds me of one of those big old black rollers, back in Oklahoma. Remember?"

Of course I remembered. The dust storms of our childhood still darkened my dreams. "Thanks a lot, Bo," I said. "You're a real comfort."

He smiled. "You worry too much, buddy. You'll get old before your time."

"The odds of a tornado actually hitting us are a million to one," Aggie reminded me.

"So were the odds of us getting hit by an avalanche," I retorted. The rumble was penetrating the concrete walls and putting me on edge: It sounded like a massive logging truck in high gear, bearing down on us.

"We'll be okay down here, no matter what," Bo repeated, raising his voice to be heard. He glanced up at the ceiling. "This old basement was built to last."

The candle flickered as the rumble became more and more deafening. Aggie began to look alarmed as well, so Bo took pity on us and held out his hands. Aggie and I seized one each, then I offered her my free hand as well. She gripped it with surprising strength, and the three of us held tightly to each other, just as we'd been doing one way or another for nearly nine decades.

We'd moved to Iowa City from Des Moines four years before, when Aggie and I were offered a dual-teaching position at the University of Iowa's Nonfiction Writer's Workshop. Neither she nor I had originally been interested in teaching at this stage of our lives, but Bo convinced us that our last few years on Earth might be better spent at something aside from scribbling memoirs and watching each other decay. We'd sold our home in Des Moines and bought a bungalow in Iowa City, close to downtown, and we were all glad we'd made the move.

Bo's mind was an ongoing puzzle for those of us who loved him. He was still more than capable of taking care of himself; he did most of the maintenance on our home and vehicles, and kept track of everything from our grocery shopping to the monthly bills. There were many days, however, when he'd repeat the same story three or four times in the course of a conversation, or when we'd find him standing still in the middle of a room, looking lost. Considering that he'd begun exhibiting signs of senility years before, it was a godsend that he was still as lucid as he was, and at the glacial rate he was slipping it was possible he'd be okay for the remainder of his life. Bo himself wasn't overly concerned, noting that he'd kept most of his marbles longer than the vast majority of our contemporaries. Physically, he was in excellent shape—which annoyed the hell out of me, as my body was falling apart.

So was Aggie's, unhappily.

My sister's mind was, as always, formidable—save for occasional lapses in her short-term memory, which she refused to acknowledge—but she'd lost a considerable amount of weight in the past couple of years, and was looking skeletal. The manic energy that had fueled her writing for so long still possessed her now and then, but she wore out easily and had a tendency to doze off at her desk. Her eyes, always large and striking, now dominated her thin face entirely; she claimed they made her resemble a slow loris, but in truth her beauty hadn't really diminished at all—it had just become less definable. Her pale skin was now almost diaphanous, and her bones were deteriorating at an alarming rate, yet her spirit—or personality, or soul, or whatever you want to call it—seemed to grow in direct proportion to her body's diminishment.

Since relocating to Iowa City, we'd taken to writing in the same room, and one day I'd watched her wake from one of her impromptu naps. As she raised her head and blinked her way back to consciousness, I could've sworn her eyes were twice as bright as usual—like she'd seen something remarkable in her dreams and was still seeing it as she sat up and smoothed her hair. I told myself I was imagining things, but as time passed the light in her eyes kept reappearing. I'd witnessed a similar burgeoning luminosity in the eyes of other elderly people, but unlike Aggie they'd all been devoutly religious types, and to see what might be described as spiritual radiance blossoming in my twin was jolting. Part of her had become a stranger, and I couldn't help but feel jealous since I was the same benighted soul I'd always been.

Happily, she was still the same old Aggie in most ways: Whenever she caught me studying her, she'd raise her eyebrows, demanding to ask why I was gawking at her like a drooling bumpkin on a street corner. I'd say something equally flattering in response, and that would be the end of it. I suspected she had no idea that a transformation was happening within her, and would only laugh if I suggested it. To tell the truth, though, the main reason I didn't mention it was that I was troubled and saddened. I feared that the fire burning within her was using her body as kindling, and would all too soon run out of fuel.

"Oh, shit, shit, SHIT!" Aggie screamed.

My ears popped as I heard glass shattering upstairs. There was a tremendous, grinding wail, as if the house, too, were screaming. I added my voice to the chorus of tortured wooden beams and besieged bricks, as several boards in the basement ceiling were ripped away, and our tiny candle blew out. Something heavy struck me in the back of the head and knocked me from my chair, but Bo and Aggie somehow kept their grip on me as a cloud of dust engulfed us; I think I was still screaming even though I couldn't hear myself over the roar of the wind. I was aware of being on the floor, with somebody on top of me, but that was all my terror allowed me to register.

The noise was appalling, world-ending, but it gradually abated enough for me to hear Bo yelling, "Hang on, it's almost over!" and at the sound of his voice I sobbed in relief. He was still holding one of my hands, as was Aggie, who was lying on me. Bo was near us on the floor, and though I couldn't see him, I could feel, through his hand, the solidity of his indomitable old body. I squeezed his fingers hard, and then Aggie's, and felt an answering pressure from both of them. After another minute or so there were other noises competing with the wind: the tornado siren still going off in the distance, police sirens, a barking dog, a car alarm down the street.

In the relative quiet, Aggie rested her chin on my shoulder and put her lips by my ear. "Thanks for cushioning my fall," she said. "That was very gallant."

My laugh was tinged with hysteria, yet it was still genuine. Somehow, we seemed to have survived a direct hit from a tornado, and though the back of my head hurt, I knew it was a miracle to still be alive. I asked Aggie if she was okay.

"Yes," she said. "Though I may need a comb."

I laughed again, more normally, and asked Bo how he was doing.

"I'm okay," he said. "I landed pretty hard on my knee, but I'm okay."

I sobered instantly; for Bo to complain about anything was a bad sign. Aggie knew this, too, of course, and she released my hand and rolled off me. I still couldn't see either of them, but I sensed her crouching at his side.

"How badly are you hurt?" she asked.

"I think my kneecap is busted," he said calmly. "I'll live, but it stings like fury."

I sat up too fast and winced; my head didn't appreciate quick movements. Getting an ambulance for Bo might be a problem. All three of us loathed the very idea of cell phones and were adamantly opposed to owning one—for the first time I was reconsidering the wisdom of this choice—and I had no idea what condition our house was in. Even if our landline was still intact and we could make a call, God only knew what our street looked like, or if anyone could get to us.

"I'll go find help," I said. I started to stand but abruptly sat again, the room spinning. "For crying out loud," I gasped. "Not now!"

"Is it your vertigo?" Aggie asked.

"Yes, and no." I fought to stay conscious. "Something hit my head after the candle blew out. What does a concussion feel like?"

"Lovely," she said, sighing. "Sit still, both of you."

I felt the rustle of her skirt against my forearm as she climbed to her feet.

"Be careful, honey," Bo told her. His voice was strained; his knee was probably on fire. "The last thing we need is for you to get knocked out of commission, too."

"Go slow on the stairs," I warned. "They could be dangerous."

"Shush, both of you," Aggie said. We listened to the sound of her voice as she made her way to the staircase. "Invalids shouldn't be so eager to offer unsolicited advice."

"Do you guys feel that?" Bo asked. "The moisture in the air, I mean." He paused. "I think it's raining in our basement."

He was right; I felt water droplets on my face. "Maybe the kitchen pipes burst."

"Nope, that's rain. Which means either the wind is still blowing crazy hard through the broken windows upstairs, or—"

"—or at least part of our roof is gone," I finished, probing the sore spot on my head. The room was no longer spinning, mercifully, but I kept still, not wanting to push my luck.

Aggie swore. "Some of the stairs are missing."

The staircase was crude, with a lead pipe handrail on one side, and unfinished boards for steps, loosely connected by steel L-braces. It was sturdy enough, ordinarily, but for all we knew now it could look like a pretzel.

"Stay off it, Aggie," Bo ordered. "It might not hold you."

"Contrary to popular opinion, my darling," she said tartly, "I'm not an idiot. I found a broom, and I'm going to—"

"—to fly back to your coven?" I offered.

"That's terribly amusing, Isaac," she said. "I was praying your brain injury might have rendered you speechless, but no such luck. For your information, I'm going to use the broom handle to ascertain the stability of the stairs."

The taps of the handle against wood and metal sounded like a drunken version of Morse code—*tock tock ping ping ping tock tock tock*—slowly ascending the staircase.

"Dammit, Aggie," Bo said. "Please come back here and wait for someone to find us."

"Don't distract me," she said. "The second and the fifth steps are gone, but the handrail is perfectly secure, and—oh, dear."

"Oh, dear, *what*?" Bo and I both demanded.

More tocks and pings, then a pause. "I believe the step closest to the door is intact." She had to be at least halfway up the staircase, or she couldn't have reached so far with the tip of the broom handle. "But several steps before that appear to be broken. Maybe if I—"

"Agnes Dahl!" Bo snapped, more rattled than I'd ever heard him sound before. "Get your ass back down here! Don't you dare try to go to the top, when you can't even see what you're doing!"

"Don't be stupid, Aggie!" I added.

A series of exploratory taps followed before she responded. "There's no need to be rude, you two. I know it's only your chauvinistic way of expressing concern for my welfare, but I'm fine." The taps descended the staircase. "The truly humbling thing is that ten years ago I could've climbed over that gap as if it weren't even there."

Half a minute later, her knobby knee collided with my spine; I reached up to take her hand, guiding her back to a sitting position between Bo and me. "Now what?" I asked.

"Now we wait for someone to find us," Bo said quietly.

"You sound dreadful, Bo," Aggie said. "Don't be manly, please. Tell us how to help."

"There's not much you can do, unfortunately." There was a long pause. "The pain isn't pleasant, but it's bearable."

The floor beneath us was cold concrete. It was also cloudy with dust, and I sneezed.

"Gesundheit," Aggie said. "Bo, do you think we're in danger of the house collapsing?"

"I doubt it," he answered. "The ceiling support beams are solid oak, and they run the width of the house. We should be fine."

"I sure hope you're right," I muttered. "The refrigerator is directly above us, and I've already got a bit of headache."

He laughed in spite of his knee, which made me feel better.

We listened for a while to the sounds drifting down through the broken floor; the wind had calmed enough that I could hear the rain, then a man's voice yelling something in the distance—perhaps a block away.

"Maybe if we screamed our heads off, he'd hear us," Aggie suggested.

An unwelcome childhood memory surfaced in my brain. "Remember getting trapped under the bathtub after the avalanche?" I asked her.

Her leg was against mine, and I felt her shudder. "Don't remind me." She paused. "You wet yourself, as I recall."

"I sure did," I said. "And I would've done the exact same thing a few minutes ago, if I hadn't just used the facilities."

Bo stirred. "My dad and Uncle Johan found you two, didn't they?"

Not surprisingly—given our present circumstances—the night of the avalanche in Utah was clearer to me in that moment than it had been for years. "Nope," I said. "Some other guys got to us first, but your dad and Johan came along right after that."

We all fell silent again. Eighty years had passed since that life-altering evening, yet I still vividly recalled watching my mother rocking baby Hilda in a chair as Aggie and I bathed in the cast-iron tub that would save our lives. That room, too, had been lit by candlelight—until hell paid us a visit and snuffed out our candle and so much else.

"Dear Lord," Aggie now said, her voice a little shaky. "I hadn't thought of that night in forever, but now it's all coming back to me."

I should've known she'd be reliving it, too. I reached out in the darkness and touched her shoulder, then Bo's wrist, grateful beyond words that at least this time around no one I loved had died.

A cat's yowl interrupted my reverie; Wotan had apparently survived the tornado as well. Aggie called out to him, and he yowled louder, sounding as if he were peering down at us through one of the gaping holes in the basement ceiling.

"Oh, good, we're saved," I said drily.

Aggie snorted. "Show some respect for poor old Wotan. He *is* the god of death, after all."

"Think we can trade our souls for a ladder?"

"Aggie's idea to holler for help is a good one," Bo said. He led us into our first round of screams, howls, and hoots, but other than the silencing of Wotan there was no response. Bo cleared his throat. "We'll try again in a bit. The rest of the neighborhood probably isn't in great shape, either, but somebody's bound to come by sooner or later."

"It's humiliating to require rescuing from our own basement," Aggie said. "Ty and Karen will never let us live it down."

"I could've sworn it was Dad and Johan who found y'all," Bo said.

Aggie and I both sighed; when Bo became fixated on historical details, it meant his mind was slipping out of joint.

"Nope," I said. "But they weren't far away."

Between further bouts of yelling for help, there was nothing to do but talk, so we did. I gossiped for a while about Danny: The last time he'd written, he said he was living with a fellow theologian, though he doubted their relationship would last. He swore he still thought of me every day, as I did of him, but we both knew that we'd likely never see each other again. At this point, we were resigned to being pen pals—which I supposed was better than nothing. (We'd split up six years before. Our age difference was part of the problem—I couldn't bear to saddle him with caretaker duties when I got too old to look after myself—but the main issue was how much I missed my family. For better or worse, Danny's heart was in Italy and mine was in Iowa, and we could no longer make it work, though God knows it wasn't for a lack of trying.)

After I finished talking about Danny, Aggie complained about the kids and how she felt they were mucking up their lives. They were still out east: Ty was engaged to a woman twenty years his junior; Jamie was attending Boston University as an art major, where he'd apparently fallen in love with his roommate's fiancée; Karen was semi-retired from Hunter College, and had recently begun an affair with a married office mate.

Bo asked again if his father and Johan had found Aggie and me after the avalanche, and Aggie patiently set him straight.

We yelled once more for help, then reminisced about people we'd loved and lost through the years: Elias and Johan, first and foremost, but also parents, friends, lovers, ex-spouses—the list of those no longer with us was getting far too long. As we talked, however, it occurred to me that to be old, injured, feeble, and in the dark, is not such a dreadful thing, really—at least not if the two people you care about the most in the world are still with you.

"How much longer do you think it will be before someone finds us?" Aggie asked during a lull in the conversation. "If somebody doesn't show up soon, I may need to use Wotan's litter box."

"Let's hope the lights don't come back on while you're doing that," I said. "I'd rather not have to gouge my eyes out."

"Would you prefer I piddle on the floor like a savage?" she asked.

I snorted. "No, you're right. Piddling in a cat box is far more civilized."

Bo laughed. "Y'all are pretty funny. We should hang out down here more often."

The only sounds we could hear outside at the moment were sirens in the distance, but we tried another group scream anyway, to no effect. Aggie sighed.

"Do either of you remember the time the power went out at

our first apartment in Des Moines?" she asked. "We didn't have any furniture yet because we'd just moved in, and we were all sitting on the floor in the dark, just like this. Remember?"

I told her no, but Bo surprised me. "Sure I do," he said. "Johan was there, too, and it was a summer night. When the electricity crapped out, we were playing pinochle and listening to the radio. The radio died and we just kept singing."

I shook my head, puzzled as always by how his memory phased in and out. When it was working, it was far better than mine.

"I forgot about our singing," Aggie said, "but I remember the game we made up since we couldn't see our cards anymore." Her fingers sought my hand in the darkness, startling me. "Here, take this, Isaac."

She set something on my palm; it was our extinguished candle. "What am I supposed to do with this?" I asked. "We don't have any matches down here."

"We're going to pass it around as soon as I can recall the rules of the game. We used Johan's hat back in Des Moines, but the candle will work just as well."

"Sounds like a real hoot," I mumbled.

"Don't be a spoilsport."

"We were singing 'Pennies from Heaven,'" Bo said, "and Johan was the only one who knew all the words. The rest of us just made them up as we went along." There was wonder in his voice. "I remember everything."

I sighed. "I'm glad somebody does."

"Okay," Aggie said. "Here are the rules. Isaac starts by passing the candle to his right, but after that any of us can switch directions at any time and give it back to whomever they just got it from. If you do that, though, the person you give it back to gets to insult you. Got it?"

"Seriously?" I asked. "Who was the moron who invented such a juvenile game?"

Aggie laughed. "It was you."

"I most certainly did not."

"Just pass the candle, Isaac."

It was an idiotic way to kill time, of course, but none of us could resist giggling like preschoolers when the insults began to fly: *Maggot eater. Floozy. Foot fetishist. Closeted nose picker. Unhygienic ape. Bottom feeder. Muppet fondler.*

We were all cackling uproariously when a loud knocking from upstairs made us all jump. "Hello?" It was a man's voice, coming from somewhere near the front door. "I'm a police officer. Anybody in here?"

None of us responded for a long moment, stunned by the sudden recollection that we still needed help. Perversely, I found myself a little disappointed to have our fun interrupted.

"We're downstairs!" Bo finally yelled back. "But be careful! I think a lot of the floor up there is gone!"

A pause as a flashlight beam began probing gaps in the boards above our heads, apparently searching for us. "I hate to tell you this, sir," the officer replied, "but a whole lot more than the floor is gone."

In the faint light provided by the darting flashlight, I could now see both Aggie and Bo, though only in silhouette. They seemed to be looking at me, too, and something about the thinness of their necks and the narrowness of their stooped shoulders reminded me forcefully how vulnerable they were, and all at once my eyes filled with tears, taking me by complete surprise. I told myself that I was just feeling maudlin because of everything we'd been through in the past couple of hours, but I knew it was more than that. We'd survived this night, thank God, but one day soon—regardless of how much we loved each other, or how tightly we held on to the life we'd shared—our luck was going to run out, and we'd have to say goodbye.

Stop it, I chided myself, hurriedly wiping my eyes and hoping that neither Bo nor Aggie saw me doing it. *What matters is that we're fine right now.*

"What's left of the place?" Bo called back to the officer. "That was one hell of a twister."

"Looks like it got about half the house. Your roof's completely gone." The flashlight beam found us, blinding each of us in turn. "Everybody okay down there?"

"One of us may have a concussion and my knee's a little banged up, but otherwise we're good, thanks," Bo said. "Can you get us out of here? Some of the stairs are missing and I don't think we can make it out without a ladder."

"The fire truck's just down the street. I'll radio them and we'll get you out right away."

"The sooner the better," Bo said. "I can't see the support beams above us to check for damage, so I'm not really sure how safe it is down here."

"We'll get to you as fast as we can. I'll be right back soon as I talk to the fire truck."

The flashlight disappeared, leaving us blind again.

Aggie nudged my arm gently—she must've caught me wiping my eyes—and I grunted in disbelief when I realized she was trying to pass the candle. I took a deep breath, then accepted the silly damn thing from her, unable to keep from smiling a little in spite of my sadness and fear. Of course she still wanted to play. We might not have a home anymore, and God only knew how much time we had left together on the planet, but at least we could fire off childish insults at each other and share another laugh or two before our game was finally over. It was who we were, after all, who we'd always been. I handed the candle back to her, just to make her happy.

"Gangrene breath," she said, chortling.

DAY TWELVE

August 24, 2014. Napa, California.

God, how I miss being warm.

The older I get, the more lizardlike I become: cold-blooded, scaly-skinned, easily frightened. Slow metabolism. Watchful, darting eyes, seldom blinking. Blending in with the scenery. Sleeping often, but only in brief snatches. Dreaming troubled lizard dreams.

God, how I miss sleeping through an entire night.

It's 2:13 A.M., and I'm shivering under my blankets. The moon is hovering above a skylight in the middle of the room, so I don't bother with the lamp as I swing my legs out of bed and feel for my slippers with my toes. It's colder than it should be for California in late summer, and I'm thankful I remembered to toss a robe at the foot of my bed before going to sleep. Once I'm up and shuffling down the hall to the bathroom, my goose bumps subside to a tolerable level.

In four more years—if I'm still breathing air rather than dirt (or eternal hellfire, as Aggie would gleefully snark if she were here)—I'll have been alive for a century. It's funny how little I care anymore if I make it or not. I keep my indifference to myself, of course, to avoid aggravating the sensitive souls among my family and friends, many of whom view my approaching mortality as a character flaw.

Ty, Jamie, and I are in Napa Valley, sightseeing. I've always wanted to come here. I've visited dozens of utopias for wine lovers elsewhere in the world—including Sonoma, just down the road—but somehow never got to Napa before. We're staying at a vineyard called Holy Waters, owned for generations by the family of my old friend Stephen Waters, the photographer I worked with in Vietnam. The main house on the property, where our rooms are, is the size of a small castle, with four floors, elegant patios front and back, and an enormous wine cellar. We're sharing the place with Stephen's oldest grandson and his family, as well as their head winemaker and two apprentices, but even so, Ty, Jamie, and I have the second floor to ourselves.

I'm wide-awake after I finish peeing, and rather than returning to bed and staring at the ceiling till sunrise, I decide to go exploring. The hallway is lit by a yellow night-light, and I creep (lizardlike) to the staircase, not wanting to wake Ty or Jamie, whose heads would explode if they saw me on the stairs unsupervised. Their anxiety about my welfare is more than justified by my questionable balance, brittle bones, and propensity for vertigo, yet I'm not as helpless as they believe, and if I go slowly and keep at least one hand on the banister at all times, it's unlikely I'll end up in a broken heap at the bottom of the staircase.

It's pathetic that this is the riskiest thing I've attempted in years.

My destination is the ground floor, where there's a wine tasting room for the public, a visitor's center, and a large kitchen. The steps are darker than the hallway, but I can still see where to plant my feet, thanks to a window halfway down the staircase. I go slowly, one tentative step at a time, and clutch the banister with both hands—death may not scare me, but hip replacement surgery isn't on my bucket list. Once I'm safely on the ground floor, I shuffle to the kitchen and flip on the light, blinding myself.

Holy Waters often hosts large gatherings, and the maple table in the center of the room seats fifteen people. The refrigerator and stove are equally oversized. Stephen's grandson, Simon, the owner of the vineyard—has repeatedly insisted that we make ourselves at home, so I take him at his word, poking around in the cabinets and fridge for a snack. Armed with a cutting board, knife, summer sausage, and a block of blue cheese, I wander down the hall to the tasting room, lusting after a glass or two of an excellent ruby port that's made right here on the premises.

Most of the organs in my body have become feckless allies or outright traitors, but my liver, miraculously, remains faithful.

The tasting room lighting is soothing, muted by mahogany paneling and wood floors. I unload my armful of treasures on the bar, find the bottle of port and a glass, and climb laboriously on a stool to feast. Given that I can't sleep, there are worse things to do in the middle of the night; I slice the sausage and cheese with some complacency, eyeing a row of wine bottles on a shelf behind the bar.

"I figured I'd find you here."

I swivel on the stool in surprise, almost falling. Ty's leaning against the door frame, rubbing his eyes and looking torn between amusement and annoyance. Like me, he's wearing pajamas and a robe, but he's barefoot.

"Ty Morgan Dahl!" I snap. "Are you trying to kill me?"

"Of course. I'm in your will, remember?" He walks over and mounts the stool next to mine, reaching for a slice of sausage. "I got up a minute ago to make sure Jamie was still breathing, and noticed you weren't in your room."

"What's wrong with my great-nephew?"

"He had a few too many glasses of wine after you went to bed."

"Poor kid." Jamie almost never drinks alcohol and has no tolerance for it. "Is he okay?"

"Sleeping like a hungover baby, but he puked up everything in his stomach first. The highlight of the evening was when he had angel hair pasta hanging from his nose."

I laugh. "Did you take a picture?"

"Sure did." The corners of Ty's mouth twitch, reminding me of his mother. "Just think of the fun we'll have tomorrow when we show it to him." He steals a taste of my drink and reaches over the bar for his own glass. "That's damn good port."

"Yes, it is. Don't hog it."

He studies me. "So why are you up at this hour of the night, old man?"

"You're not exactly a spring chicken, yourself," I remind him, deflecting his question. "In fact, you're damn near an octogenarian chicken."

"Not for three more years. I'm practically an infant, compared to you."

We sip and chew in companionable silence, listening to the house's night noises: the hum of the refrigerator down the hall, a ticking wall clock, a strong breeze pressing against the windows. We finish the sausage with regret, and he goes to the kitchen to find more; I refill our glasses when he gets back, then raise mine in a toast.

"To debauchery," I say, "in the wee dark hours of the night."

It was a toast Aggie made every time we all got together, and Ty's eyes meet mine as our glasses chime. His heart hurts, too, I know, but we both smile.

"*L'chaim*," he murmurs.

Aggie told me that the most aggravating part of dying as an old lady, sick in her bed, was that it was such a cliché. In the notebook she kept at her side at the hospice, I found a list of ways she would have preferred to go, including:

—*drowning, after being mistaken for an orca and harpooned by a sadistic Inuit whaler*
—*electrocution, from a faulty, supercharged, lithium-ion dildo*
—*sneezing with enough force to expel brain tissue at the speed of light*
—*simmering in a creamy garlic sauce until fork-tender*

She left her notebook to me in her will, so a lot of what she wrote was for my entertainment. Up until the last few days—when she had enough morphine in her system to sedate an ox—her prose remained distinctive, cogent, opinionated, funny, and infuriating: in short, vintage Aggie. Bo was too addled after she was gone to understand much of what I read to him, but he liked listening to the familiar flow of her words.

I have not written about either of their deaths before, nor do I wish to do so now. Suffice it to say that Aggie died of bone cancer at ninety-two, and Bo from pneumonia at ninety-three. Aggie knew me until the end; Bo didn't. Several years have passed, but I'll never wrap my mind around the fact that they're truly gone. After the tornado destroyed our bungalow in Iowa City, we moved into an assisted-living cottage, where I now live alone. I still catch glimpses of them all the time, from the corner of my eye—Aggie sits at her desk, writing, while Bo haunts the front stoop, whistling to himself and watching the world go by, much as Uncle Johan used to do when we were kids. I know these are only phantasms, of course, by-products of an old man's loneliness and grief, yet I gladly welcome them. They get me through the day.

Ty, Karen, and Jamie remain in New York, but it's a rare week that goes by without all three of them checking in via phone or Skype. Karen is flying out to join us here in Napa next weekend, and then we're all heading up to Portland for an art gallery opening that Ty is helping to promote. They're all amazing people, and I adore them. I continue to crawl out of bed every morning against my better judgment, mainly because they want me to, and I love them too much to let them down.

But they're not Aggie and Bo.

Isaac, Aggie wrote, *since you're now reading my notebook, it's safe to say I must be dead. I would never allow you to read it otherwise, and you wouldn't dream of sneaking a peek without permission, as you're too honorable (and/or self-righteous) to sneak. I always assumed I'd outlast you, because (A) I deserved to, and (B) your unhealthy obsession with mortality should've been the death of you years ago. That said, I'm relieved to be proven wrong. You may be tedious, overweening, shallow, pompous, inconsiderate, prudish, confrontational, and dim-witted, yet strangely enough I've grown rather fond of you, and I'm grateful I won't be there to see the Grim Reaper slap you silly.*

I have a few demands to make.

(1) Bo's mind is unlikely to last longer than a month or two, at most, though his heart may continue to beat for millennia. Regardless of how untethered from reality he becomes, however, you must be there with him at the end, to guide him home. Hold him tightly, as I would, and remind him how much he has been loved—and always will be—by all of us. He's allowed to forget everything else, but not that; please, never that. Accordingly, you are forbidden to die before he does. Call this an unreasonable edict, if you wish, but I'm serious: Don't leave Bo alone in the world.

(2) Now that I'm gone, Karen is likely to offer to move back to Iowa, to babysit you. Do NOT let her make that sacrifice, under any circumstances. She has always been too willing to set

her happiness aside for the sake of those she loves, and this self-lessness, though admirable, has hurt her work. (Remember how little she accomplished during Jamie's adolescence?) I'm aware she's a pigheaded senior citizen used to getting her way, but she adores New York and would be miserably unproductive anywhere else. Convince her you'll be fine without her, whatever the cost to yourself. I was wrong to crucify you for moving to Italy with Danny all those years ago, and I know it sapped your strength to have your heart in two places. Spare yourself the pangs of a guilty conscience and be kinder to Karen than I was to you.

(3) Ty and Jamie, thankfully, seem to have patched up their relationship, but they are still wary of each other. They would greatly benefit from spending more time together, but I fear they'll never do so unless you coerce them to join you for various outings, family vacations, etc. Our Ty is a dear man, but he's become too serious in his old age, especially when it comes to dealing with Jamie. Remember how lovably infantile he used to be with Elias? He's lost touch with that less forbidding version of himself, and you must help him rediscover it, by whatever means necessary. I recommend investing in a sturdy pair of forceps, to assist him in pulling his head out of his anus.

(4) My last demand concerns you, and only you, and I find myself reluctant to continue. I worry you'll read this and believe the morphine made me go soft at the end, but so be it; there are things that must be said. But where to start?

Isaac. My brother, my twin, my nemesis, my foil, my rival, my asylum cellmate, my biological hair shirt. What will become of you when Bo and I are both gone? You're so accustomed to being part of the six-legged, three-headed creature that we've always been; whatever will you do with two-thirds of yourself missing? I foresee you lurching around the cottage in your underwear and bathrobe, reeking of red wine and dried sweat; I see dust piling up on your computer and desk; I see unanswered mail and unread newspapers on the porch step; I see the assisted living nurse strapping you down for daily sponge baths and force-feeding you Jell-O.

It's not a pretty picture.

You have work yet to do, and you must find the will to do it. I'm aware I've frequently maligned your writing over the years, but I only did so because it was good sport to watch your face turn purple. My true opinion of your worth as a writer—oh, dear Lord, this is excruciating—is that your narrative voice is lovely; your clarity and insight are often staggering. (Don't gawp like a startled chimp at this morsel of flattery; I'm simply puffing up your ego to hold your attention.) Indeed, I have never questioned your talent, nor your commitment to your work, but far too often your heart goes AWOL.

If you can abstain from drinking yourself to death, you may last a few more years. I fervently pray that you do, as you'll need at least that much time to fix the sorry mess of an autobiography you've been furtively scribbling in your room. I found what you've written thus far (you should learn to hide your personal papers better), and it does little justice to the extraordinary life you've led. The last thing the world needs is yet another traditional, erudite autobiography from a well-traveled "man of letters." Your previous books and articles have chronicled, exhaustively, the people you've known, where you've been, and what you've seen, and while much of this information is objectively fascinating, YOU'VE ALREADY WRITTEN IT.

I beg you to start over. Select ten or twelve memories—an evocative distillation of your life, nothing more. Utah and the avalanche should be your first chapter, I believe, but then I'd suggest leapfrogging through time, with a decade or so between each chapter. This will allow you to explore the scattershot richness of your past, without getting bogged down in minutiae. Don't fret if an occasional memory isn't historically earthshaking; ordinary moments often resonate the most.

The Isaac Dahl that I know, and love ever so dearly, is a moody, neurotic, charming, flawed, silly, clever, and precious man. THAT is the Isaac Dahl who needs to appear in this book of yours. Not the journalist, historian, and essayist, but Isaac Dahl, the human being. Don't go the full monty, however—be a coquette, and reveal only the pieces of yourself that matter the most: family and friends, work and play, love and death. Allow your readers to resurrect the missing pieces of you in their imaginations, and they will not easily forget you, nor any of us.

I don't know about you, brother, but at this point, I'll take whatever immortality I can get.

P.S. You'll no doubt be tempted to amuse yourself by portraying me as an unhinged harpy, but beware: I'm sharpening my claws in the afterlife.

"It's cold down here," Ty says, yawning. "How about we go back up to the tasting room?"

"In a bit," I tell him. "I'm feeling adventurous."

We're in the Holy Waters cellar, surrounded by dozens of sixty-gallon barrels of wine, stacked on their sides in racks from concrete floor to wood ceiling. The room is clean and well-lit, banishing shadows to the corners. One wall is clear glass, with an entry door; the other walls are rough stone. Stephen Waters, my old photographer, used to talk all the time about his family's vineyard, but I'd never dreamed it was such a sophisticated operation. The cellar is climate-controlled and somewhat chilly; I assume it's an optimum temperature to mature the wine for bottling. I cinch up the belt of my robe and shiver, glad I'm not barefoot like Ty as we wander arm in arm down one of the long, wide rows of the cavernous cellar.

Ty glances at his watch. "It's 3:22 in the morning, and I, for one, am more than a little inebriated. Can't this safari of yours wait for a more civilized hour?"

"Don't be a party pooper." I stop to catch my breath, looking around. "I don't know why I never came here to visit

Stephen when he was still alive. I would've loved to have seen him again."

"I'm sorry I never met him," Ty says. "Elias always said the two of you saved his life from the Klan in Mississippi."

"Stephen gets the credit for that. I was too busy soiling my britches to be of much use." I shuffle forward again, tugging Ty after me. "Stephen was the only reason any of us got out of that mob alive. He was like a pissed-off grizzly, and no one had the balls to take him on."

All at once, I'm reliving the ugliness of that long-ago day, including Stephen's arrest. The ACLU got him released from jail, finally, but it took three weeks, and he came out half-starved, squalid, and looking ten years older than when he went in. Soon afterward, we were back covering the war in Vietnam, where we stayed until we couldn't take it anymore. I asked to be reassigned, but Stephen quit the news business altogether, swearing that once he made it back to Napa he'd never leave again. We kept in touch for a while, but only in letters, and when I'd heard he died recently, I'd felt compelled to come see his home. Looking around now, I smile sadly, missing him.

"You made a good choice, buddy," I murmur, too quietly to be heard over the soporific whirr of the cellar's ventilation system.

"Beg pardon?" Ty asks.

I sigh. "Stephen thought I was crazy to still want to be a reporter after Vietnam."

Ty's snort is eloquent. "I believe Mom might've said something similar, once or twice."

"Just every day of her life." I breathe deeply, enjoying the smell of oak and red wine in the air. "She accused me of being an adrenaline junkie."

"She didn't really mean that. She knew you were just trying to make a difference, and she loved you for it. We all did."

His arm is warm and strong, linked with mine, and as usual,

I'm grateful to be with him. He may not be Bo's flesh and blood, but he inherited much of Bo's matter-of-fact sweetness and sensitivity. I rest my hand on his as my mind wanders. "Did you see those pictures of the *Houston* in the news a few days ago?"

He raises an eyebrow. "Of course. We already talked about it, remember?"

"Nope." I forget so much these days that my memory lapses no longer bother me. "I haven't been sleeping very well since they found her."

Less than a week ago, the wreck of the USS *Houston* was finally discovered, seventy-two years after she went down in the Java Sea. Seeing photos of her broken hull at the bottom of the ocean, overgrown with rust and coral, deeply upset me, dredging up memories of the last time I'd seen her, the day before she sank. I can still conjure her crew as they'd looked when I disembarked—exhausted and filthy, but unbeaten, even after the harrowing night they'd all just gone through. I can feel Alan Weintraub's strong hand in mine when we said goodbye; I can smell the overpowering stench belowdecks of gun grease, engine oil, human sweat, and urine. My friend Paulie Morse survived the *Houston*'s sinking, of course, and my first thought was of him when I saw the pictures. I knew if he were still alive that his memories would be far worse than mine, so I'd finally attempted to track him down, as I'd been telling myself to do for years. I was too late, however: All I found was his obituary.

"I'm amazed you can sleep at all, with everything you've seen," Ty says. "Back when you first wrote to us about your time on the *Houston*, Mom read your letter aloud to Uncle Johan, Karen, and me. She left out the parts that were only for her and Johan, though, so Karen and I stole it from her dresser, and read it all. It gave us nightmares for weeks."

I smile. "Idiots. Did you ever tell Aggie?"

"We didn't have to. Karen and I woke up that same night at

the same damn time, screaming bloody murder. We both still have matching handprints on our butt-cheeks from the spanking Mom gave us."

We reach the far wall of the cellar, where a giant fermentation vat sits, squat-bellied and peaceful as a buddha in lotus. I rest my back against it; more worn out from this late-night stroll than I care to admit. "Okay, that's more than enough adventure for one night," I say, scratching my chin. "Want to go back to the tasting room and open another bottle of port?"

He leans against the vat, too. "I thought you'd never ask."

An explosive CRACK from somewhere deep beneath us shatters the silence of the night, making us both jump. A second later, the ground buckles and heaves, and we stumble, helplessly, lurching into each other. The overhead light flickers as I fall on all fours, yipping in pain when my knees hit the concrete; Ty trips over my shins and ends up flat on his back. We gape at each other in terror and astonishment as a dozen or more wine barrels tumble from the racks. Most break apart, but several of them begin rolling wildly around the room.

"SON OF A BITCH!" Ty wails, trying to sit up but unable to recover his balance. "IT'S A FUCKING EARTHQUAKE!"

Across the room, the glass wall and doorway shatter with a shrill, staccato scream. A three-hundred-pound barrel takes flight from a rack and sails at least twenty feet, smashing against a wall and spraying red wine and wood splinters; the oak fermentation vat beside us splits along a seam, instantly drenching me with a sweet-and-sour geyser of lukewarm Chardonnay. I make a feeble effort to crawl to Ty's side, but tip over before I get there, landing hard enough to knock the air from my lungs. Another barrel flips by us, end over end, and I whimper as it misses Ty's head by inches. The earth heaves me against him, and I clutch him tightly in a vain attempt to protect him.

"We have to get to Jamie!" he cries.

"We can't! We have to wait it out!"

Once again, I'm helpless to save myself or the people I love. I scream in fury, but of course it does no good; there's no stability left in the world, nothing to hold on to but each other. Unbelievably, I realize that Ty has begun laughing hysterically, his cheek against mine.

"What natural disaster is next for you, Isaac?" he shouts. "A flood? A volcano?"

The absurdity of my very long, very strange life hits me, too, and suddenly I'm laughing with him. What else can I do?

"It's my first apocalypse without Bo and Aggie!" I yell back. "Looks like you're my new dance partner!"

And just like that, it's over. The world bucks and kicks one final time—making me squeal between laughs—then it drifts back to sleep. The ensuing quiet in the room is eerie, the only sound that of spilled wine trickling down a drain in the center of the floor. Ty stirs and we slowly disengage from each other. His pajamas are soaked with wine, too.

"Christ on a crutch," he grunts. "You okay?"

I move my arms and legs experimentally. "Everything still works, I think. You?"

"A few bumps and bruises." He climbs unsteadily to his feet, groaning, then helps me up, and we stare around the room. The wreckage is near absolute. In less than twenty seconds, the cellar has been turned from the pristine, organized heart of a vineyard into a pile of sodden, sticky debris. The racks are crippled, tottering carcasses; half the wine barrels are destroyed, the rest scattered here and there—flotsam from a shipwreck.

"So," Ty says, "that's what an earthquake feels like." His eyes are wide with shock. "How big was it, do you think?"

"Big enough, that's for damn sure." I shake my head to make my brain work. "We better find Jamie fast, and everybody else, too, and get outside, before any aftershocks come along." I glance at the carpet of broken glass on the floor across the room, where the door to the cellar used to be, then I look down at Ty's bare feet, and my sodden slippers. "We'll cut ourselves to shreds getting out of here, though."

A voice calls from upstairs, and we both relax a little: It's Jamie, and he sounds okay, if a trifle panicky. Ty yells back, and a minute later Jamie trots down the cellar stairs, followed closely by Simon Waters, Stephen's grandson and current owner of the vineyard. Jamie is wearing nothing but boxer shorts and sneakers; Simon is in sweatpants, boots, and a pullover jacket. They jog toward us—it's a long way from the stairs to where we're standing—but we warn them off before they reach the broken glass.

"What the hell are you guys DOING down here?" Jamie demands, skidding to a halt. "You scared the crap out of me when I couldn't find you."

"Isaac wanted to go exploring." Ty gives me his arm and we start looking for a way through the ruins. "That's a nice outfit you've got on, by the way," he tells Jamie.

Jamie looks down at his slim body sheepishly. "I was in a hurry."

Simon's face is anguished as he stares at the shattered remnants of his wine cellar; something about the set of his shoulders reminds me of his grandfather, though he's nowhere near as stocky. He's a young man in his late twenties like Jamie, but at the moment he could pass for fifty.

"Oh, God, Simon, I'm so sorry," I tell him. "This must be devastating for you."

He has tears in his eyes, but he swallows hard and shakes his head. "Could be a hell of a lot worse. At least no one's hurt." Jamie offers to go find our shoes, but Simon stops him. "We better just carry them," he says. "It's not safe down here and we need to get out fast."

They tiptoe with care through the glass minefield, and Jamie hugs us both when he reaches us. His olive-colored skin is paler than usual, owing to fright (or perhaps alcohol poisoning). Ty outweighs me by twenty pounds, so he ends up piggyback on Simon, while Jamie and I debate the best way for him to carry me. I no longer outweigh him, but I'm at least six inches taller—so we eventually decide a fireman's carry is our best bet. He drapes me over his naked shoulders like a stole, then follows after Simon and Ty. He's small, but quite strong.

"Oof," I grunt. "You're too damn bony. Your left shoulder is giving me an appendectomy."

He's panting a little from the strain. "Yeah, well, guess you should've put on . . . shoes before wandering around a strange basement . . . in the middle of the fucking night."

"Language, son," I scold. "Watch out for the—"

"I see it, old man. Shut up and let me concentrate."

"You'd make a lousy fireman."

"Ninety-six-year-old baby," he complains. "I'm putting you back where . . . I found you."

The exasperation in his voice tickles me, as does the indignity of being toted about like a wet sack of rice in my stinking nightclothes, with my scrawny, ancient buttocks pointed at the ceiling and my liver-spotted forehead bouncing gently and repeatedly off Jamie's right bicep. Ty and Simon reach at least temporary safety, and as I watch my elderly nephew clamber down from Simon's back and hobble toward the stairs, I begin laughing like a fool, realizing something that surprises me almost as much as the earthquake.

I'm not ready to die, after all.

I may change my mind tomorrow, or the next day, but right now I'd like to live a while longer. Not because life is beautiful—it is sometimes, of course, but other times it's ugly beyond belief—nor because I'm afraid of the dark, nor eternal damnation, nor even of the pain and suffering this body of mine may endure before I'm dead and buried.

I want to keep living today, simply because I seem to have

found myself in another story. What happens when we reach the top of the stairs and go outside under the stars? What will things look like when the sun comes up again in a couple of hours? I have no idea, and the uncertainty, as much as anything, is the hook for me. I'll no doubt sit with Ty and Jamie, and we'll call Karen to let her know we're fine; I assume we'll gather with fellow survivors, and grieve with Simon's family for their losses, and do what we can to help, if anything. I imagine I'll eventually nod off, however—hopefully somewhere with an overstuffed armchair next to a roaring fire—and dream about what has been, and what is, and what else may come along between now and nightfall.

I want to see how this story ends.

AUTHOR'S NOTE

No, I wasn't stoned when I came up with the idea for this book.

Truly.

Regardless of how plausible it might sound, I was absolutely NOT sitting on my couch in sweatpants and a wine-stained hoodie, smoking a joint and shoving fried cheese balls into my mouth while mumbling things to my cat like: *Hey, how about I start my next book in 1926, when the main dude is just eight years old, then jump eight years in the future for the second chapter, then just keep on jumping eight years for every chapter after that until he's old as hell, and along the way I'll toss his butt in an avalanche, a dust storm, a naval battle, a movie about Cinderella, and other random crap like that? Want a cheese ball? These freakin' things are awesome!*

I only wish my creative process worked like that.

I began plotting out *The Very Long, Very Strange Life of Isaac Dahl* in the summer of 2014. The only reason I know this is because I found the following note scribbled in one of my notebooks:

August 31, 2014. Historical novel.

First person, past tense. Early childhood to old age.

Each chapter eight years apart, starting at age 8, ending at age 96, so 1926 -2014.

Twelve chapters, roughly twenty pages each. Each chapter a day in history.

Different location each chapter. Recurring characters, new people in each.

Narrator is writer/journalist/gay.

Much of this note now mystifies me. How did I decide on an eight-year gap between each chapter? And why twelve chapters with approximately twenty pages each? I must've had a good reason for such a specific format, but I can't remember it.

What I *do* remember is spending a lot of time Googling the years I'd chosen. Once I settled on twelve true-life events and/or settings that interested me—not an easy task, given how much fascinating stuff occurs on planet Earth at any given moment in history—I dug deeper into my choices, in chronological order, finding out as much as I could about each before working out how my characters might fit in the timeline.

Things went pretty smoothly until all the preliminaries for the book were done and it was time to start writing. I opened my laptop and was faced with a blinking cursor at the top of an empty first page, and I thought the same thing I always do when I get to this point in telling a story: *So now what?*

I like everything about writing except the actual writing.

I'm joking, of course. I love writing.

Sort of.

I love looking up weird facts on the Internet or reading amazing books about a subject that interests me. I love traveling to lovely locales I haven't seen before: This book alone took me to Provence, Tuscany, and Napa Valley. I love immersing myself in memories of places from my past: Horseneck Beach in Massachusetts, the Varsity Theater in Des Moines, and the loft apartment of dear friends in NYC all made an appearance in this novel. I love that I work at home, seldom wear shoes or set an alarm clock, and still get to pretend I'm a semiproductive member of society. I love that there are people in the world who seem to enjoy my books, and I know I'm enormously lucky to earn a living this way.

But do I love the writing itself?

The paragraph above (that you just read in approximately ten seconds) took over an hour to write. If all the paragraphs in all my novels were equally time-consuming—and if I were masochistic enough to add them all up—I'd likely drown myself in the bathtub at the realization of exactly how much of my life I've spent agonizing over things like whether it sounds better to say "*the* bathtub" or "*my* bathtub."

But yes, I love writing.

Sort of.

I submitted the manuscript of *The Very Long, Very Strange Life of Isaac Dahl* to my editor on January 4, 2022. That's nearly eight years after I first started writing it. Not all of that was hands-on work; the first draft spent two full years in solitary confinement—banished to a desk drawer for bad behavior—while I cleared my head by writing a less cantankerous novel. Still, six years is a significant chunk of time, and astonishes me in retrospect.

What kind of person willingly surrenders so much of his/her/their daily existence to play make-believe? Why would most authors rather do this kind of work than almost anything else? What's the motivating force behind the desire to write a book that (A) may never get published, and (B) even if it does, could very well get torn apart by the critics? Are all novelists raging egomaniacs? Or just delusional dreamers, hoping to write the next *Beloved* or *Moby Dick*?

I have no answers to these questions, but I'm okay with that. I figured out a long time ago that it's better for my mental health to not know why I do what I do.

I've always wanted to write a book that followed one character from childhood to old age. Once I began Isaac Dahl's story, however, he insisted on bringing his twin sister and his best friend along for the whole journey. I wasn't sure at first this was a good idea—it wasn't my original intention—but he convinced me his life wouldn't be nearly as interesting without them. He was right, of course: The odd love triangle of Isaac, Agnes, and Bo ended up being the heart of the novel. As I was writing, all three of them kept doing and saying things I didn't expect; God only knows how many times I had to change a scene to accommodate their quirks, moods, and whims. It was sometimes aggravating, but I'm so glad they got their way: They made me laugh, cry, and rethink my assumptions about the nature of family and friendship, and I enjoyed their company immensely.

The hardest part of finishing a novel is losing touch with imaginary friends like these. After spending so much time together, it's often painful to let them go, but the good thing is that there's always the next book—and the next set of playmates to fall in love with. I actually can't wait to meet the new batch.

What can I say? Fiction writers are fickle creatures.

—Bart Yates, June 26, 2023

THE VERY LONG, VERY STRANGE LIFE OF ISAAC DAHL

ABOUT THIS GUIDE

The suggested questions are included to enhance your
group's reading of Bart Yates'
The Very Long, Very Strange Life of Isaac Dahl

DISCUSSION QUESTIONS

1) *The Very Long, Very Strange Life of Isaac Dahl* has an unusual structure for a novel, skipping eight years ahead in time from one chapter to the next, with each chapter detailing a day in the life of Isaac Dahl. Did this non-traditional approach to storytelling work for you as a reader?

2) The three main characters in the book—Isaac, his twin sister, Agnes, and their best friend, Bo—have a unique bond that lasts a lifetime. Is there a particular scene that stands out for you as a good example of the closeness of their relationship?

3) Many of the chapters in this novel are based on actual historical events, such as the 1926 avalanche in Utah, or the 1982 raising of the *Mary Rose* in England. What historical incident do you think affected Isaac the most? When was he the most at peace with himself?

4) In addition to Isaac, Agnes, and Bo, there are dozens of interesting characters in the book, some major, some minor. Do you have a favorite among this large supporting cast, and what did you like about them?

5) If you were telling a friend about the plot of this book, what would you say? Is there an overarching theme, and if so, what is it? Family ties? The passage of time? Mortality? Friendship?

6) In spite of their intimacy, Isaac and Agnes are always verbally sparring. Why do you think this is? Is one more to blame than the other for their often-antagonistic relationship?

7) Of the twelve days from Isaac's life that he tells us about in this novel, which interested you the most? Did you prefer the days that revolved around major historical events, or the ones that were primarily about the Dahl family?

8) There's a lot of sadness in this book, but also quite a bit of humor. What was the saddest part for you? How about the funniest?

9) All the chapters in this novel are written in past tense, save for the very last one, which is in present tense. Why do you think the author chose to make this switch at the end?